# COUNTERFEIT
# KILLING

### A NOVEL
### BY
### MEL GOLDBERG

## ACKNOWLEDGEMENTS
My thanks to Chapala Writers for listening to many of these chapters and for their guidance and perceptive critiques.

Also by Mel Goldberg

**Poetry:**
*The Cyclic Path*, 1990
*Sedona Poems*, 2001
*A Few Berries Shaken From the Tree* (haiku), 2011
*If We Survive*, 2011
*Memories*, 2013
*Seasons of Life* (haiku) 2013

**Prose:**
*Choices*, (A Novel), 2003 reprinted 2011
*A Cold Killing* (short stories), 2010
*Catch a Killer, Save the World* (A Novel) 2013
*Embracing the Fog* (short stories) 2015
    Wth James Tipton, Robert Dryden, & Antonio Rambles

ISBN-10: 0-9827345-7-3
ISBN-13: 978-0-9827345-7-5

# CHAPTER ONE

The impact of the bullet dropped Stanfield Margason to his knees. He clutched his chest and gasped, "You!" On his knees, he squinted up in surprise at the man dressed in a black tee shirt, black jeans, and shoes covered by hospital slippers. "What the hell are you doing?"

The second and third shots missed as the pistol recoiled slightly, the bullets shattering panes in a large glass window. But the fourth and fifth shots hit Stanfield in the lower chest and abdomen. He fell slowly backward, his head bouncing on the carpeted floor. As he lay sprawled on his back, his eyes fixed in a sightless stare toward the ceiling, his blood bubbled out in odd geometric shapes from the three gaping holes.

Half an hour earlier, Stanfield had eaten dinner with his estranged wife, wealthy heiress Cathy Willock, in the dining room of the Aster Road mansion in which he once lived with her. After the meal she had invited him to his favorite room, the library, where hundreds of books filled the bookshelves. "We can have an after-dinner drink and sign the divorce papers.

"Finally. So that's why you invited me. You know I shouldn't be here."

"Don't worry about that Order of Protection. It was merely a piece of paper. I had my lawyer draw up the agreement to include maintenance of ten thousand dollars a month you wanted. Until you get your inheritance."

As they entered the library, Cathy walked quickly to the bar at the far end of the room. She muttered to herself, "I need that drink." She poured two ounces of Glenfiddich single malt in a tumbler.

Stanfield had stopped in front of the floor-to-ceiling window and looked out over the twinkling lights of Phoenix. He had turned when he heard a sound behind him of books falling from a shelf, surprised by the sneering man in black wearing socks but no shoes. In his gloved hand he held a Czech 9 mm Luger. "Good thing you kept it in the hiding place behind the Dean Koontz novels."

After the five shots, Cathy stood frozen, staring at the man with the gun whose jaws were tight, his mouth set in a grimace. He stood silently looking at Stanfield's body, the gun still pointed toward space Stanfield had occupied before he fell. As if she suddenly thawed, Cathy drew an audible breath, covering her open mouth with her hands. "Oh my God. What did you do?"

"What do you mean by *what did I do?*"

"He promised to give me half of the inheritance when he got his money."

"You mean his father's money?  And what would I get?

Expecting to inherit his father's five hundred million dollar estate, Stanfield had not led a productive life. He had partied through three universities, but never finished.  He had dabbled in several financial enterprises, all unsuccessful. Although he received a generous yearly allowance from his late father's trust, he often found the amount insufficient.

Well known in wealthy societies in the United States, several countries of Europe, and parts of Africa, Stanfield's abiding objective in life had always been to have fun.  Of medium height and slender, he carried himself with an arrogant air which invited comparison to Fred Astaire, although Stanfield had neither the liveliness nor the intellect.

2

Inheriting his late father's estate required Stanfield demonstrate to the trustees that he had created a responsible and legitimate career before he reached his forty-fifth birthday, the age at which his father had earned his first million. At the start of his forty-fourth year, Stanfield had felt immense pressure to accomplish something.

Now Cathy and the shooter stared at the unmoving man who lay bleeding on the floor, his head several feet from the broken window. Then like a cornered fox looking for an escape, Cathy's eyes darted from the body on the floor to the man holding the gun. "My God, what if someone heard?" Her voice, nearly inaudible, squeaked, high pitched. "I think I'm going to throw up." She turned her face away.

"A bit late for remorse now. This was the plan, wasn't it?" His mouth downturned in a scowl, his eyes narrowed.

"I. . . I suppose so." Her voice trembled.

"What stupidity. You lure him to dinner to discuss the divorce and the maintenance, and he takes the bait like a mouse going after cheese in a trap." He paused and handed Cathy the gun. "You better fire one shot into him."

"But he's already dead, isn't he?"

"I think so, but the police can determine whether or not you've fired a gun. And your fingerprints have to be on the gun. Put one into the cheap bastard's heart."

"I don't think I can." Tears began to form in her eyes. "This isn't like target shooting."

"You have to, Cathy. Otherwise all this is for nothing. It has to be self defense, remember."

She took the Luger and inched over to the body, careful not to step in the blood seeping from his chest and soaking into the carpet. When she leaned over his body, the pungent, musty odor of blood mixed with urine filled her nostrils, causing an involuntary spasm of her stomach. For a moment she thought she might vomit on top of him, but she sucked in her breath, positioned her arm about two feet over his chest, clenched her teeth, and fired one shot. Cathy winced as the impact of the bullet caused Stanfield's chest to move slightly and then he lay still, all his grandiose ideas silently sliding into the abyss of death. Cathy straightened up, tears clouding her vision. She walked back to the bookcase and dropped the gun on the floor next to the scattered books.

"Now we need to shatter the window. Did you put your dressmaker's dummy in the closet like I told you?"

In her foggy state, his voice struck her like a bright light. She wiped her eyes with the backs of her hand and nodded. Walking to a door between the bookshelves, she opened the closet and rolled out the life size dressmaker's dummy, supported on a metal stand with four small wheels. She pushed it into the center of the room, its wheels leaving tracks in the carpet. "What about my prints on it?"

"It's your dummy. They should be there."

He removed Stanfield's shoes and slipped them on his own feet. Pulling the mannequin up from its post, he carried the figure outside to the large window, raised it over his head, and heaved it. The many-paned window exploded, showering shards of glass and pieces of wood over Stanfield's body. The dummy landed on the body and rolled to one side, smearing its side with blood and pushing the blood on the floor in a wider pattern.

He then returned. At the door, he slipped on his own shoes, and walked back to the library. Replacing Margason's shoes, he picked up the dummy, put it back onto its stand, and hoisted both over his shoulder like a sack of wheat.

"You're getting blood on your clothes."

"Who gives a shit. No one will ever see these things again. But that son-of-a-bitch has treated me like an outcast for the last time." He walked back toward the door. "Fortunately for us, he didn't have the guts to go through with that casino purchase."

"Where are you going?"

"I have an idea for this thing. Things should be quiet this early on a Saturday morning. You keep to the plan. All the dishes into the dishwasher. Vacuum the carpet where he walked. Remember. He crashed through the window threatening to kill you. He was acting crazy."

Once Cathy Margason heard the front door close, she vacuumed the carpet from the dining area to the library. Then she gathered all the dishes, glasses, and utensils, placed them in the dishwasher and set the dial on high heat. She wiped the table and chair where Margason had sat. Finishing all her cleanup chores, she hurried upstairs to her bedroom to lie down. This death was messy, unlike when her grandfather had died peacefully in his sleep and her father had called people to take care of everything.

She had never seen so much blood. Thankful she didn't have to clean up his mess, she shuddered, the sight and smell imbedded in her mind. To have had a hand in such an enterprise was ghastly. She started to shake and wanted a martini but knew drinking might mess up the plan. Instead of another drink, she took time. Time to collect her thoughts and calm down. Time to look properly distraught instead of agitated. Lying in bed, rehearsed the story in her mind of self defense from an estranged and abusive husband who had threatened to kill her.

Three hours later, she called the police.

# CHAPTER TWO

At three AM, Detective Aaron Guerevich's cell phone played its tinny *Hatikvah* tune and buzzed on the wooden dresser, waking him. Calls that early in the morning usually meant bad things had happened. Someone shot or killed. Saturday. The sabbath. *Shabbos* his father would have said, using the traditional old Sephardic Hebrew pronunciation. *Shabbat* in modern Hebrew. Picking up the phone, he imagined the frown on his father's face. His father would not have answered the phone. It would be considered work on this day of rest and prayer, the holiest day of the week.

Guerevich did not believe it was possible to be part of a modern American society and still live according to the strict interpretation of Jewish Talmudic law. His father had become upset when Guerevich said that Jews who lived in the ghettos of Poland or Russia kept the Sabbath because they had no choice. Their lives otherwise would have been unbearable, without meaning. For most modern Jews the sabbath had become another day. Like a block of stone rolling down a hill, its edges had become rounded.

Guerevich still considered himself a religious man. Although his father disagreed, Guerevich believed he had a moral obligation, as well as a civic requirement, to violate some religious prohibitions. While Jewish law prevented any manner of work on the Sabbath except to save lives, religious authorities allowed doctors to work on the Sabbath. Guerevich considered his occupation in the same category as a doctor. *I also deal with life and death.*

Stumbling from bed, he flipped open the cell phone as the tune started a second time, hoping the sound had not awakened Ann Berendt, asleep with her warm back next to him.

"Guerevich," he whispered.

"There's been a shooting, Aaron. We have a body." The voice belonged to Robert Kipinski, Ann's cousin and head of the third shift Scottsdale Police Evidence Collection Team, now popularly called CSI like the TV show, instead of its official acronym SPECT.

"Where, Kip?" Guerevich half mumbled, pulling a pad and pencil from the night stand.

"At the Stanfield Margason residence.   11635 W. Aster Road. Margason's dead.  I just got here."

"Is the M. E. there yet?"

"He's on his way."

"I'll be there soon as I can, Kip."   Guerevich refrained from mentioning he'd had very little sleep.  He and Ann had gone to bed at ten but didn't get to sleep until well after midnight.   Somehow it seemed tacky even though Kipinski, Ann's foster father, had introduced them.  Ann and Aaron had been together for four years, although each kept a separate residence.

Guerevich quietly got dressed, putting on the same white shirt, dark trousers, and suit jacket he had thrown on the chair the night before.

Ann opened sleep-heavy eyes. "What happened, Aaron?"

"Someone got killed.   Someone named Stanfield Margason."

"Who?" she murmured.

"I need to go.  Get back to sleep."

Ann nodded her head and smiled slightly in assent. "No doubt I'll get all the details later at the lab."

He saw his tie on the dresser and decided to leave it. Looking as rumpled as Peter Falk's Columbo, he leaned over the bed to give her a kiss. She put her arms around his neck and pulled him to her, kissing him passionately. Then she let go, pulled the covers up to her neck, and rolled to her side, her back to him. He let himself out of the apartment, refreshed by the cool night air. He stopped at an all-night diner for coffee. *No rush. The dead never complain* Driving the nearly deserted streets of Scottsdale, he felt no need for a siren or flashing lights.

He wondered if the circumstance of this killing was murder or self defense. In Yeshiva he had studied the Jewish concept of *din rodef,* the law of the pursuer. *If someone is pursuing another to kill him, such a person may be killed by anyone if the pursuer refuses to stop.*

Half an hour after receiving the call, Guerevich arrived at the house, which appeared to be a mansion rather than merely a residence. Entering the house through a side entrance, he followed the sound of voices to where the body of Stanfield Margason lay on the floor. The pungent odor of dried blood hung in the air like the stench of old cigarette smoke. He waved to Robert Kipinski.

Kipinski pointed to the body and waved away Tom Stone, his assistant and the forensic photographer. "Tom, y'all can get more photos after I bring Aaron up to date."

Kipinski never let anyone forget his Texas past.
Wearing his usual black Stetson hat, jeans, and boots, he responded to the name of Cowboy. He took pains to look like the stereotype of an old western lawman. His sand and gray brush of a mustache hung over his upper lip and down at the corners. As he walked toward the body, his boots left impressions in the deep pile of the carpet.

Guerevich pushed his new glasses higher on his nose and ran his right hand across thinning reddish-brown hair. "Stanfield Margason?"

"Yup. And that's exactly how we found him. Flat on his back, covered with glass and pieces of wood from the window. Four entry wounds to the upper torso. And y'all look at this. One smack over his heart."

Guerevich looked at the body in silence, thinking as always about his Torah studies at the Yeshivah, the orthodox Jewish secondary school. Touching a dead body, even being in the same room, made him religiously unclean. Being unclean would cut his soul off from Israel when the Messiah came. In his ten years with the Scottsdale Police Department, he had always been unclean, but that was one of the compromises he had made with life as a detective in the twenty-first century.

Kipinski looked up at the younger Guerevich, taller by four inches, and continued speaking. "Y'all look like you're still asleep. You get any rest at Ann's?"

"Not a lot." Guerevich could feel his ears getting warm and knew his face started to flush.

Kipinski smiled. "Don't worry about it. Still soloing?

"The bureaucracy moves slowly. Actually, working alone seems to suit me."

"That's a formula for trouble but I can't argue with you?" Kipinski pointed to the shattered window and looked back at the body. "You really think he broke into the room through that ten foot glass window."

"Maybe in desperation, Cowboy. Or high on something." Guerevich looked around the large book-lined, grey-carpeted room and smiled. "Looks like a library. Maybe we should start looking for Colonel Mustard."

"He was definitely shot. But let me know if y'all find a knife or a candlestick."

Guerevich stared at the body on the floor. He pushed his glasses above his forehead and rubbed his eyes.

He ran his right hand through his hair again, shook his head, and looked down at Kipinski, who squatted next to the body.

The dead man lay with his head toward the broken window. His legs described a reversed numeral four, with his left leg crossed over his right. His lightweight tan sport jacket lay open, exposing a white shirt covered with drying blood stains. His navy wool trousers were up around his calf, exposing alligator loafers and no socks.

Kip pointed at the body. "Them clothes ain't the type you wear for a break-in."

"How long you think he's been dead, Kip?"

"Hard to tell for sure. Three hours, maybe four. The M. E. can tell better."

"Three or four hours. Wonder why they waited so long to call?"

Kipinski stood and folded his arms over his bulky kevlar vest. His gray eyes scanned the body again, then walked to the broken window and touched the pieces of wood with his gloved hand. "The mullions make the window weak, easier to break."

"Mullions?"

"Yeah. Those wooden bars that separate the glass into those two foot by two foot sections."

"How'd you know what they were called?"

"My father did a lot of carpenter work around the ranch. I used to work with him on my time off until he

decided he wanted to retire."

"Well, it doesn't matter now. Did anyone talk to the shooter?"

"A little. Said she came down to get a book when he crashed through the window, screaming he was going to kill her, and she shot him. We were waiting for you to question her officially. She's lying down in the master bedroom, upstairs. She's pretty upset."

"Who is this 'she'?"

"The guy's wife. She said they were separated. Claimed she had a restraining order on him. That and a Czech 9 mm Luger, which we already bagged."

Guerevich looked at the photographer, still standing to one side. "Get plenty of pictures, Tom."

"We always do."

Kipinski nodded. "That way things won't get nasty later." He walked over to Tom and they spoke in quiet tones. Kipinski pointed to several places around the room.

Tom's flash went off enough times to make Guerevich see the book-filled walls of oak shelves as a strobe light show. He paced off the distance from the broken window to the bookcases, directly across the room. Several books were scattered on the floor under a space on the book shelf where they apparently had been lined up. With a gloved hand, he ran his fingers over the volumes still on the shelf as if he were looking for a specific book. Imagining he heard the crash, he quickly spun around, trying to reenact a startled woman turning and firing the Luger.

*It had to happen fast. The gun must have been in easy reach or even in her hand when he broke through. If he broke through."*

He could smell the dusty books, and wondered if they were for show or if anyone had read them. The rows of shelves reminded him of the bedroom wall in his father's house, filled with hundreds of books on Jewish biblical commentary which his father consulted constantly. Guerevich had read many of them but his father, a Talmudic scholar and teacher of history, had studied and virtually memorized every one of them.

He left the carpeted library area and walked back to the foyer. His shoes clicked on the tiles in the huge room with its twenty foot ceiling and massive chandelier.

A young uniformed officer stood in front of the ten foot entry doors. "Quite a place. My two car garage is smaller than this," he observed.

Guerevich nodded. "Doors locked?"

"Locked when we arrived."

Guerevich turned and walked toward the winding staircase. "I assume these lead to the bedrooms on the second floor?"

"Yes sir."

Guerevich motioned for the young man to follow him.

"Something you need, Detective?"

"Yeah. I'm going upstairs to question the shooter, and I need you to come with me."

"I don't think I'd be much help. This is my first homicide."

Guerevich felt like a father asking his son for assistance. "You don't have to do anything. Just be there. I'm sure at the academy you learned never to question a suspect alone. Especially a woman."

"I get your meaning, Detective."

"Name's Aaron Guerevich. What's yours?"

"McNulty. Jack McNulty."

"Glad to meet you, Jack. Well, let's get to it. The first few hours are the most important. Maybe we can get some answers and be home in time for breakfast."

# CHAPTER THREE

Guerevich and McNulty climbed the stairs side by side. Guerevich still felt a slight tug each time he raised his right leg, a constant reminder of the bullet he took in his thigh the year before in a drug shooting which had claimed the life of his long-time partner. He clamped his teeth and shook his head to dodge the memory. The ache reminded him that he was now forty-two in a career which accelerated the aging process.

"Your father happy you're a cop, McNulty?"

"Yeah, he is. He tells everyone how I finished at the top of my class. Maybe it's an Irish thing. I'm waiting to hear about my application to the motorcycle traffic division."

Guerevich smiled at the shorter, uniformed man. "My father wanted me to become a doctor or a lawyer. Ten years as a detective and he still reminds me. It's a Jewish thing."

McNulty looked puzzled. "Yeah, maybe."

On the occasions when they spoke, Guerevich's orthodox father Avram always mentioned his friends' sons and daughters. "They have careers and families, doctors, lawyers, even a rabbi." But the younger Guerevich believed the dangers of being a cop precluded having a family, although his relationship with Ann made him rethink his position regularly.

He looked to the top of the winding stairway and remembered reading about this area of Scottsdale. The few remaining houses like this one had been built by copper mining barons before 1930. From the outside, this house looked like a small hotel or a bed and breakfast. It reminded him of one of the old North Shore mansions along the Lake

Michigan in Evanston, not far from where he had grown up in Chicago. Things change. The synagogue on Sedgwick Street where he had celebrated his Bar Mitzvah had become a Baptist Church, yet it still had the Hebrew inscription of Deuteronomy 6:4 in the white stone arch over the doorway.

"This stairway is right out of Tara," Guerevich noted as his feet sank silently into the deep-pile carpet at the top of the stairs.

"What's Tara?"

"It's a mansion. From a novel, *Gone With the Wind,* about the South during the Civil War."

"I never read that one. My folks have the DVD of the movie."

"Yeah. A bit dated, but a great movie."

They paused at the top of the stairs and looked down a long hall. They could see eight doorways, all with closed doors.

"Probably eight bedrooms," said McNulty.

The last doorway, the only one with a double door, had a uniformed officer posted outside. Guerevich and McNulty walked down the hall toward him.

McNulty waved to the guard. "Hey, Don. Detective Guerevich is here to interview the shooter."

The guard took a step forward. "What're you doing here, Jack? Who's at the front door?"

"It's secure. He asked me to be the observer when he questions her."

Guerevich approached the door and knocked.

"Who is it?" came a weak reply.

"Detective Aaron Guerevich and Officer Jack McNulty, Scottsdale police. May we come in? We need to ask you a few questions."

"Oh, yes. Of course. Please."

Guerevich pushed opened one of the heavy doors and walked into a bedroom as large as his condo.  Thirty feet ahead of him, the floor-to-ceiling windows flanked French doors which led to a deck.  Beyond the deck he saw heavily wooded grounds, the edge of the guest parking lot, and the pond.  In the early light of dawn, glowing purple/gold above the horizon, the sky and the silhouette of the evergreens reflected in the water.   Although it was late October, there were no golden-leafed maples of his Chicago childhood, no red-tipped oak leaves to warn of approaching winter.

Dwarfed by the room, the California King bed with four posts and a canopy, occupied a small space in the center of the right-hand wall.  The woman lying with her legs crossed on top of the duvet wore red and gold silk pajamas, her feet covered in matching open-toed slippers.  Long flaming red hair spread across the pillow and her arm lay across her forehead. Her light olive complexion told Guerevich her red hair came from a salon.  She raised her head, watched him for a moment, and then sat up in bed and extended her hand, fingernails painted to match her outfit.  He walked to her and took her limp hand in his.  Her right hand felt cool, and she placed her left hand on top of his.  The unmistakable strong scent of gardenias tickled his nose.  Guerevich marveled she could look so placid a few hours after shooting her husband.  Like Delilah after she had ensnared Samson.

"I'm Mrs. Stanfield Margason," she whispered in a hushed, heavy voice.  "But please call me Cathy."

Guerevich nodded. "Thanks for seeing us."

"Oh, please.  No need to be apologetic.  I'll tell you everything I can. You may sit at the writing table."   She pointed to a small chair and mahogany pedestal table with three flared legs about twenty feet from the bed.

Guerevich looked from the table to the bed. "Would you mind if I bring the chair closer to the bed. That way. . ."

"Of course. I wasn't thinking."

"Let me get it." Officer McNulty picked up the chair and carried it to the side of the bed. When Guerevich sat, McNulty stood slightly behind and a few feet to his left.

Guerevich crossed his legs and noticed a small food stain on his right pant leg from the vegetarian pizza he had eaten the night before. He picked at it with his fingernail, and then looked at the woman on the bed. Using a technique designed to make people being interrogated more comfortable, he reached up to loosen his tie, but remembered he wasn't wearing one. He took a small note pad from the inside pocket of his jacket.

"You do have the right to have an attorney if you want one."

"Do you think it's necessary?"

"That has to be your decision."

"I don't think I'll need one. I have nothing to hide."

Guerevich noted Mrs. Margason declined an attorney. "Can you tell me exactly what you remember?"

"Well, I wasn't able to sleep. Sometimes when I have a touch of insomnia, I go to the kitchen to get a glass of warm milk. They say it helps - you know, the tryptophan. Then I decided to read for a while and went to the library to select a book. That's when I heard the crash. When I turned around, Stan was on his hands and knees there, in front of the broken window, covered with glass. I guess he must have been dazed. After a moment he got to his feet and started coming toward me, shouting he was going to kill me. That's when I shot him. Three times."

"Do you normally carry a gun when you get a book to read?"

"Oh, no. The gun has always been kept on the bookshelf, hidden behind the signed first editions of Dean Koontz. I knocked down some of the books getting the gun. After I shot him, I became so upset I didn't know what to do. Once I calmed down, I called the police."

"How long did it take you to calm down?"

"I don't remember. It may have been an hour or two."

"You dialed the full number for the police? Why not 9-1-1? Or an ambulance?"

Cathy adjusted her position in the bed. As she sat up straighter, the top of her silk pajamas slipped, revealing her cleavage. She smiled and made no attempt to pull up the top.

"There was no need. Those are for emergencies when someone is injured and needs help. I knew he was dead."

"How could you tell?"

"I placed as an alternate in pistol for the American squad at the Pan-American Games." She raised her right hand and pretended to shoot. "He lay there and didn't move."

"So he threatened to kill you? Can you tell me exactly what he said?"

"He didn't just say it. He shouted." She paused and sighed. "I don't remember his exact words. He called me some vile names and came toward me shouting 'I'm going to kill you.'

"Did he have any reason to threaten you?"

"He's changed ever since he started hanging around with a Las Vegas crowd. We were separated. I planned to file for divorce because of his recent violence toward me. He knew he'd have only his trust allowance until he could collect his full inheritance.. We've been living on that and my trust for the past few years."

"Your trust?"

"Yes. My maiden name is Willock. Of the California Willocks." She stopped, as if waiting for some sign of recognition.

Guerevich wrote something and waited for her to continue.

"The California department store chain. You know, Willocks, the May Company, Macy's."

"Oh, of course."

"Until Daddy sold out and retired."

"And his selling out upset you?"

"Oh, no. Before he died, Daddy set up my trust fund and bought me this house and remodeled it. I have more than enough money. I think that's why Stan married me."

"You're quite a bit younger than your husband."

"Yes. I was only twenty-two when we married."

She stopped abruptly, reached for a tissue from the box at her side and dabbed her eyes.

Guerevich continued. "Sometimes unfortunate things happen. You mentioned Mr. Margason's inheritance."

"Stan's father made a lot of money in oil with the Gettys in California. He wanted Stan to earn his own way, so he set up the bulk of the inheritance with two conditions. Stan couldn't touch the money until he turned forty-five. The other condition was Stan had to become a successful businessman in his own endeavor. Stan turns forty-five, sorry, would have turned forty-five next year, so he faced a lot of pressure. He really hadn't done much with his life."

"I see. So his lack of success troubled him?"

"I didn't think so at first. Then about a year ago he started to change. He started going to Las Vegas and staying for weeks at a time."

"Did he tell you why?"

"He said he had a project, a business deal. He was trying to buy a small casino using the inheritance he planned to collect, although he wouldn't get any money for almost a year. That way he hoped to show the trustees of his father's estate he was a successful businessman." She dabbed her eyes with the tissue again.

"I can understand. How much did he hope to inherit?"

"About five hundred million dollars." She paused as if waiting to let the amount sink in. "That is if he can. I mean if he had been able to show he had a successful career."

"That's quite a lot of money."

"Yes, it is. But then he started acting like a spoiled child. He turned mean. One time I went with him to a business dinner. In the restaurant with a few of his Las Vegas friends, everyone started drinking and the conversation about women turned crude. They all spoke with accents. Mexican, I think. Or Italian. They started talking about which women's physical attributes were most appealing to each of them, as if I weren't there." She covered her face with her hands and shook her head. "I didn't like the conversation, so I got up to leave. He grabbed my wrist and forced me back into my seat. He shouted I could leave when he told me I could and they all laughed."

"That must have been very unpleasant."

"It was. When we got home, we had an argument and he raised his hand to slap me. I told him to get out. That's when I got the restraining order. About two months ago."

"I see. Back to this incident, was anyone else here when the shooting occurred?"

"No, I was home alone."

"Well, you've been very helpful." Guerevich stood. "Thanks for talking to me under such difficult circumstances. I don't have any more questions for now, but I would like one of the forensic techs to come up and do a GSR test, if you don't mind."

"I don't mind at all. I know about gunshot residue tests from TV. When you fire a gun, small particles from the explosion are deposited to your hands and clothes."

"Exactly."

The bedroom door opened and the guard let in a woman with a briefcase. The tech took a piece of adhesive tape, pressed it to Cathy's hand and fingers, and attached it to a small, square plastic plate which she placed in an evidence envelope.

The tech smiled at Cathy. "Thanks, Mrs. Margason. We'll also need the clothes you were wearing when you shot Mr. Margason."

Kathy looked up at Guerevich. "Well, anything I can do to help. It's so awful. I - I feel so strange." She took a deep breath.

"Strange?"

"All mixed up inside. I feel a little satisfied he's gone. But sad and sick, too. As a child, I saw a mean dog in the neighborhood get hit by a car. It's the same kind of feeling."

"You'll have to come down to the station to complete the processing."

"I don't understand. I've told you everything. I admitted I shot Stan. What more do you want?"

"You need to be processed and fingerprinted and there's a lot of paperwork to be completed. It's standard procedure."

Her lips hardened into a slight pout, and her smile disappeared. She swung her feet over the side of the bed and stood up glaring silently at Guerevich, her arms folded across her chest, the top of her head even with his neck.

"In that case," she clipped her words, "I will call my attorney. Now, I need to get dressed. Will you leave the room, or do you want to watch me?"

She marched slowly toward the dressing room as Guerevich and McNulty walked toward the bedroom doors.

"You sure went easy on her," whispered McNulty.

"I got the information I wanted. You often get information from people by listening to what they say and hearing what they don't say." Then he turned to Mrs. Margason. "Have him meet us at the booking."

She stopped, her hand on the doorknob, turned her head back toward Guerevich, and spoke slowly through pursed lips. "My attorney is a woman. I'm sure you'll enjoy meeting her."

The two men left Cathy Margason's bedroom and walked down the hall to the stairs, their feet again leaving impressions on the deep pile carpet.

"I don't know what help her attorney will be, even if she is a woman." McNulty smiled as he and Guerevich walked down the stairs. "She confessed to shooting him."

"She only admitted she shot him in self defense. It's not quite the same thing as a confession. Anyway, thanks for your assistance."

"No thanks needed, Detective. Besides, this gives me a chance to learn hands on, something they can't teach

at the academy."

"Thanks again. There are times when questioning someone can get messy without a partner."

"But why are you working alone? I thought it's against department policy."

"Long story.   The short version is my partner got killed in a drug shootout last year.  I haven't found anyone I feel comfortable with yet.   Or who feels comfortable with me."

# CHAPTER FOUR

When they reached the bottom of the stairs, McNulty went back to his posted area near the front door and Guerevich returned to the library. Tom Stone had stopped photographing as the medical examiner bent over the body. Robert Kipinski, Cowboy, sat at a small library reading table a few feet from the body. Next to him on the floor a partitioned metal briefcase held hand-marked evidence envelopes in every slot. Cowboy took perfection to a high level. His thoroughness had become legend and his testimony at trials was usually unimpeachable.

Guerevich walked to where the body of Stanfield Margason still held the center of attention and stopped next to Cowboy. "Hey, Kip, looks like you're going to run out of evidence envelopes."

"Maybe. You can never collect enough evidence. Some lawyer will always try to come up with one minor bit he thinks we should have collected but didn't." Cowboy put down his pen and looked up. "What'd she say?"

"I got her admission, but I think it's bogus." Guerevich dragged over a chair and sat across from his friend.

"I suppose she said that he broke through the window threatening to kill her."

"Yeah. And she made a point of telling me her lawyer's a woman."

"What difference does that make? Man or woman, I've got the evidence and it doesn't change."

"What's your opinion?"

"I can't make a final analysis until I've examined all of it, but for my money, I agree with you. She's lying. Her story has a bigger hole than the window. Unfortunately, we did find his shoe prints outside the window."

"And the dirt on his shoes?"

"Also matches, but the position of the prints is all wrong."

"What do you mean?"

"A guy goes to break through a window, his feet would be turned so his shoulder breaks through first. His prints show he walked up to the window. You'd expect him to take a little run." Kipinski rose and waved his hand in the direction of the broken window, as if he were pushing it away. "Look at all the glass on top of his body. There's no way he crashed through in the middle of the night. Coincidentally, just as his estranged wife comes down to get a book, knowing the gun was behind it." He walked the few feet to the body, looked down at it, and shook his head, his jaw muscles twitching, his mustache bobbing up and down.

"For the sake of argument, let's say he stood outside and when he saw her through the window. . ."

"He just lost it?" Kipinski cut him off. "He put his head down, and dived through. I mean, here's a guy who probably never did anything physical in his life. He's a bit on the thin side. A wimp with freshly manicured fingernails, the resort type. You believe he's the kind of man who'd bull his way through a window? No way." Cowboy walked around the body, pushed his hat back on his head, and pointed to the body again. "All that glass on top of him tells a different story."

Guerevich paused and looked at the body again. Oscar Plant, the Medical Examiner, walked into the room. He bent down to take the body temperature. Brushing away a few fragments of glass with a gloved hand, he opened the dead man's shirt enough to push in the stem of what looked like a large meat thermometer.

"Based on his liver temperature," Plant asserted, "he's been dead about four hours. The autopsy'll tell us more about exactly what killed him."

"He bled out," countered Guerevich. "Didn't that do it?"

"Probably. Four shots and enough blood here to suggest he did. I won't know conclusively without more tests. Take a look."

Oscar Plant kneeled down and opened back the dead man's jacket to show the wounds. Using a pencil, he pointed to each blood stain. "You can see where the bullets entered. One entered here, to the upper right chest, just below the collar bone. One just below the rib cage, also on the right. And one went into his abdomen, just above the belt line. One bullet looks like it could have pierced his heart."

"Four? She told me she shot him only three times. Can you pinpoint the trajectories?" asked Guerevich.

"Maybe, once I get him in the lab." The Medical Examiner stood up again. As he walked through the doorway, he poked his thumb over his shoulder, pointing toward the body. "He'll let me know everything. The dead

always have stories to tell."

Cowboy and Guerevich were left alone with the body,

"Well, Aaron, no one in his right mind is going to believe her story."

"Probably not. You know it doesn't matter what anyone would believe. Especially when he threatened her and she had a court order of protection to keep him away."

"She didn't need any court order. She had her protection in her hand. Tell me, when did an order of protection prevent a man from injuring or even killing his wife?"

The Medical Examiner returned to the room with two assistants, one of whom removed Margason's personal items from his pockets and put them into a large clear plastic bag. "You ready for us to bag him, Cowboy? You need anything else before we do?"

"Not from me. You think of anything, Aaron?"

Guerevich shook his head.

"Well, we'll get him over to autopsy." Plant motioned to the men waiting in the doorway. "Okay, guys." He turned to Guerevich. "You want the personal effects now or later?" Without waiting for an answer, he handed Kipinski the bag with Margason's wallet, keys, money, and a folded envelope.

Guerevich looked again at the prone form of Stanfield Margason, covered in glass shards, his face now a cold blue-gray. The two men in white jump suits with the words Medical Examiner's Office stenciled on their backs bent down and rolled the body into a large black bag. After they zipped it closed, they placed the bag on the lowered pop-up stretcher, raised it, and wheeled the dead man out of the room, with Plant leading the way. The photographer put his camera into a large bag and left the room as well.

Guerevich and Kipinski looked at the space vacated by the body. It seemed to be outlined in broken glass, the way a stencil blocks paint spray around a cutout, leaving the center relatively clear and allowing the shape of the cutout to remain.

"There you are, Aaron. A guy comes crashing through a ten foot window and gets shot, he doesn't clear a space to fall."

"You don't have to convince me, Kip."

Kipinski continued as if Guerevich had said nothing. "It gets worse. There should have been some serious cuts on his head and hands."

"Defensive wounds?" Guerevich, put his hands up in front of his face.

"Absolutely. Even if he'd been drinking. It's an instinctive reaction, like blinking. That is if he's alive when he goes through the window."

"You're not saying someone threw him through the window after he was dead? You know what strength it would take to throw a hundred and fifty pound man through a window? And dead weight at that."

"Dead weight is right," agreed Kipinski. "No, that's not what I'm saying. But even dead he'd show scrapes and have glass stuck in his clothes. No, he was shot before the window was broken."

"We'll have to wait for the M. E.'s report before we can make any definitive conclusions. And with five hundred million at stake, no one's going anywhere."

Guerevich walked to the broken window and looked at it again. Then he turned and walked toward the back door through which he had entered.

Cowboy closed up his evidence briefcase and followed him. " Go get some sleep. You look pretty bad."

"I'm getting too old to get by on three hours any more. Maybe I can catch Ann for breakfast. Did you recover any of the bullets?"

"We found two outside. The guys used our new state of the art metal detector. They found one buried in the dirt and one in a tree."

"That's two. There were four entry wounds."

Kipinski walked to the space where the body had lain. He brushed away some shards of glass. "Hey, look at this. Here's one of the bullets. It's in the floor. It must have been under the body."

"Can you pry it out?"

"Yep. One of those shots had to come from directly above him. It was probably the shot to the middle of his chest."

"She shot him after he was dead?"

"Maybe he was still alive when she fired. Plant'll be able to tell."

Guerevich shook his head and whistled. "This case gets stranger by the minute. Let me see his personal effects."

Kipinski handed Guerevich the evidence envelope. Inside were the wallet with three hundred seventy-two dollars in bills, the keys, some change, and two envelopes folded in half.

"We got the folded envelopes from the right back pocket of his pants."

Guerevich opened the first envelope, which contained a hand-written note on paper with the letterhead of a Las Vegas attorney. The note confirmed a meeting in two weeks explaining it would take that long to get all the paperwork together and the task would be expensive.

Guerevich handed the note to Kipinski. "Doesn't say what paperwork or how expensive, but lawyers don't work cheap. I'm sure Margason knew. Probably had something to do with the casino purchase his wife told me about."

Guerevich stood quietly for a moment trying to visualize Cathy Margason standing above the body, aiming directly over his heart, and pulling the trigger on the semiautomatic Luger. Given the domestic cases he had worked on, he experienced no surprise a woman could kill a man with whom she had been intimate. Some people take their anger out on inanimate objects, like a wife scissoring her adulterous husband's clothes. But there are those who take a more direct approach. And Cathy Margason, nee Willock, fell in the latter category.

"This other envelope has something that's odd. Seven crisp new hundred dollar bills with consecutive serial numbers."

"Why would he have the new bills in an envelope and not with his other money?"

"That's something we'll have to find out."

"Maybe Ann can lift some prints from the envelopes when she gets them at the lab."

He waved goodbye to the posted guards and headed to his car. Driving back to Ann's, he fought sleepiness and thought about the money and the letter in the envelopes.

He walked quietly into Ann's, removed his jacket and shoes, and fell asleep on the sofa. His mind became a movie screen filled with the sight of Stanfield Margason lying dead on the floor. In a fitful dream-scene awash in red and black, Margason rose from the floor and floated toward him, pointing to his wounds, like the ghost of Macbeth's father.

# CHAPTER FIVE

Light streamed through the blinds when Guerevich woke to the smell of eggs frying. He rubbed his eyes and sat up. Then he looked at Ann in the kitchen.

She smiled at him. "Looks like you had a bad night. Or should I say early morning. You were tossing and mumbling something when I walked by earlier. Why'd you sleep on the sofa?"

"Didn't want to wake you." He moved his head from side to side to eliminate the stiffness. "Strange case. Stanfield Margason's wife shot and killed him."

"The name sounds familiar. Who was he?"

"One of the really idle rich. He had about five hundred million, only he couldn't touch it."

"Couldn't touch it? Then why'd she shoot him?"

"He and his wife were separated. She claimed self defense." Guerevich got up and walked to the bathroom. As he emerged drying his hands, Ann slid the fried eggs onto a plate and set it on the table.

"That should make it easy," she said as she put a plate with two toasted bagels on the table. "Why don't you have breakfast and then get some sleep. You're no good to

anybody as tired as you look."

"Depends on what you have in mind. You're pretty sexy in your work clothes."

Ann pulled the dish towel from her shoulder and threw it at him. Her work clothes consisted of a large pink sweat shirt with a smiling dog stenciled on the front, a pair of loose fitting jeans, and a knock-off version of Reeboks.

After pouring herself a cup of coffee, she walked to the table, sat down and buttered half of a toasted bagel.

Guerevich sipped his coffee and put his cup down. "You just having toast and coffee?"

"I'll get something at the lab. Maybe a boiled head or a finger."

"Very funny. Speaking of funny, there was something strange about her admission. She said he crashed in through a large window although the evidence tells us that wasn't possible. And she waited three hours to call after she shot him. And when I questioned her, she freely admitted the shooting."

Ann picked up her coffee and held it. "So he didn't come in through the window. How'd he get in? I know. She invited him and he came to the house so she could shoot him."

He put the last of the egg in his mouth and went to the coffee table to retrieve his notebook. Then he sat at the table again and flipped through several pages. "She had a restraining order."

"Maybe she called him to patch things up."

"Right. Then when he gets there, she shoots him, breaks the window, and claims he crashed in through it."

"It is a bit strange."

"It gets stranger. We also found new hundred dollar bills in an envelope in his pocket along with a letter from an attorney relating to the purchase of a casino in Las Vegas. You'll see everything when you get to the lab. See if you can lift some prints from the envelope."

"Sounds like you've got a real puzzle, but I'll see what I can do." Ann walked into the bedroom, returned with a jacket, and started toward the front door.

"Going in early?"

"I'm not scheduled 'til noon, but I've got some errands to run before I get to work."

After she left, he walked into the kitchen to get another cup of coffee. The unmistakable aroma of meat cooking enticed him to look into the crock pot on the counter. A large roast covered by small potatoes, carrots, and celery was starting to simmer.

*"Looks like a stew. That's something I know I can eat.* He recalled at least one host's discomfiture at a dinner where he ate only the salad and vegetables because the entree had been a pork roast.

As he got ready to leave, the phone rang and he let the machine record the call. A man's voice spoke in a robotic monotone, "Tell Detective Guerevich it was self-defense. No need to dig any deeper."

He stared at the machine, as if he expected more, but the whirr and click told him the message had ended. He immediately dialed star 69 and got the callback number. He called the station and had Danny Sanchez check. The call had come from a pay phone at the Sky Harbor Airport in Phoenix. He locked Ann's door and walked to his car, thinking about Margason and the phone call.

He wondered how the caller knew Ann was working on the case. In fact, she hadn't been assigned to it yet. The speaker didn't address her directly but had to know she would give him the message.

Driving to work, he thought about Cathy Margason. *She plays cool, but is a bit naive if she believed her order of protection would get her case dropped or get her a suspended sentence if it ever gets to court.* Guerevich knew her lawyer would tote out a complete bag of tricks because money was involved. But other people had to be involved in Margason's death, and Guerevich was determined to find out who.

At his office, he did an internet search into the Margason investments and learned that George Ginderer was Stanfield Margason's financial advisor and the trustee of the estate. He decided a visit to Ginderer might give some background to Margason's finances, but that would have to wait until there was an evidence plan for the murder.

At eleven fifteen, Guerevich's desk phone rang.

"I just walked into the lab and I saw all the evidence bags." Ann's voice had an edge. "Is all this stuff piled on my desk from the Margason case?"

"And hello to you, too. It is if it's marked *Margason*. By the way, thanks for breakfast. I only wish you could have stayed."

"Then I would have been late for work."

Guerevich smiled. "I want to meet with the trustee of Margason's estate as soon as you have something for me. Let me know when you do."

"I have a couple of other case files on the fire ahead of this one. You think I sit around all day waiting for your work?"

"Seems like this one has a pretty high priority."

"Your case will be handled just like all the others, in the order it came in." Her statement continued its unmistakably irked tone. "However," she continued, more calmly, "if you can clear it with Escobedo and Robby, this one might go to the head of the line. Then I can give you my full attention."

"I love your full attention. Thanks again for breakfast. Why don't you come to my place for dinner. It's the least I can do." He thought about the roast in the crock pot.

"Least you can do is right. You're not going to make mac and cheese with cream of mushroom soup again, are you?"

"It's a healthy vegetarian meal."

"Call it whatever you want. It comes from a box and a can, so I'll pass. Come back to my place tonight. Before I made your breakfast, I put a roast in the crock pot. I'm sure you knew. It should be perfect by six. And if you want horseradish sauce, pick some up on your way over."

"So that's what smelled so good. If you call Escobedo, she'll clear your work load and I'll see you tonight."

One of the office clerks put a copy of Cathy Margason's sworn statement on Guerevich's desk. "She came in with her attorney, Judith Westerly, about 9:30 and signed it in front of Captain Escobedo."

"You know Westerly?"

"Only by her reputation as an activist lawyer. She smiled a lot but didn't say much."

Guerevich had never met Westerly, but he also knew her reputation as a hardheaded women's rights activist. "Just what I need. Turn this case into a battered-woman, self-defense battle."

He leaned over his desk and read the statement, which differed from what she had told him the night before. The statement now affirmed she had fired all four shots. She admitted she had first told Guerevich there were only three, but after she had thought about it, she said she clearly remembered four.

She had been arraigned, had surrendered her passport to the court, and had been released to the custody of her attorney after posting ten percent of a $250,000 bond.

That night, after dinner, Guerevich stretched out in the recliner he had bought for Ann's apartment. Six months earlier, when he suggested she ought to have a recliner, she had told him if he wanted one, he'd better buy one. He did, and paid extra to get fabric that matched her decor.

Ann cleared the dishes from the table and placed them in the sink. "Did you hear that message? I heard it when I got home. What the hell's going on? How'd they know? I didn't even know I had the case until today. Why didn't they just call you? Dammit, I don't like this mystery shit."

Ann's rapid-fire questions made Guerevich understand the message had unsettled her. She still wanted to believe these things just didn't happen in Scottsdale. He wanted to pursue the subject, but didn't know what to say without sounding condescending or trivial. Instead he asked if she needed help cleaning up.

"Not your kind. There's only room for one here if we're going to get any dishes done. Stay in your recliner and talk to me." She forced a smile. The last time he had helped her clean the small kitchen, they had started fooling around and didn't clean up until the next morning.

He removed his shoes, put his hands behind his head, and leaned back. "Did you go over the Margason file?" He hoped to shift her mind from the call to her research.

"Margason's bio and profile are in the folder. What the hell's with these people?" Her yellow rubber gloves squeaked against the glasses as she put them in the dishwasher. "They have more money than Gates and they have to kill someone? I don't get it."

"Neither do I. Guerevich laughed. "Maybe inherited wealth means never having to say thank you. But that kind of money usually means problems." As he opened the folder, Guerevich was silently thankful he had grown up in a strict religious environment. From the time he was old enough to remember, he had been required to earn the things he wanted, which caused him to appreciate everything he had.

He read through Margason's bio. The man had grown up in wealth and luxury. For all his life, his wants had been satisfied. His mother had died in an accident just after he turned ten, and his father had left him in the care of housekeepers. He wrecked his first car, a Corvette, when he was sixteen, escaping with a broken arm and collarbone and a few bruised ribs. He wrecked his second car, a Mustang, a few weeks before his seventeenth birthday when he drove off the highway into a cotton field at night in Maricopa. In both accidents he was charged with reckless driving, but not DUI. His high school grades were mediocre. Guerevich saw the pattern. Margason's father, Philip, traveled much of the time and guilt caused him to indulge his son with everything the young man wanted.

"Have you read this bio?"

"I did. And with the kind of money his father had, no one would have dared to tell young Stanfield there were things he couldn't have."

Guerevich's study of psychology in college taught him that this kind of childhood led to overconfidence while it masked feelings of anxiety and powerlessness. Young Margason grew to manhood in the shadow of his father, developed a dependent personality, and dropped out of several colleges. Clearly, he had trouble accomplishing anything, because at age forty-four, he had never managed to get a job or have a career.

Guerevich had read several articles about people growing up in great wealth with absentee fathers. Like Margason, none had any direction in their lives. In an interview printed in a popular psychology magazine, one young man who had inherited great wealth said he had no reason to get out of bed each day. When the interviewer asked why, the man responded, "What's the point?"

He put the folder down and shook his head in disbelief. "What a wasted life. All he accomplished was to get himself murdered."

"I thought you said his wife claimed self defense. I mean, she asserted he broke into the house threatening to kill her and she shot him. He owned the gun, and the tox report indicated he'd had some wine. He'd also eaten less than an hour or so before she shot him."

"So she invites him for dinner and then shoots him. Talk about the spider and the fly." She finished loading the dishwasher and stood up.

"Well the report indicated his shoes matched the impressions in front of the window. The dirt on them matched as well. The only fingerprints we could lift from the envelope were Margason's. No DNA from the glue. We processed some prints from the books on the floor through the Integrated AFIS. Some were Cathy Margason's, which we expected. We got a hit on another one, George Ginderer, Margason's financial consultant. We only got some smudged prints on the bills."

"Margason didn't have a weapon. No knife, no gun. I'm sure his wife shot him, but I'm not convinced she did it alone. She's not hardened enough. I think someone else either helped or did it."

"What makes you think that?" Ann scrubbed the heavy, brown glass liner of the crock pot and placed it in a dish drainer to the side of the sink.

"The divergent shot pattern." Guerevich closed his eyes and made a gun with his fingers, aiming at the ceiling. "She said she hit him three times, and then changed her story. We know there were six shots fired, because six rounds were missing from the magazine. We found two outside. She claimed to be an expert with a pistol, but this wasn't target shooting.   When you fire fast at someone attacking you, you don't take time to aim, yet four shots hit him and two missed.   She hit him once in the upper right shoulder, once just below the rib cage, and once in the abdomen, and declared she knew he was dead after she shot him in the chest."

"Maybe she looked after he fell on the floor."

"Could be.   But someone else could have fired the gun and then handed it to her, like the Hoffman case, where the woman's boyfriend killed her ex for the insurance money and gave her the gun to get her prints on it."

"What do you think happened?"

"If someone else fired three shots into Margason and gave Cathy the gun so her prints would be on it, she must have shot him as he lay there, just to get GSR on her hands. The bullet that pierced Margason's heart penetrated the floor. That had to be the fourth shot.   Maybe she didn't remember because she didn't pull the trigger four times."

"He seemed to be worth more to her alive. It's not my area, but what's her motive?" Ann removed her gloves and wiped her hands on a towel before walking into the living room.

"That's what I have to find out.   Maybe there are five hundred million motives.   In an odd reversal, you're right. He'd be worth more to her alive than dead."

He yawned and stretched, then asked her to research all three people.  "I especially want to know more about the former Cathy Willock and George Ginderer.

Ann promised to see what she could dig up on them. "I also plan to check Cathy's phone records for the previous two months.  She sat on the arm of the sofa to explain part of the Medical Examiner's report.  "The bullet that caught him in the upper right shoulder traveled down through his lung, and lodged near the third dorsal vertebra. We recovered the other two from his body. The bullet recovered from the dirt had microscopic glass fragments along with dirt and organic material. You dug one from the floor. Do you want the rest of the report?" She slid onto the sofa, slipped off her shoes, and put her feet up.

"Only what I need to know," responded Guerevich. He moved to the sofa and reached over to rub her leg.

"Well, the GRS report indicates she definitely fired the gun. Her prints were on it. There were particles of gunshot residue taken from her right hand consistent with the Luger and primer residue from her left." She leaned back and covered her eyes with her arm.

Guerevich put her feet in his lap. "Other things can give similar results, can't they?"

"I've read some types of fertilizer can. And without the electron microscope to verify the findings, we can't be positive. We really need that scope. If we send the work out to San Diego, any decent lawyer would be sure to question the findings and try to convince a jury she might have been out doing yard work. And with her money, she'll have the best lawyers money can buy,"

"Like she got out there with her Mexican landscapers and messed up her hundred dollar manicure digging in the dirt. Without gloves."

"What's the difference. She did admit she shot him." Ann pulled her feet up under her and sat up. "And here's an odd piece for your puzzle. According to the M. E., the bullet that killed him was probably the one to his heart."

"What do you mean?"

"I mean he lay there bleeding to death, but he might not have been dead when the bullet pierced his heart. And it came from very close range, not more than a foot according to the powder residue on his clothes."

"That means if she fired the heart shot, she's the one who killed him."

"Technically, yes."

Guerevich moved closer to her on the sofa. She turned and leaned her head on his shoulder. "I'm really tired. What're you doing tomorrow?"

"I'm going to *Shabbat* morning prayer service at Beth Joseph synagogue. Schneider called me. They're having a hard time rounding up ten men for a prayer *minyon* nowadays."

"The youngest man at Beth Joseph is 75, but those old men still won't count me because I'm a woman. At least I'm counted at the reform services."

"I feel comfortable at orthodox prayer services. I just can't get used to the violin and piano at the reform synagogue."

"But you're willing to eat in restaurants and buy meat at Safeway. When are you going to put both your feet on the same side of the fence?"

"I don't want to argue about it. It's what I grew up with. Do you want to come with me?"

"What, and sit in the back behind a *mechitza* curtain? No thanks. When I go to temple, I want to be able to hold the the Torah like a human being, a full member of the congregation. Some of those men are such hypocrites. You can smell the bacon on their breath." Her tone had the icy edge of anger. She moved to the far end of the sofa, her arms crossed.

Guerevich sat up and looked at her. "Okay, okay, I get it. But there's another reason I want to go. Those men might be old, but they remember the past. The fact is David Schneider owned a big department store in Phoenix until he sold out to Sears and retired. He might be able to give me some background on the Willocks or the Margasons."

"That's a long shot. You think their minds still work?" She put her feet back in his lap. He began to massage them.

"Those guys still tell stories about the old days, when the downtown drew crowds to shop. Before the malls killed them."

"I'll take the malls, thanks. They're cleaner and you can park. Why don't you make some coffee. I could use a cup."

Guerevich gently pushed her feet from his lap and got up. After he started the coffee, he walked back to the living room and smiled. The smell of brewing coffee trailed after him. She crinkled her mouth into a half smile. "You staying tonight?"

"Tigers couldn't drive me away." He smiled. "Lions maybe, but not tigers."

He sat next to her on the sofa again. She scooted toward him until she seated herself on his lap. Tenderly, he kissed her shoulder. Then he slid his lips up her neck to her ear, as his hand slid under her blouse to touch the warm skin of her back. He slipped his hand under her bra strap. She sat up and reached behind her, her arms like butterfly wings, undid the clasp, and then melted back into his arms. With one arm, he cradled her, his other hand moving slowly up and down her now unobstructed back. She put her head on his shoulder, her face nestled in the warmth of his neck. With his other hand, he found the softness of her breast, running his thumb slowly back and forth over her erect nipple.

She stood and took his hand in hers. "C'mon, the coffee'll wait," she asserted, and led him into the bedroom.

The problems of the murder, the five hundred million dollar motive, the bullet in the heart, and the hundred dollar bills melted away like a block of ice in the Phoenix August.

The stream of water ran to a small corner of his mind, forming a puddle to be toweled up another day.

# CHAPTER SIX

The next morning, Guerevich woke early. The dresser clock glowed 5:45. For a few minutes, he lay motionless with his eyes closed. Although it was the Sabbath and he planned to go to the synagogue, he could not free his mind from the questions floating around in his head. Why had Margason's wife waited three hours before calling the police? And why did she call the police and not 9 1 1? Why was Margason shot through the chest at such close range that the bullet went through his heart and into the floor? Even alive, he couldn't have touched the five hundred million for almost a year. How could Cathy or Ginderer or anyone else profit from Margason's death? Guerevich wanted answers to pin to the bulletin board he had formed in his mind. Even after many years in law enforcement, he still had difficulty understanding money as a motive important enough to cut off a man's life, given the dark chasm of what lay beyond an already short span.

He eased quietly out of bed and stood for a moment in his pajama shorts and tee shirt looking at Ann as she slept. As he stood next to the bed, Ann opened her eyes, smiled, and closed her eyes again. Her relaxed face showed none of the daily stress-lines she hated so much.

After he showered and shaved, he found a relatively wrinkle-free white dress shirt and tan dockers. As he sat on the side of the bed to tie his shoes, Ann turned toward him, her face partially buried in the blankets.

"I don't know why you go to synagogue to pray. I'm not even sure you believe in God."

"That doesn't matter. We don't pray to God to ask for something. We *daven*, which is praying, yet not praying in the usual sense. Even the origin of the word is lost in antiquity. We give praise and thanks for what we have." He looked into her eyes and touched her face. "And I am thankful for what I have."

"So am I. I'll see you when you get back." She closed her eyes and rolled to her side with her back to him.

He walked to his car in the parking area, drove to Beth Joseph Orthodox Synagogue on Bethany Home Road, and parked on East Rovey Avenue, about three blocks away. Under his arm he carried his blue velour bag with his prayer shawl and yarmulke inside. Walking to the synagogue, he tried to shed the week's events, which weighed heavily on his mind.

As he entered the building, Harry Schneider walked up to him to shake hands. "Shalom, Aaron. Good to see you. You make nine but with the Torah we have a minyon."

Guerevich shook Schneider's hand, looking down at the older man whose slightly bowed body barely came up to Guerevich's shoulder. The mottled, wrinkled arm the man proffered was a stark contrast with his own muscled forearm. "Good to see you too, Harry. How's the hip?"

"Can't complain. It hurts when I do. It also hurts

when I don't." Harry smiled at his little joke.

As they walked down the short hall to the sanctuary, Guerevich was struck by the smell of age in the building as if Isaac or Jacob might suddenly appear. The boards of the wooden floor had separated in places. Mustiness hung like a great chandelier, suggesting ancient ideas, beliefs Guerevich thought seemed incongruous with the twenty-first century.

The segment of the Torah, *Parashat Noach,* read for the October shabbat morning was the weekly portion in the annual cycle of Torah reading, the story of Noah, from Genesis, called *Beresheet* in the Hebrew Bible. The full portion covered the life of Noah from the time after the flood to the building of the Tower of Babel after Noah's death.

In the six verses after the flood ended, Noah planted a vinyard, drank wine, got drunk, and lay naked in his tent. Ham, his youngest son, saw his father and told his two brothers, Shem and Japheth, who took a garment, put it on their shoulders, and went in backward to cover the nakedness of their father, not wanting to see the old man in his shameful state. When Noah awoke, he discovered what his youngest son had seen. He cursed Ham, saying that Ham's son, Canaan and by extension Canaan's offspring, would forever be servants.

Guerevich knew the story, having heard and read it many times, but today as he listened to the reading, the curse had a greater impact on him than it had in the past, reminding him of the alienation between him and his own father. Although they spoke periodically, Guerevich had not seen him for several months. Guerevich thought his father considered him like Ham, a disrespectful son. Each time he spoke to his father, they disagreed. Avram expressed disappointment in both his son's life style and his occupation.

Guerevich wanted the aura of peace the Sabbath should bring, but anger kept taking bites from around the edges of his thoughts. After prayer services, he approached Harry Schneider, whose old blue serge suit, shiny at the seat and elbows, was slightly wrinkled, his white shirt open at the collar while his gray striped tie hung loose around his thin neck. From under his black fedora, white tufts of hair stuck out like gnarled fingers. He put a mottled hand on Guerevich's arm.

"*Nu*, Aaron, you still playing cops and robbers?"

"Not playing, Harry. It's pretty serious. There are people who do bad things and need to be stopped."

"Oy, it's such a different world than when I was young," Harry shook his head. "It was all I could do to make a living. Who had time for craziness. That, I read about in the papers. I see you're working on the Margason case. Such a tragedy."

"Yeah. Say, Harry, when you had your department store in Phoenix, did you know the Willocks or the Margasons?"

"Who didn't? I only met the Willocks a few times. Business things, you know. But the Margasons, they were different."

"How so?"

"Philip Margason was a true philanthropist. He gave money to everything - symphonies, museums, you name it, he could always be counted on to give. Had his name on every charity list."

As they spoke, a few other members of the congregation walked past and they exchanged greetings and *sholoms*. Guerevich and Schneider joined the group walking toward the outer doors. Outside, the brightness of the day erupted.

Guerevich put his arm on the old man's shoulder.

"Want to get a cup of coffee and a bagel?"

"Good idea. I'm ready for lunch."

They walked in silence to the small coffee shop at the corner, found a table, sat down, and ordered.

"So you and old man Margason were friends?"

"Not really. Let's say Philip and I were close acquaintances. We didn't run in the same circles. In those days there was a clear separation between Jewish and Christian social groups. He made his money in oil, with Getty as I remember."

Their coffee came and Guerevich put cream in his coffee and pushed the small container toward Schneider.

"No cream for me, thanks. I had pastrami with my eggs this morning."

Guerevich took a sip and continued the conversation. "What about his son?"

"The one who was just killed? Stanfield. What a shame. It's good his father isn't around. To tell you the truth, I was surprised. The newspaper said he beat his wife, but I found it hard to believe."

"Why?"

"He had a good heart, but the boy had no direction. He was an easy-going kid."

"Kid? He was forty-four."

Their bagels came with the non-dairy margarine. While they buttered their bagels, they continued talking.

"You're right. He was a grown man, although I haven't seen him for years. I remember when his mother died. He had to be about ten, I think. And Philip traveled a lot of the time, so Stan was raised by hired housekeepers. Good women, I'm sure, but afraid to tell him no."

"That's too bad."

"You're telling me. Once, Philip and I were at a charity luncheon and he told me he didn't know what to do about his son. He was fifteen, I think. I told him he should send Stan out to work in the oil fields, like he did. I felt it would give the boy some appreciation of what his father had accomplished. But he told me he didn't want his son grubbing in the mud. He wanted more for him."

"Did Stanfield run with a bad crowd? Did he ever have problems? You know, did he ever get in serious trouble?"

"I don't think so. He was confused. I think he was waiting for his father to acknowledge him, to treat him like one of those charities, so he never did anything really bad. Too afraid of his father. He just had too much given to him."

"It's too bad Stanfield's father couldn't do anything."

"He tried to use his money to straighten Stan out. Especially after he got a girl pregnant. He was nineteen, I think. Frank, no, Franklin they named him. After Philip's grandfather. Philip insisted the two of them get married, but that lasted only a year or so. When she left Stan, she got a good settlement. That's when Philip set up the trust for Stan."

"Which he couldn't touch until he turned forty-five."

Harry dipped part of his bagel in his coffee and took a bite. "That's right. The story didn't make the papers, but it was common knowledge. I thought it was a mistake to force the boy to wait so many years."

"What do you know about the boy, Franklin?"

"I think he lived with his mother. Until about ten years ago, when Stanfield married the young Willock girl. A real beauty, but I heard she was a little wild, spoiled. You know what I mean. Had her own money, but Philip didn't trust her. When he died, the last of the really big downtowners went."

"Thanks, Harry."

The bill came and Guerevich paid over Schneider's protests. "Harry, you've been a great help. It's the least I can do."

"Oy, sometimes I talk too much. I'm an old man, still living in the past."

"Not at all. You've been very helpful. Sometimes background information like that is important. Do you live far from here?"

"Just a couple of blocks. It's a nice day to walk."

They left the coffee shop and Harry started to walk away, then turned toward Guerevich. "Good to see you, Aaron, Say hello to your father for me."

"I will when I see him," replied Guerevich, thinking it might be a long time. Walking the three blocks back to his car, he tried to think about his father in happier times, but remembered only the aloofness, the distance between them, probably like Philip Margason and his son, Stanfield. *I'll treat any son of mine differently. I'll take him to baseball games, football games, even if the games were played on Saturday. And I'd never be too busy to pay attention to his activities.*

Guerevich decided not to take the Parkway, knowing at this time of day the traffic would be bumper-to-bumper. He took the surface streets, enjoying the more leisurely drive through the North Mountain Preserve.

He called Ann from his cell phone as he drove, telling her Margason had a son, Franklin, who had been raised by his mother until Stanfield married Cathy Willock. He asked Ann to research the young man's past to find out if he had a record, juvenile or adult.

The next morning, he walked into Ann's office and she gave him a folder marked "Franklin Margason," which contained a two page summary of the young man's life. Ann had been unable to get his complete juvenile record opened, but she had been able to secure public arrest records and a few transcripts. It didn't surprise Guerevich when he read fifteen-year-old Franklin had left his mother to live with his wealthy father and stepmother. Wealth often causes people to do things that defy logic. Franklin had graduated from high school with an unimpressive scholastic record. He had placed third in his junior year in the regional wrestling competition, but had not pursued the sport. He had lived at home for two years after high school while he attended Glendale Junior College but never completed his Associates certificate. He moved out on his own when he was twenty but never held a steady job.

As an adult, he had been arrested twice for speeding and possession of drugs, once for disorderly conduct, and once for assault in a bar. Every arrest had resulted in a fine and a suspended sentence or community service. In the bar brawl, he had punched another man hard enough to break his jaw and send him to the hospital with a concussion. Several witnesses were deposed, and all stated the injured man had started the fight. The incident never went beyond an arrest and release.

Between the lines, Guerevich saw Stanfield's money at work. The fines for speeding had been paid quickly and quietly. The drug possession charges resulted in two six-week rehab stays. The assault victim, a local plumber who had no insurance, had all his medical bills covered. The damage to the bar as a result of the fight had been repaired. Shortly after the incident, Franklin bought an interest in the bar but never really worked there. Guerevich understood Franklin's resentment, the acting out caused by Stanfield's money.

After reading the two pages, Guerevich considered how Franklin might fit into this puzzle and wondered why Cathy Margason never mentioned the young man's existence.

*If Stanfield dealt with Franklin the way his own father had dealt with him, the kid might have a strong motive to be involved.*

# CHAPTER SEVEN

On Monday, shortly before seven AM, Guerevich arrived at his desk, one of eight arranged in two equal rows of four. Stained coffee rings were partially covered by the large desk calendar which boasted its own stains and penciled notes. He spread several eight by ten photos from the Margason crime scene on top of the calendar and examined each of them with a round magnifying glass. After a few minutes he put the glass down and stared at the photo of Stanfield Margason lying on his back, his head about ten feet from the broken window, his arms spread out away from his sides. The glass shards on top of the his body confirmed the window had been broken after Margason went down, but nothing else in the photo shouted "Look at me. Here I am." Undoubtedly he had been shot and had fallen backwards, and his body had not been moved. Another photo showed the books on the floor, which suggested they could have been knocked down to retrieve a gun hidden behind them as Cathy Margason had said. The strewn books could have been staged, knocked down after the shooting. George Ginderer's fingerprints were on one of the books. The financial advisor had to be involved. Margason had been shot four times, but Cathy Margason originally stated she fired only three shots.

Guerevich returned to his earlier theory that someone else, possibly Ginderer, had fired the bullet into Margason's heart at close range from directly above him. The more Guerevich thought about it, the more logical it seemed. Only three people had a strong motive for Margason's death. One was Cathy Margason herself. The other was Franklin, whom Cathy Margason had not mentioned. A third was George Ginderer, who might also gain financially.

But Margason had not met the provisions get his own inheritance, so Guerevich could not imagine a motive for Franklin or Cathy. In all likelihood, neither of them would be able to get any of the five hundred million. After examining the photos for half an hour, he picked up the phone and called Ann at her apartment.

"For God's sake, Aaron, it's not even 7:30 yet. I just stepped out of the shower."

"Need help toweling off?"

"What am I supposed to do. Stand here wet and wait for you?"

"Just a thought. Did you get any more information on the Margason case yet?"

"Give me a break. Considering I only had half a day on Friday, I got a lot. My notes are at work. I'll call you when I get to my office."

He heard the click and then the silent line. *She admitted she shot him. The question is how many times.*

He hung up the phone and walked down the flight of steel-tipped stairs and out the safety door to the Silver Spoon Coffee Shop around the block where the regular morning waitresses knew him.

Guerevich knew that one of the waitresses, Diane, had been divorced from an abusive husband. She had a faint scar across the bridge of her nose extending to her right cheek in testament. Although she always appeared happy and friendly, he thought of her as hardened from street-wise experience.

She was fortunate to have a job. At a recent department meeting on domestic violence, he had learned nearly half of all homeless women on the streets and in shelters were escaping domestic battery.

The statistics on battered women had surprised him, even though he considered himself well-informed. Most women never filed police reports. And those who did file reports were often abused again. Forty per cent of the women who needed emergency-room treatment for violent injuries had been beaten by a husband or boyfriend. Over a million women each year were assaulted or murdered and the few who took radical steps and ended their suffering were often found guilty of murder since they took action when their husbands or boy friends slept..

As he entered the restaurant and walked to an open table in Diane's station, he imagined the condemnation of his father who would never eat in a restaurant that was not strictly kosher.

Guerevich sat and thought about Cathy Margason. *Was she one of those abused wives who took matters into her own hands? To be granted an Order of Protection by a judge, she had to have proved she been physically abused and that Stanfield was her abuser. Having money and a good attorney no doubt helped the process.*

He waved to Diane and watched her fill a carafe with coffee and walk toward him.

"Morning, Detective Guerevich." Diane turned over the cup on the table and filled it with coffee. The biting smell made him smile. She set the carafe on the table and took a pad from the large side pocket of her skirt. "Usual this morning?"

"Yeah. Veggie omelet, Diane."

"Veggie omelet," she repeated, writing on the order pad.

"Today I'd like a toasted onion bagel with cream cheese instead of regular toast."

"You got it." She turned and walked to another table where two men had just sat down. Guerevich sipped his coffee and listened to the clatter of dishes and calls from the cooks to the waitresses to pick up their orders. He tuned out waitresses and customers chatting about their lives and retreated into his thoughts.

*It's odd that Cathy never even mentioned Franklin. He's got to be involved somehow. And George Ginderer. The financial advisor somehow fits into the puzzle, too.*

He took out a pad and made some notes to review later. Two other detectives entered and waved hello to him but sat at a table by themselves.

He put his pad aside when Diane brought his breakfast. The first bite of the bagel covered with cream cheese took him back to his childhood when every Sunday his father brought fresh bagels from a kosher bakery and made a breakfast of scrambled eggs and lox.

When he finished his meal it was just past 8:30. Ann wouldn't call until about ten. He went back to his office and made some calls to get Cathy Margason's phone records. Then he called a friend in the juvenile department, hoping to get a little more information on Franklin Margason.

"People with too much money," he said aloud. "Maybe it drives them crazy."

"You talkin' about the Margason case?" came the scratchy alto voice of Danielo Sanchez, with whom Guerevich sometimes partnered, the only detective on the Scottsdale police force from the Dominican Republic. Sanchez was the kind of man everyone turned to look at when he entered a room. He had a golden brown complexion and stood six feet four inches tall, two inches taller than Guerevich. Sanchez intentionally wore size large tee shirts that were slightly small for him. With his buffed chest and large biceps, his muscles stretched the fabric.

Guerevich nodded. "Didn't see you sitting there, Danny. Just going over my notes again and waiting for Ann to call."

"When you gonna marry that girl?"

"She keeps saying it's too soon after her divorce."

"How long's it been?"

"Three years."

Sanchez picked up his cup and walked between the row of desks toward the back of the office. The coffee urn roosted on top of a gray filing cabinet against the back wall.

At 10:20, Guerevich's phone rang. Ann told him she was on her way to a staff meeting but she would meet him at two o'clock for a late lunch at Michael's Pizza to go over the information she had.

Guerevich hung up the phone and went back to reading his notes and staring at the photos. He looked again at the glass shards on the body. The shattered window panes and pattern of the broken glass meant whoever did it had to use a large object to break the window. And again he wondered why Cathy had never mentioned Stanfield's twenty-five-year-old son. He googled Stanfield Margason and started putting together a folder, printing information he pulled up on the internet. Everything confirmed Stanfield as a man who relied on a limited trust income and who exploited others' assumption that he would inherit his father's wealth.

He left, went to the police gym, and lifted weights for an hour. Lifting gave him a euphoric feeling, a feeling of victory over an imaginary adversary. After he showered, he headed to Michael's Pizza. He liked Michael's, because they had several varieties of vegetarian pizzas.

Arriving at Michael's at ten minutes to two, he took a small table, and ordered a diet coke with no ice. Then he sat back to watch the people. At two, he walked outside to the vending machine, bought a newspaper, and glanced at the headlines.  At two fifteen, the waiter came by with a pitcher to refill his water glass.

"Are you Aaron Guerevich?"

"Yes.  I'm waiting for a lady to join me."

"I know, sir.  A man asked me to deliver this note at exactly two fifteen."

The waiter handed Guerevich a sealed envelope and then left.  Guerevich opened the letter and read the small bold computer print.

"Ann will be unable to join you. Margason's death was self defense. There is no case here. Let dead dogs lie."

He looked around the restaurant, knowing his scan was useless.  After a few moments, he put the letter down.  As soon as did, his cell phone buzzed and he answered.

"Aaron, it's Ann," she declared in a hoarse whisper before he could say anything.

"Where are you?"

"I'm at home."

"At home?  What's going on?"  Realizing he sounded anxious, he calmed his voice, not wanting to tell her about the note.  "Did you forget you were going to meet me?"

"I'm a little shaken, but okay."

"Shaken?  What happened?"

"I had the scare of my life earlier.  About one thirty, two big men came to the lab and said you'd been in an accident and they were to take me to you at the hospital. They wore suits and had official police IDs, but now I think about it, they looked around as if they were nervous and anxious to leave the building.  I thought it had to do with your accident."

"Ann, what're you talking about?"  Now he had to work to steady his voice.  "What accident?"

"After I got in their car they just drove me home. You hear me. They drove me home." Her voice had a quivering edge to it. "I knew they made a mistake when they turned north on Scottsdale, because the hospital is the other way. I asked them what they were doing, but neither one said a word. Aaron, they knew exactly where I live."

"Did they do anything? Say anything? What did they look like?"

"They were in their forties, a little over six feet and about two hundred fifty pounds. One had dark blond hair and sideburns and the other looked tan. What's so strange is they didn't do anything except drive me home. When we stopped in front of my apartment building, the driver said he felt sorry Stan Margason was dead, but his death should be called a justifiable homicide, and there was no reason to pursue the case. The other one nodded in agreement and said you'd know what he meant."

"Did they do anything to you?" he repeated his question loud enough to get stares from a few other patrons of the restaurant.

"No. It was eerie. They told me to get out and to call you at the restaurant. I still have the shakes. I don't understand what the hell's going on."

"This isn't New York or Chicago. This is Scottsdale, dammit." Guerevich threw a dollar on the table and started

for the door, his cell phone still at his ear.

"Aaron, I have no idea who these people were. The lab is secure, but anyone can walk in to the reception area. And with their IDs, they were buzzed into the lab. I... I feel so vulnerable."

"That's just what they want." He sprinted toward his car. "Call Kip and have him tell Captain Escobedo what happened. You need to file a report."

As he spoke, Guerevich unlocked his car, slid in, and started the engine.

"What'll I say? That two men lied to me and drove me home?" Ann lowered her voice. "I got in their car willingly."

"Stay there. I'm on my way over. Don't worry about your car. We can get it later. And I'll pick up your notes. Are they in your briefcase?"

"Is that all you can think about? The goddamn notes? Why don't you take the notes home and read them yourself."

"Sorry. I wasn't thinking."

"You care more about this case than me. Don't bother coming over. I can manage without you."

"Ann. . ."

"I mean it. I got along just fine before I met you, and I can get along without you now."

Guerevich heard the connection terminate. When he set his cellphone in the cradle, the readout was dark. As he drove, he nearly shouted her name to speed-dial her number and began speaking the moment that she picked up. "Ann, I said I'm sorry. The notes can wait."

He heard sniffling, and waited for what seemed like several minutes. Then he heard her voice, weak and fragile. She told him to pick up her briefcase next to her desk and get the notes in a folder marked *current* in the top drawer of the file cabinet. "Maybe it'll give me something to do besides feeling so scared I want to vomit. But I'm still pissed about your priorities."

The silence as Ann hung up her phone told Guerevich she had ended the conversation again. Within fifteen minutes he was at the lab and had picked up her notes and briefcase. Twenty minutes later, he unlocked her door. He saw her sitting on the sofa, staring at the floor, a cup of tea getting cold on the coffee table. He dropped the briefcase on the floor, walked to her, and sat next to her on the sofa. As soon as he sat down and wrapped his large arms around her, Ann folded against him like a week-old newspaper.

"I'm okay," she mumbled into his chest. "It was just so weird. At first, they scared me. I thought something had happened to you. Then I became scared for myself. I never felt so creepy, sitting in a car with two big mutes. Like they want you to know they could get to us."

"What did they look like?"

"They were white and big. Tall. At least two hundred fifty pounds each. Suits and ties, with longish hair. That should have been my tip-off. One fair and one dark. I didn't pay as much attention as I should have because I thought they were cops."

"This case gets stranger by the minute. Who'd want to do that? Do they think we could back off because they threaten us? Do they think the case will just go away? All this does is tell us the killing wasn't the self-defense Cathy Margason wants us to believe." He held her tighter and stroked her hair.

"And there's a lot more we don't seem to know," she stammered into his shoulder.

Guerevich mentioned it might be wise for her not to continue on the case.

"And who'll do the forensics?" She looked up at him and smiled, tears forming little diamonds in the corners of her eyes. She pounded her fist lightly on his shoulder. "I'm still angry at you, but you know I'm the best damn forensics researcher you ever slept with."

"You mean the only one."

"You better say that. Besides, if they want to get to you, they'll go through me anyway. I might as well stay on the case with you."

For fifteen minutes, they sat there holding each other, not saying anything. After she felt calmer, she pulled back from his embrace. He got up to heat more tea.

"I did get some information before I was kidnapped."

"Kidnapped?" He walked back to the doorway to look at her. "Is that how you feel?"

"What else can you call it? My God, they walked right into the lab. They had badges and IDs."

The tears started forming again. She wiped them away with the tissue in her hand. As she looked at Guerevich, the tears slid down her cheeks. He returned to the sofa and sat next to her again. She started sobbing and turned away. A moment later, she threw herself at him, her face pressed against his chest, her breath exploding into throbbing spasms, like a thumb struck by a hammer. He held her and remained silent until her rhythmic pulsing subsided. After a few minutes, she got up, walked to the bathroom, and returned with a box of tissues, wiping her eyes and blowing her nose.

She forced a smile and sat on the sofa again, facing Guerevich, legs drawn up under her. "Maybe I'm being too dramatic." She shook her head vigorously. "I'm okay now."

"I'm sorry I wasn't there. I don't understand how they knew I left for lunch and where I went."

"All they had to do was watch. You signed out, didn't you? Where we meet for lunch has no top-secret clearance. And cell phone conversations are notoriously public." Ann paused and snapped open her briefcase on the coffee table. "Anyway, I told you I got some information today. I'll feel better when I get my mind working." She removed a large manilla envelope. Taking out several sheets of paper, she spread them out on the coffee table.

She had learned Cathy Margason was exactly the person she claimed to be, living on her trust from the Willock fortune. Her income netted her three hundred thousand dollars a year. Her expenses, unfortunately, were considerably more, and at the rate she spent money, her trust would be exhausted in fewer than ten years. Ann held up her cup as she looked at the pages.

Guerevich stood and took it from her hand and walked toward the kitchen. "Meaning she had to draw more principal each year to maintain the life style she and Stanfield had developed. You'd think the trustees would warn her."

"The trust is held by a corporate bank." Ann went on to explain what she had discovered about George Ginderer, the financial planner. Stanfield had no money of his own except for the yearly hundred thousand allowance set up by his father Philip, who had appointed Ginderer as the trustee. Ginderer served as one of the three people who would make the decision on whether or not Stanfield actually had a career when he turned forty-five. Four years earlier, at age forty, Stanfield had tried to have the terms of his father's will overturned, claiming forty-five years was too long to wait. His attorney had argued that Stanfield had a career as a travel counselor, that a career constituted the work a person chooses as his occupation. Although Stanfield had no office, he regularly advised friends on European travel arrangements and protocol. Ginderer, arguing the contrary for the trust, had maintained a career consisted of a sequence of work activities in which one engages to earn a livelihood. In the absence of payment, the court agreed advising friends could not really be considered a career, merely a friendly gesture.

Angered by the court's decision, Stanfield had instituted a financial review of the manner in which Ginderer handled the estate's investments, charging Ginderer had used money for personal affairs and had altered the books. Ginderer received one hundred thousand dollars a year for his services, an amount far less than the estate earned. The audit had turned up no improprieties.

Phillip's will also made a financial provision for Ginderer. In the event Stanfield Margason failed to have a career, or died before reaching the age of forty-five, Ginderer would receive a severance of ten million dollars. The remainder of the estate would be divided among several hospitals and colleges.

Ann had been unable to dig up any information about how the death of Stanfield Margason would significantly improve Cathy's finances. If he died before collecting his inheritance, she would get a single settlement of one million dollars.

The kettle whistled and Guerevich placed green tea bags into two cups and poured the hot water. He carried the two cups to where she sat on the sofa. "Meanwhile, here's another cup of hot green tea."

She smelled the pungent aroma and set the cup on the coffee table next to the pages of data. "Here's what I can't figure. She couldn't collect on something he didn't even have yet. He wouldn't have been able to get his inheritance for another year. In addition, he'd have to be successful, not to say alive to collect it. She would have been better off to keep him alive and then divorce him after he collected. Even if she only got a fourth of the estate, she'd have netted over one hundred million."

He sat next to Ann and put his arm around her shoulder.

She leaned back into his arm. "You staying tonight?"

"Tigers couldn't drive me away."

"I know." She half smiled and looked at him with tear-shining eyes. "Lions maybe, but not tigers."

"I think I'll go out to the mansion again tomorrow morning. I need to revisit the crime scene. Maybe looking at it fresh will fill in what seems to be missing."

# CHAPTER EIGHT

The next morning, as Guerevich drove Ann to the station to pick up her car, he insisted she file a report about the abduction with Captain Escobedo.

"What's the point of that? What can she do about it?"

"It'll make the event official. And I'm sure she'll understand how upset you are."

He parked in his space in the lot, walked Ann to Escobedo's office, and stood outside when Ann went in.

Seated in the Captain's office, Ann told Escobebo what had happened and how foolish she felt. The captain insisted that Ann meet with the computer sketch artist to develop drawings of her two kidnappers.

When Ann went to meet with the artist, Guerevich explained his belief to Escobedo that there had been more than one shooter in the Margason case. "She couldn't have done it alone. That Margason woman's not strong enough to have thrown a large weight through the window. And she's got enough money to hire anyone to do anything."

"You're probably right. You know that'll change everything from a wife-shoots-abusive-husband affair to a possible homicide. Follow up on that and see what crawls out from under the carpets."

After he ended his conversation with Escobedo, Guerevich went to the sketch artist's office. Ann had just finished and was closing the door. He took Ann's hands and pulled her toward him. When he hugged her, the smell of her warm body began to excite him and he kissed her ear.

She pulled away and smiled. "I have to get to my lab." She touched his face. "I'll see you tonight." She walked toward the end of the hall and the stairs that led up up her lab. As she got to the door and put her hand on the bar, she turned. "Who's going with you to the Margason place?"

"I thought about asking Sanchez, but he's so damned intimidating. I'm probably going to go alone."

"That's not smart." She walked through the doorway and left him standing alone.

The word stung a bit reminding him of something his father had often said. "Smart is not one of your best qualities. Intelligent, yes, even brilliant. But not always smart. To be successful in this world, you have to be intelligent and smart. Emphasis on the smart."

Guerevich knew department policy was designed to prohibit the lone ranger approach. It was especially important since Cathy was an attractive woman. But he believed he could take care of himself and ignored the trouble he could get into with the department. His solitary, low key approach, which others derisively called his Columbo technique, had worked well in the past. Making Cathy feel comfortable, as though he just happened to stop by, would catch her off guard, which would make her likely to tell him more than if she felt badgered.

His successes in working alone outweighed the disadvantages. He loved the convenience and even the excitement in discovering pieces of information and fitting them into the puzzle he was putting together in his mind. He had most of the edges in place. Now it was a hunt for the middle pieces.

Working alone he didn't have to listen to someone else's personal problems or have his own train of thought derailed by another's assessment of a situation. He didn't have to deal with another person's mistakes. The mistakes he made were his alone, and he was willing to take responsibility for them.

He relied on his ability to examine a problem objectively and understand more than one side, a technique learned during his years in religious school. He had excelled in Talmudic methods for argumentation, scrutinizing both real and imagined religious issues. He recalled the times he thought he had correctly analyzed a religious problem, when his mentor asked the dreaded 'but what if' question. The procedure had enabled him to resolve complex secular problems which made questioning people second nature to him.

But he was also aware of the problems which could arise in a one-on-one interview at her house, especially with no lawyer present. Anything she said might not be admissible in court. The pajama incident in her bedroom could have turned out to be disastrous if McNulty had not been there as an observer.

Before driving to the Aster Street mansion, Guerevich phoned Kipinski. "Anything more on the Margason case?"

"Not really. The bullets were definitely fired from the Luger. And the prints on it were hers, palm print on the handle and finger print on the trigger. There's no doubt she fired the gun. There were also some smudges that might have been old prints. Of course, they could also have been caused by normal cleaning."

"So we can prove she shot him and he didn't break in. I don't want to arrest her until we find out who else is involved. The prints on the book?"

"We traced it through Arizona AFIS. They definitely belonged to George Ginderer. He'd been an economics teacher before he went into financial consulting, so his prints were in the state database. We're also trying to track down cotton fiber particles on some of the glass shards, but they'll probably turn out to be from Margason's clothing."

Driving to the Margason residence and fighting through the stop-and-go traffic on Cactus, Guerevich tried to figure out what Franklin and Cathy would gain by Margason's death, and how George Ginderer fit into the puzzle. The more he thought about the situation, the more he believed Ginderer had the clearest motive. Ten million dollars. And the financial advisor had means as well as opportunity.

When he saw a black Mercedes SEL 450 in Cathy's circular brick driveway, Guerevich drove past. He parked his unmarked, white Crown Victoria a block away on 114th Street, and walked back toward Aster and the immense house. He scrawled the license plate number of the Mercedes in his notebook. Looking ahead as he trudged up the long walkway from the driveway toward the house, he saw curtains in the entryway window close quickly.

He reached the front deck, rang the bell, and waited on the Mexican paver tiles. A young, round-faced, Filipino woman, smelling of fresh soap opened the door. She wore a dark dress and uniform pinafore. When he asked to speak to Mrs. Margason, the woman explained that Mrs. Margason had guests in the dining room.

"Hello, Detective." Cathy Margason walked toward the foyer where Guerevich and the housekeeper were standing. "Thank you, Sandria." Cathy turned to Guerevich. "You might say I rather expected you." She turned to the young woman. "It's okay. I'll handle this."

The young housemaid nodded briefly and walked quickly away.

It was obvious that Cathy wore nothing under her pink sweatshirt, and her bare feet protruded from beneath tight-fitting stretch jeans.  Her red hair, pulled back into a pony tail, had a wet and shiny appearance.

Cathy smiled at Guerevich. "Please come in.  I hope I won't need my lawyer this time."

"Well, it's still up to you.  I just need to examine the crime scene again and tie a few loose ends together."

"Before you do there are some people I want you to meet."  The smile caused her eyes to crinkle as she caught him looking at her breasts.  She led him through the foyer past the winding staircase and into the dining room.

The large oak table had three places set and an array of partially eaten food, suggesting people had either been interrupted at breakfast or had just finished eating.  The smell of fresh-ground coffee hung in the room.  As Guerevich entered, he saw two people, a young man standing, arms folded across his chest, and an older seated man who appeared to be about fifty.  He recognized them both from photographs.  The young man could have been a clone of his recently dead father.  His shoulder-length light brown hair appeared damp.  The same height as Guerevich, he wore jeans and a tight navy blue tee shirt that exaggerated his weightlifter's chest.  He stood leaning slightly backwards, feet apart, hands at his sides. Wound around his right forearm, he sported a snake tattoo with its head ending at his wrist, mouth open, fangs ready to strike.

The older man, George Ginderer, thinner across the shoulders, smiled at Guerevich, as if waiting for him to speak.  His graying full head of hair had been stylishly cut.  He wore a crisp white shirt, a muted tie, and navy slacks.  Guerevich saw a summer-weight, tan cotton blazer draped over the back of the chair where he sat.

"Detective Aaron Guerevich, I want you to meet Franklin Margason and George Ginderer.  Frank is Stan's son from his first marriage. George is our, or should I say was Stan's financial consultant."

Guerevich moved toward the young man to shake hands, but Franklin's hands never moved. George stood to shake hands, giving a tight-lipped scowl at Franklin.

"What's all this about?" Franklin addressed his question to Cathy Margason, whose smile morphed into a frown. Franklin's alto nasal voice rasped across Guerevich's ears and didn't match his muscular body.

"Frank, Detective Guerevich is working on the death of your father." Her jaws tightened.

"What's the point?" Franklin spoke to Cathy as if Guerevich were not there. "It was self defense, wasn't it? You told them you shot the son-of-a-bitch when he attacked you, didn't you? What more do they want?"

Ginderer nodded his head and glared at Franklin. "Frank is very upset about the death of his father. Aren't you, Frank. It was such a shock. Cathy's is taking medication to calm her down. Prescribed by her doctor, of course."

Guerevich looked at Franklin. "The papers may have reported self-defense, but there are still some circumstances we have to investigate."

"Circumstances?" Franklin leaned toward Guerevich, dropping his arms to his sides and pushing his lower jaw outward. "You mean you don't believe Cathy. You think she's lying?" Franklin's lips tightened until they disappeared into a pursed sneer.

Guerevich returned the young man's look with a blank stare, not wanting to make a bad situation worse. Franklin sat down and tilted his head to one side, making the dangling silver cross in his left ear bobble. He sat silently waiting for Guerevich's response to his question.

Guerevich refused to be pushed to anger. "Well, Mr. Margason, it doesn't matter what I believe or don't believe.

We have to gather all the information before we can make a final determination. The medical examiner is working up his conclusions from the autopsy, and then we can make an official report."

"Who gave authorization for an autopsy?" Cathy Margason's pursed lips matched her wrinkled brow.

"It's standard procedure. The medical examiner orders one whenever there's a shooting death and there are questions surrounding it." Guerevich remained matter-of-fact. He knew his statement wasn't completely true. The medical examiner usually notifies the next of kin first. Guerevich didn't want to provoke a confrontation.

"Questions surrounding it? Who the hell has questions?" Franklin's voice rose in anger.

Cathy jumped in. "I don't care about standard procedures. No one gave permission for any autopsy."

"I understand how you might feel, Mrs. Margason. But in a death like this, an autopsy is always required by the Medical Examiner. Even without permission." As he spoke he was thankful they weren't Jewish or he would have had to contend with the religious precept that prohibited a post-mortem examination as a desecration of the deceased.

"That's a joke," snarled Franklin. "Maybe you didn't notice, Detective, but if you had, you might have discovered the cause of my father's death. Shot while breaking into a house. Where he had no business to be." He started to walk toward the doorway and stopped in front of Guerevich, who purposely didn't move aside, forcing the young man to stop, an intimidation strategy.

He looked at Franklin. "The forensic evidence indicates some person or persons broke the window after your father had been shot. Some large object was thrown through the window while your father lay dying on the floor."

Guerevich just guessed at the large object, but he wanted to see their reactions to his statement. When Cathy and Franklin looked at each other, her eyes opened a little wider registering surprise. Franklin's eyes took on a hard look and closed slightly, as if he were squinting into the sun. Ginderer shrugged his shoulders and looked confused. No one said a word. Guerevich continued before they had a chance to regain their composure.

"By the way, do any of you know why Mr. Margason would have new hundred dollar bills in an envelope with a letter from a Las Vegas attorney?"

Franklin looked at Cathy. His jaws clamped and unclamped so hard the muscles in his cheeks twitched.

Cathy looked surprised and stammered. "I, uh, I don't know where Stan got any of his money. He did have some business dealings in Las Vegas. As I told you the other day, he'd been keeping bad company." She paused and looked at Franklin, as if waiting for him to respond.

"What difference does it make where he kept his money." Ginderer's voice broke the momentary silence. He cleared his throat. "It's not illegal to carry hundred dollar bills, is it? I have a few in my wallet right now."

"I just wondered why he didn't keep the bills in his billfold with his other money, as you do, Mr. Ginderer. It seems odd that. . . "

"That's ridiculous." Franklin regained his self-assurance, and cut Guerevich off. "It's just another stupid police tactic to waste time. Just don't keep us waiting too long, Detective. We have a funeral to plan for, and it'd be so nice to have a body to put in the casket. Now, if you don't have anything else, I have to go." He maneuvered around Guerevich. When he reached the doorway, he turned his head back toward Cathy. "I'll talk to you later."

"Call me this afternoon?" she asked, with a hint of pleading in her voice.

"No doubt we'll see each other again, Detective." He walked out of the dining room toward the front door and didn't look back.

"I really must be going as well, Cathy," said Ginderer. "Again, my condolences. If there's anything I can do, call me. Nice to meet you, Detective. Here's my card. If you need any financial information, let me know. I've been with Mr. Margason and his father before him for quite a few years."

Ginderer took his jacket from the back of the chair and walked to the doorway. "Thanks for the breakfast, Cathy. Keep me informed about the arrangements."

Cathy nodded as he left. She sat down at the table.

"Franklin's an interesting young man," said Guerevich. "I take it he and his father didn't get along. How long have you known him?"

"Since I married Stan. After we were married, Frank came to live with us. He had just turned fifteen. Hard to believe it's been ten years."

"And how old were you when you married his father?"

"Twenty-two. I was a little younger than Frank is now. Stan had just turned thirty-four. Would you like to sit down? Can I get you anything?" Her tone became more confident once Franklin left.

"A diet coke, if you have one cold. No ice." He

hoped asking for a drink would cause her to relax further.

"I'll get you one. Why don't we sit in the kitchen. The housekeeper will want to clean up here."

As they walked toward the kitchen, Guerevich considered the early morning breakfast involving Cathy, now a self-made widow, and Franklin, a grieving son who seemed to dislike his father. And George Ginderer, the financial planner. Maybe all three of them were somehow involved in Stanfield's death.

"Did you have a pleasant breakfast?" Guerevich asked as they walked out of the dining room.

"As pleasant as possible under the circumstances. They, uh, came over early. We were meeting to discuss the funeral arrangements." She led him through double swinging doors into the kitchen. They crossed a tile floor into a room that looked like a restaurant prep area with a small, well-worn, pine table. The smell of fried food and disinfectant hung in the air like a fuzzy shadow from a distant light.

"Please sit down. If you're going to ask me questions, I probably ought to call my lawyer."

Guerevich sat in one of the six replica Amish farm chairs. "That's your decision. Before I re-examine the library, I would like to ask a few more background questions."

"I can only reiterate what I've already told you." She took a can of diet coke and a bottle of mineral water from the restaurant-size refrigerator. Using a spoon, she pried open the can of coke and poured it in a glass, setting the empty can on a stand next to the refrigerator. She poured the mineral water over ice in another glass.

"You must do quite a bit of entertaining here."

"We did. Stan designed the kitchen. I'm not much of a cook."

"You seem to know where everything is," Guerevich observed.

"I know where a few things are. The kitchen help prepare most of the meals." She walked around the stainless steel island and returned to the table.  As she set down the drinks, Guerevich took out his notebook.

"I'm surprised you don't use a recorder."

"Easier to summarize ideas as I write them down, instead of later," he responded.

"There must be a problem or you wouldn't be here." She smiled slightly as she sat across from him and folded her hands above the table.  Her demeanor and flushed face suggested a high school student caught smoking in the bathroom.  "Detective Guerevich, I really think my lawyer ought to be here."

"Sure.  Call her.  I can wait.  After all, there's not really a problem, Mrs. Margason."  Guerevich said as took a sip of coke.

"Cathy, please."  Her smile broadened and she passed a hand over her hair.  For the first time Guerevich noticed her straight, even teeth.  Without makeup on her wrinkle-free face, she didn't look any older than Franklin.

"Yes, of course.  Cathy.  Just some bits of information I'm trying to clear up.  You have no idea where the hundred dollar bills came from?"

"None at all.  Maybe they came from his Las Vegas friends."

"I'll check that out."

"I'd like to call my attorney."

Guerevich continued without pausing.  "Now, you originally stated you fired three shots, yet later in your statement, you said you clearly remembered four.  We found one of the bullets in the floor, under the body, indicating it had been fired from directly above the victim."

"I think we should wait until my lawyer gets here."

"I'm just restating what you already alleged."

"I'll call her from the other room."

While Cathy left the kitchen to phone her attorney, Guerevich poked into the cupboards and looked in the refrigerator. The cabinet under the sink contained only cleaning supplies. He peered into the trash bin and moved things around with his pencil. Beneath a pile of crumpled paper, he saw the scrap of a partially burnt document just as he heard Judith Westerly arrive. It had been twenty minutes.

As they walked into the kitchen and sat at the table, Westerly asked Cathy if Guerevich had harassed her. He assured her he hadn't, but merely wanted to ask again why Cathy originally said she fired three shots fired and later changed it to four when six shots had been fired.

"Well, in the confusion, I did say three." She sat at the table and her lawyer stood slightly behind her. Cathy's smile disappeared and she swallowed, although she hadn't touched her drink.

"Maybe you don't understand her terror, Detective," declared Westerly, leaning forward, her hands on the table. "She feared for her life. Stan broke in acting like a crazy man. Shouting and carrying on. But later, she clearly remembered firing four shots."

Cathy unfolded her hands and dropped them into her lap.

"So you fired three times as he stood and once as he lay on the floor?"

"No. Yes. I. . .uh, I'm not sure. I think I fired three times as he stood facing me, and once as I walked toward him. It all happened so fast."

"When you walked toward him, he must have fallen before you fired the fourth time. That would explain the bullet in the floor."

"I really can't remember his exact position when I fired each shot."

Westerly interrupted. "Hold on, Detective. He broke in through the window and she shot him. What more do you want?"

"Let's not continue with the broken window scenario. All the glass on top of the body tells us someone broke the window after he was down. What really happened?"

Cathy stood up and walked across the room to the deep double sink, placing her hands on the edge. "No. He broke in through the window," she maintained, although the conviction in her voice had weakened, like a child clinging to a fantastic story to explain a broken vase. "It was a very traumatic experience." She covered her mouth with her left hand and shook her head.

"I don't think you should answer any more questions, Cathy."

"Was Franklin there at the time?" Guerevich pressed on, ignoring Westerly.

"No." The word leaped from her mouth almost before Guerevich finished his question. "No, Franklin wasn't there. I don't know where he was. Out of town, probably."

The mention of Franklin's name caused her ears to turn the color of her hair. Guerevich asked about George Ginderer.

"George wasn't there either. He had been there earlier in the day to discuss my financial problems in the event I divorced Stan."

"That's enough," protested Westerly. "I think this discussion is over. You're just fishing now. My client has nothing more to say."

"No more questions. But I will need a phone number

and an address for Franklin."

"I'll get it for you. It's in my address file on my laptop." She left the room with Westerly and Guerevich took the opportunity to retrieve the partially burnt scrap of paper from the trash bin. He picked it up by a corner and opened it on the table. The e-mail fragment had been sent from *fmarg@aol.com*. Only the words, *You did what had* and *Leave the rest* were visible. The remainder of the page had been charred. Guerevich placed the scrap into his notebook, returning to sit at the table just as Cathy and her lawyer reentered to the room.

Judith Westerly walked to the table, threw him a sheet of paper and folded her arms. "Here's his address and phone number. Is there anything else, Detective? Cathy has a busy day ahead of her. She has to make preparations for the funeral."

Guerevich looked at Cathy. "Did Franklin ever speak to you about his father? Or e-mail you?"

"What do you mean? Why would he?"

"You two are close to each other in age. Did he ever confide in you about his feelings toward his father?"

"He and his father were close. Just because he lived with his mother until he was fourteen, there was no bitterness between them, if that's what you're driving at. And Stan was a concerned father."

"I'm sure. But we need to examine. . ."

"We're done, Detective," declared Westerly. "It's time for you to leave."

"Certainly. I understand. I just need to revisit the crime scene for a few minutes, and then I'll see myself out."

"Thank you." Cathy, her arms hanging loosely at her sides, did not move.

Guerevich got up and started for the doorway. "One last thing. We'd like to examine your laptop. Would you mind if I took it along with me to the lab?"

"As a matter of fact, I would. I need it today to complete the letters I'm writing. There are people who need to be notified about Stan's death."

"Without a warrant, she's under no obligation to give you anything," added Westerly.

Guerevich thought about the scrap of paper in his pocket. "I could get a warrant," he responded, addressing Cathy directly. "Then you'd be without your laptop for quite a while. However, If I take it now. . ." He paused. "And you said you'd do whatever you could to help."

Westerly looked at Cathy. "Is there anything on the computer you need? Any e-mails?"

"I always delete my e-mails after I read them."

Westerly turned to Guerevich. "You people love to create an incident even when there isn't one. Her husband is dead and she admitted to shooting him. But that's not good enough. You have to play Sherlock Holmes and look for clues even if there are none. In the interest of speeding up this so-called investigation, I'm advising my client to give you the damn laptop. Just tell us how soon she can get it back."

Cathy stomped out of the room and returned with a Macintosh Powerbook. After she set it on the table, she glared at Guerevich. Tears of anger glistened in her eyes. "There it is. I've got a headache and I'm going to lie down. Examine whatever you want and show yourself out." She turned her back to him and left the room.

"I think I'll accompany you to the crime scene, Detective. Just to make sure everything is on the up-and-up."

"You are more than welcome, Ms Westerly." He pulled a handkerchief from his pocket. Placing the cloth over one edge of the Powerbook to cover his hand-print, he picked it up, put it under his arm, and walked to the library. The room was still taped off.   He looked at the few books still on the floor beneath the bookcase where Cathy said the Luger had been kept.  Several others were at the lab.

Guerevich thought as he walked around the room. *If Ginderer placed the books on the floor, that's how his prints got there.*

"Are you satisfied?" asked Westerly.

"I am.   Nothing's changed."   He smiled at her. "Well, that's all I need here."  He left the library and walked back to his car. *Cathy said she always deleted her emails, but I heard emails can live forever on a hard drive.  We need to find out how it can be made to spit them out and any other information in there.*

# CHAPTER NINE

Before Guerevich returned to his office, he went to the forensics section of the building, and climbed up the flight of stairs with the lap-top in the evidence bag under his arm. He smiled at the secretary in the reception area, and she buzzed him into the lab. At the end of the aisle, Ann sat at her desk, her head supported by her hands, a medical examiner's report spread out in front of her. He walked toward her, past a maze of whirring and buzzing machines, past the floor mounted microscopes on his right, and tables with machines he didn't recognize. A dark computer screen sat next to a blood separator used for determining DNA.

"You file the report?" He placed the evidence bag in a clear spot on one side of her desk.

Ann didn't raise her head. "Yeah. Now there's an official record of my stupidity."

"So you think it's stupid to be worried about me enough to get kidnapped?"

"That's not what I meant and you know it." She stopped reading and looked up at him. "I was more worried about you than about myself. I imagined you lying in some hospital bed with God knows how many broken bones or bullet holes."

"I know," was all he could manage, her comment causing him to turn away momentarily to hide the moisture in his eyes. As he swallowed the tightness in his throat, he touched her shoulder, angered such a traumatic event had happened to someone he loved, guilty that he was involved in a case that could jeopardize her safety. He also knew her talking about it would constitute a kind of therapy. Keeping emotions repressed could cause inner turmoil which might explode at the most unlikely moment.    "Anything about those two bozos?"

"Of course not. You think they're going to come back to say 'sorry for the inconvenience'?" She shook her head and closed her eyes.

"What did Escobedo say?"

"She couldn't believe I'd got into a car with a couple of strangers without first checking with the hospital.  She put out the description of the car and the drivers and said she'd see about getting me some time off if I want.  Without pay, of course.  I considered it for -- let's see -- about three seconds. We're in this together."

Guerevich grinned, took her hand, and pulled her gently out of her seat and into his arms, giving her one of his great bear hugs.

"I don't mind telling you I was scared," she mumbled into his chest.  "But I was more worried about you."  She pushed him away, her voice strong and adamant.  "I'm not going to turn and run."

He wanted to tell her he had been afraid as well. Afraid she had been injured or worse, that he had lost her forever.   He believed in being honest, although he didn't reveal every detail of his feelings.   Losing a loved one because of police work was one thing no one spoke about but every cop feared.  Good men fell victim to depression or became devastated and left the force after an innocent wife or child had been threatened or victimized by some punk wanting to get revenge.

He understood Ann didn't give in easily.  She was not the type to quit, to fold under pressure.  He remembered the time she had been badgered when she gave forensic testimony.   When a lawyer asked the same question three times, she politely reminded him that the definition of insanity was repeating an action and expecting a different result.   She could boil skulls and take fingerprints from exhumed corpses, but she had become vulnerable.

She looked up at his face.  Tears had formed in the corner of her eyes.   "Just don't take me for granted.  It's the one thing I couldn't stand."

"What makes you think I'd ever do that?"

He moved toward her again.   She stood without moving from her desk and put her arms around his waist as he enfolded her in his arms again.  For a minute, they held each other, drawing comfort from the hugs.   Then she pushed him away, wiped her eyes, and looked at the bag he had placed on her desk.

"What's in there?"

"Cathy Margason's laptop.  I want you to search it for e-mails she received or sent.  Here's a scrap of an e-mail I found in the Margason's trash."

"You went through their garbage?"

"Not quite.   I found it in a wastebasket in the kitchen.  Maybe there's something we can use."

Ann shook her head and took the scrap and waved it in front of his face.  "You know any information from this won't be admissible in court."

"I don't care.  It might give us another piece of the

puzzle."

She told him to take the laptop down the hall to Martín Velez in Scottsdale Police Information Technology Services.  If any message had been sent or received, Martín would be able to find it.

"He's the new tech from Mexico, isn't he?  I haven't met him yet."

"He's not new and he's not from Mexico.   He's Colombian.   And he really knows his stuff.   The last computer case we had, he found information no one thought could be retrieved."

Guerevich felt some hunger pangs and looked at his watch. "Want to grab some lunch?"

"Not today. Too much work. And you just keep bringing me more." She turned around, returned to her chair, and pointed at the printout. "I'm learning a lot about Cathy Margason. She's a piece of work. I'll tell you all about it tonight." Then she pointed to a file box with several large evidence envelopes. "But apparently, I still get to work on a hit and run case as well. Want to help me examine some paint we scraped off the victim's clothes?"

"No thanks."

"Besides, I brought a tuna salad. It's in the big cooler."

"With all the other crap you keep in there?"

"Right next to the boiled heads and the vats of blood. What's the problem? The rule here is don't eat anything if it's unmarked and don't drink anything that looks like apple juice. Now get out of here and let me work. See you tonight."

Guerevich's cell phone buzzed. Escobedo wanted to see him immediately. He walked downstairs to the Captain's office and found her pacing in front of her desk.

Escobedo craned her neck to look up at him. "Just stand right there, Guerevich. What the hell do you think you're doing?" The blue vein on Escobedo's forehead stood out against her flushed face.

"What're you talking about?"

"Be quiet. I just got a call from the superintendent about your visit to the Margason residence. Did you really take her laptop? Without a warrant?"

"It's material evidence in the investigation. She invited me in and gave it to me voluntarily. Her lawyer agreed I could take it."

"I don't care who said you could take it. Who do you think you are? Some goddamn hotshot private detective working the case all alone? You trying to get yourself an unpaid vacation? And don't give me that shit about Bobby getting killed last year."

Guerevich stared at he floor. He knew department guidelines prohibited detectives from working without partners except in emergencies, and this was not one.

"If you want a desk job," Escobedo railed on, "I can arrange it. Otherwise, you take Sanchez along the next time you go to the Margason residence or have any dealings with anyone connected with the case. Or any other case. As of now, he's your new partner."

Guerevich opened his mouth to argue, but thought better of it. He clamped his teeth shut and nodded in agreement. When he was dismissed, he went back upstairs to the lab.

Ann was standing at one of the microscopes. She turned as he approached. "You look like someone just kicked you in the balls."

"Escobedo just assigned Sanchez as my partner. He's a good man, but I've gotten used to working alone." He put his arm around Ann, squeezed her shoulder, and picked up the evidence bag. Without saying another word, he walked out of the lab and down the hall to the door marked SPITS, Scottsdale Police Information Technology Services. The joke among detectives was that the department literally spits out information.

Opening the door to the windowless SPITS room, he saw a chubby man just hanging up the phone. He was seated on a wooden swivel stool, his back to the door. To the man's right spread a row of work tables which held several computers in various stages of disassembly, along with spider webs of wires, several things that looked like speakers, and various other pieces of equipment Guerevich could not identify. Holding a tiny screwdriver in his right hand, he spun around in his stool and slid his bulk off the stool to face Guerevich as the door closed. Few people ever entered, so this department had no waiting room, no secretary, and virtually no security.

Nearly a foot shorter than Guerevich, the clearly Hispanic man outweighed him by fifty pounds. At thirty he looked forty-five with thick graying hair that hung in straight lines to his shoulders. The small round glasses on his pudgy face made him look impish.

"Good morning." Smiling, he spoke nearly unaccented, Midwestern English. He put his screwdriver down on his workbench and looked up at the taller man. "You must be Aaron Guerevich. Ann called and said you were on your way over."

"And you must be Martín Velez, champion computer sleuth." Guerevich approached and the two men shook hands warmly.

"Call me Marty. I'm happy to meet you face to face finally. Ann told me you had a problem with a laptop. What can I do to help you?"

"There may be some deleted stuff on this laptop I need in the investigation of the Margason murder. According to Ann you can find things on computers other people say can't be found."

"I do my best. Let me tell you, my friend, nothing is ever really deleted from a computer unless you erase the hard drive, which no one ever wants to do. Part of the magnetic field can be degaussed if someone knows how to do it.  But the field can't be reduced to zero.  What do you need specifically?"

"I need to know the e-mails that have been sent and received."   Guerevich opened the envelope and slid the titanium Mac powerbook from the bag to a small space on one of the tables.

"That's an old one.  Do you know if it's a G4?  Even the old Mac OS ten system is Unix based, and. . ."

Guerevich held up his hand.  "I don't understand a word you're saying.  What I know about computers is you boot them up, and hope they do what you want them to do."

"Aaron, my friend.  You really need to understand more about computers."

"It's like my car, Marty.  I turn on the key and it starts.  If it doesn't, I call someone who can get it to start.   The world has become very specialized.   The last man who thought he could know everything was Francis Bacon, back in the 1600s."

"And I thought you wouldn't have anything to do with bacon, Aaron."  Velez chuckled at his little joke.

"Very funny.   You know something about Jewish dietary laws?"

"Of course.  Just because I'm from Colombia doesn't mean I know nothing about the world.   There's a large Jewish population in Bogotá near where I went to school for a while.  Besides, I have been in this country for many years, going to school and working.   I have met many Jewish people."

"Sorry.  Anyway, how long before you can get to this.  It's a priority."

"I will have whatever's on this by, let's see, give me two days."

"Two days?"

"Takes time. I'm not a magician. That is a screw driver, not a magic wand. First I have to discover if the original messages have been written over. How long since the e-mails were written?"

"A few days. Maybe a week."

"That may not be too bad. The longer the time, the worse it is. Maybe I can have something for you this afternoon."

"Okay. Do whatever you can. I'm heading over to the deli for some lunch."

Velez looked at his watch. "Lunch sounds good. Come with me and we can talk. It's only about ten blocks to a wonderful place called *Restaurante Colombian*. I'll drive and you can buy me lunch. I haven't had their *empanadas* for at least two days."

Guerevich grimaced at the humor, but he waited while Martín laughed, grabbed his jacket from the wall peg, and waddled to the door.

As they walked down the stairs and out to the parking lot, Guerevich paced his steps to those of the shorter man. Velez pushed a button on his key ring and Guerevich saw lights flash and heard the locks click open on a three-year-old, black Nissan Maxima. When they entered the car, Guerevich marveled that the inside looked new. Velez drove out of the lot and turned left, telling Guerevich he was going to love the food.

Aaron wondered what he had gotten himself into. Although he had been raised orthodox, he often ate in restaurants, but unlike many Jews he knew, he could never bring himself to eat pork or shellfish, and he wouldn't even eat foods if he didn't know their ingredients. He thought about what he'd be able to eat. At the worst, he could order a salad. More importantly, he had concerns about what a Hispanic computer tech could do to help him.

# CHAPTER TEN

Martín drove his car into what looked like an alley between a liquor store and a gas station, stopping at a gravel parking area with five cars close together. He maneuvered his car into the small remaining space between the last car and a hedge. A cement delivery dock with several wooden steps led up to the partially open door back that had a hand painted sign: *Restaurante Colombian.*

Guerevich opened the car and squeezed his body between the door of the car and the hedge, trying not to bang his head or scratch the car door.

Martín exited the driver's side. "I understand why you haven't come here to eat, Aaron. Me, I come here almost every day for lunch."

"How would I ever have found it hidden in this alley? Guerevich, not wanting to eat anything forbidden by his religion, hoped Martín could explain a few of the ethnic foods once they were seated. As they wove their way through tables irregularly placed toward an available one, Guerevich saw people casually dressed reading Spanish-language newspapers, as well as several men in suits talking on cell phones over small cups of espresso.

As they walked past a counter, Martín pointed to bread-like rolls in a glass display case. "Those are called *bunuelo.* And the golf ball-sized pastries are fritters with a sweet cheese-crumb coating."

They arrived at an empty table near a window and sat down. A boy who looked twelve immediately brought menus and two glasses of water without ice. Martín drank half of his water and set his glass down heavily. "This restaurant may be as close as I can ever get to Colombia, Aaron. I really miss it." After a few moments' silence, he shook his head, his eyes glistening. "But I never will be able to return."

"Why never, Marty?"

"For me, it is too dangerous. Besides, the Colombia I knew is gone. It is a different country, one that I would not want to return to even if I could. Friends have told me I would not recognize my home town."

"I think I know what you mean. I feel the same way about the neighborhood where I grew up in Chicago." He looked at the menu. "What are you going to have?"

Before Martín could answer, a waitress came by and stopped at their table.

"¡Hola, Martín! ¿Qué le gustaría beber?"

"Uno momento, Anita. Este es mi amigo, Aaron. Trabajamos en lo mismo edificio."

She held out her hand, and smiled slightly. "Con mucho gusto, señor. Hablas español?"

"Sorry. I only know a few words of restaurant Spanish."

Martín looked surprised. "Living here in Scottsdale? She asked what I want to drink. Then I introduced you to her, and she said she was pleased to meet you. I told her we work in the same building."

Anita smiled again, this time showing white teeth against a bronze face. Her thick black hair was pulled back against her head, exposing huge hoop earrings. Her eyes, darkened with mascara, gave her an exotic aura.

"For your benefit, Aaron, I shall order in English. Do you speak English, Anita?"

"Sí, Claro. Of course" she responded in accented English, placing both hands on her hips, wrists bent back. "I am from Bogotá, not some backward aldehuela."

Martín laughed. "Bring me a *naranjilla sorbete* and one for my friend."

After she left, he explained to Guerevich that it was a popular drink in Colombia, made like lemonade. "The juice is made from the fruit of the *lulo* plant. Even though *naranjilla* means little orange, it is not the same. It is a little bigger than a golf ball. Its inside looks like a tomato with green pulp."

When their drinks arrived, Guerevich took a sip and set his glass down. "Thanks, Marty. This is very good."

"Aaron, why do you know so little about computers since you use them almost every day?"

"I just don't have the time. When I turn it on, the screen lights up, and I do what I need to do."

"You're like all the others. As long as everything is okay, you don't care about your equipment. Do you treat your pistol that way? Never clean it? Never take care it out of the holster? Never think about it until you need it?"

"The pistol's different. It's life and death." Guerevich took another sip of his juice and looked at the plump man seated across from him. Martín looked more like a field hand or day laborer than a computer expert. He could be someone who might be able to provide important information about the killing, yet Guerevich knew almost nothing about him.

"I also have a lack of knowledge. All I know about you is you have a good reputation, and you're Jewish, so you don't eat pork."

"Also shellfish. I don't eat shellfish or any fish if it doesn't have scales."

"Why not?"

"It's part of the religious belief I grew up with. Simply told, the only meat Jews are supposed to eat comes from animals that have both a split hoof and chew a cud.

And only fish with both fins and scales. But that's only a small part of it. There are so many more rules, it would make your head spin. I don't follow them all, which has caused problems between my father and me."

"I can understand the connection to tradition. But I have to say you're missing out on some good eating."

Anita returned and Martín ordered a tropical coleslaw salad.

"Even with your rules, you'll be able to eat what I am having, Aaron."

Guerevich chose not to tell Martín about the rules regarding ritual animal slaughter.

"We can get the department to pay." Martín smiled when Guerevich looked surprised. "Relax, my friend. The bill will come to less than ten dollars for each of us, even with the *propina*, the tip. And even if I order the *empanadas*."

"You've mentioned them twice. What are they?"

"They're thin cornmeal crusts filled with meat and potatoes and some herbs, but they can be filled with anything."

"A bit like *hamentaschen*, the triangular pastry Jews eat at Purim."

Martín turned to Anita, who stood smiling with her bill pad in one hand, her pencil in the hand on her hip. He ordered a bowl of *santafenero* for each of them, explaining the chicken stew was thickened with potatoes and came with capers and avocado slices.

"Marty, did you memorize the menu?"

"My family owned a cafe in Sincelejo, the city where I grew up. That's in the north, near Cartagena. But it's also close to Montería, where the FARC had many sympathizers." Velez sipped his drink and wiped his mouth on his napkin.

"What's this FARC?" Guerevich set his glass down and leaned forward.

"*Fuerzas Armada Revolutionarias de Colombia*. The armed revolutionary forces of Colombia. Marxist radicals who want to overthrow the elected government. If my parents had been important people, they would have been kidnapped and held for ransom from the government, like Íngrid Betancourt, the pro-democracy presidential candidate in 2002."

"A candidate for president?"

"She ran on the Green Oxygen party. They also took Clara Rojas, Íngrid's campaign manager."

"What happened to them?"

"They were held for years and eventually released. The FARC exchanged them for guerrillas captured by the government, although that was supposed to be a secret. My father was only a small businessman, but he was loyal to the government. Silly as it sounds, he believed in democracy, and thought people should be free to elect any kind of government they feel is best. He also hoped someday I would take over the family business."

"Why didn't you?"

"Because when I was nineteen, the FARC assassinated my family." Martín's eyes took on a sad, far-away look. "My father had sent me to Cartagena, to get supplies we couldn't get locally. Friends told me what had happened by cell phone, so I never returned. I went to Colón, where my father had an old friend, Miguel Santiago. I abandoned my truck at the Panama border, crossed on foot, and hitched rides to Colón."

"It couldn't have been very easy." Guerevich folded his hands and placed them under his chin with his elbows on the table.

"It wasn't. I hid for two days in the jungle before I could cross. Panama has a border patrol, but it's not like here. Here, when they find you, they give you food and water and send you back. There, they take what you have before they shoot you and bury you. But fortunately, they are not very vigilant. Señor Santiago had risen to a vice presidency of the Banco Nacional de Panama. He got me identity papers and a job. I worked there for two years, keeping quiet and learning the banking business. Then I left."

"Why not stay there? You had a good job."

"I did not like Panama. Too hot and too much illegal money. And I wanted to get to the United States and as far away from Colombia as I could. For a year I walked and hitched my way through Costa Rica, Honduras, and Guatemala. In those parts of the world, people who have cars are often willing to give you a ride. I ended up in Puebla, Mexico. I stayed there for a while, worked some day labor, and learned a little English and Mexican Spanish."

"You traveled a long way."

"Not really. The distance from Bogotá to Puebla is less than from Los Angeles to Chicago. But I really wanted to come to the United States. After a few months in Puebla, I took a four-day bus trip to Algodones, where I crossed the

border to the U. S."

"You were an illegal?"

"Not the first day. I managed to get a one-day tourist visa. I didn't become illegal until the second day when I got a job in Yuma. My English was terrible, so I bussed tables and enrolled in night school. With some help from the restaurant owner, I applied for asylum, got a green card, and eventually became a citizen."

"Your English is very good. As good as most native speakers."

"Thank you. I worked on it for a long time."

"How did you become a chef?"

"Not a chef. Just a cook. When the chef walked out in the middle of a dinner rush, I got promoted. I made Colombian specialties but I couldn't make decent money. Too many Mexicans fighting for kitchen jobs. Most of them can't cook for shit, but they work cheap. Still it was better than bussing tables. I went to night school to study computers."

"Why computers?"

"There aren't many bilingual computer programmers. So there's my story, Aaron. What about you?"

Guerevich told about growing up in Chicago and attending religious schools. "My father wanted me to become a doctor or a lawyer, but neither one interested me. I wanted to become a cop like my mother's cousin. I don't know if the uniform or the power affected me. According to Jewish tradition, every man is required to perform *mitzvot*. Those are actions to help others."

"That sounds good. What about your father?"

"He wasn't too happy I wanted to perform my *mitzvot* by helping others as a cop."

"You are fortunate your father is alive even to disagree with you."

"I guess you're right. We have a strained relationship now and he never asks me about my work. We don't speak often and when we do, it nearly always ends in an argument. I only wish things could be different."

Their conversation stopped when their food arrived, and they were silent for a few minutes as they started to eat. Guerevich recalled how many months it had taken him to tell his father about his decision to study criminology and become a cop.

"Well, Aaron, you seem to be far away." Martín interrupted Guerevich's daydream. "Let's talk business. You brought me that computer because there's something on it you think the owner is trying to hide." Martín sat up and chuckled. "People think when they hit delete, the data is gone. But it's not quite that simple, my friend. Just because you delete something doesn't mean it's gone from the hard drive. Delete is like cutting labels off the folders in a filing cabinet. The information in the folders is still there. You just can't find the folders anymore unless you know where to look."

"Where does it go?"

"It doesn't go anywhere. It stays there. No matter what you do, electronic ghosts of everything stay inside the machine."

Guerevich asked Velez where he had honed his skills. "They don't have courses at college in secret data retrieval, do they?"

"Hardly. After I finished computer school at night, I went to work for a company in Seattle called EED, Electronic Evidence Discovery, finding information for legal cases when writers thought it had been trashed. People wrote things in e-mails they would never put on paper. They didn't understand information created on computers can be used in court."

"But only if it can be retrieved, right?." Guerevich stared at his empty bowl. For a few minutes he watched as Velez consumed everything left on the table.

"While we're waiting for dessert, I'll give you a couple of examples."

"That's okay, Marty, I believe you."

"No, you really must hear this. I worked on one case where some mortgage banker in Texas emailed the loan officer to find some excuse to deny a loan to a Black customer. Then she deleted the e-mail. The family and the NAACP sued the bank, and the mortgage banker discovered two things. First, hitting the delete key doesn't make a document go away. And second, e-mail is not private communication."

"So how did you find it?" Guerevich had become intrigued.

"I used a data cloning software utility I helped develop at EED to restore the deleted documents. When we gave them to the prosecution, we were able to provide not only the e-mail, but the file name, the description, the date the banker created it, where she sent it from, and when she deleted it."

"So there's no way to ever get rid of information on your computer?"

"I didn't say that. Of course there's a way. But no one wants to erase their hard drive. And since most people believe when they delete something it's gone, I should be able to find the e-mails you want. Give me a day and I should be able to tell you every e-mail sent or received by that machine. Everything."

Anita brought the vanilla ice cream and Velez finished his in three bites. He smiled at Guerevich. "And thanks for the lunch."

Martín squeezed out of his chair, wiped his mouth, hitched up his trousers, waved at Anita, and headed for the door. Guerevich sat shaking his head and then went back to the office with Velez. Then he went to see Ann in the forensic lab.

"Well, did Marty give you any help?" She kept looking through a microscope at a paint chip. "I'm glad every auto manufacturer has distinctive paint colors.   This one came from a Mercedes."

"After listening to him, I'm afraid to send an e-mail to anyone."

She looked up.  "So what's our next step?"

"I'm going to take a few days off and go to Las Vegas to try to get information about that casino sale.  If I do it on my own time, I can go alone."

"Can't you just call the police there?"

"Not for the kind of information I may need. Something odd went on, and I need to talk to an old acquaintance, a guy who used to be called Sid Goldfarb."

Years before, Goldfarb had been on the shady side of the drug culture, and he owed Guerevich a big favor.  When Guerevich wore a uniform, he had saved Goldfarb's life by arresting him in a drug killing to which Goldfarb had been a witness.   Guerevich made sure Goldfarb went to a secure cell so he wouldn't be found floating down the Salt River with a few pieces missing.

Guerevich notified Captain Escobedo, who didn't like the plan but agreed to give him some time off.   "What you do on your own time is your business."

Guerevich made reservations through Harrah's Ak-Chin casino south of Phoenix but planned to wait until he arrived in Las Vegas to contact Sid Goldfarb.   The only people who would know about his trip were Ann, Escobedo, and Cowboy.

After dinner, Ann brought up Guerevich's trip again. She told him he was foolish to go alone and asked him about Goldfarb.

"I met him in college, and we still keep in touch now and then.  He was a bit older than the rest of us, being a Viet Nam vet.  He was a lousy student.  I think he went to college because he was getting paid through the GI bill and didn't have to get a job. He had a drug problem, and after I joined the force, I got him into a treatment facility. It didn't work and when he was arrested, a background check revealed he had earned the Army Distinguished Service Medal in Viet Nam. With a gold star. That means he got it twice. He had befriended a guy in his unit, Jack Miller, who was shot up pretty badly. According to reports, Sid tried to save him. He dragged Jack through the jungle about three miles back to a medic position. Unfortunately, Jack didn't make it. Turned out Sid had carried a corpse for most of the way, but he said Jack's parents had a right to give their son a decent Jewish burial at home."

"He doesn't sound particularly religious."

"He isn't. Never was. I made sure that one condition of his incarceration was getting him the help he needed to get clean. When he got out of Maricopa, I helped him move to Las Vegas. Calls himself Tony Gold now, but I'm betting he's still got some connections."

"Yeah, and with all the wrong people. I need contact information for him just in case. These people have already tried to get you to drop the investigation. I think going alone is stupid."

"It's the best way. Anyway, I'm just looking up an old friend in Las Vegas. And believe me, I intend to move very quietly."

# CHAPTER ELEVEN

Before Guerevich could get his ticket to Las Vegas, he and Danny Sanchez were called into Escobedo's office.

"This Margason case is starting to bite me in the ass," she told them. "It's a higher profile than I imagined because of the money and people involved. The Franklin kid has threatened to take his story to the tabloids if we don't get the case closed. We need to make some progress."

Danny folded his arms. "Can't we arrest his wife? She admitted the shooting. Isn't that enough?"

Guerevich shook his head. "Not that easy, Danny. The forensic evidence contradicts her story. She may have shot him, but someone broke the window afterwards. We just aren't sure who the others are and we need to find out."

"Check out this George Ginderer, and see just how he fits into this puzzle." Escobedo looked directly at Guerevich. "And I don't want you doing another solo act. You two go together. Or you don't go at all. I've requested a search warrant for Ginderer's house."

Guerevich and Danny waited in Escobedo's office for the assistant District Attorney to arrive with the warrant.

Danny sat in the chair next to Escobedo's desk. "Bring me up to speed on this. What do we know about Ginderer?"

Escobedo opened the folder on her desk. "Ginderer was the accountant and financial consultant to Stanfield's father, Philip. According to this, his investments built the estate to its present worth of five hundred million dollars. But five years ago, after Philip died, Stanfield accused Ginderer of embezzling from his father's account to buy himself a townhouse in San Francisco.    The case was dismissed for lack of evidence, but in the deposition, Stanfield accused Ginderer of being incompetent.  He had contended that more aggressive investing would have increased the holdings by an additional fifty million."

Guerevich nodded. "You'd think a case like that would cause some bitterness.  He and Franklin looked pretty damned friendly when I saw them together at breakfast the other day.  Anything else we ought to know?"

"Just that in the event Stanfield died before he could inherit the money, the estate would be divided between three hospitals for research wings. And Ginderer would receive a ten million dollar severance."

Danny shook his head. "Ten million is a lot of money.  People get killed for a lot less."

When the warrant was delivered, Danny and Guerevich expressed their disappointment that it limited their search to financial records only.  The DA had been unable to get a general warrant for any evidence regarding the shooting.

They drove to Ginderer's house in Avondale.  As they parked across from the house, they saw a huge construction dumpster which took up half of the driveway.  One wall and part of the roof of the house had been removed, the open area covered by a heavy blue plastic tarp.

A pale woman who introduced herself as the housekeeper met them at the door.  Millie Alverson, a slight woman in a shapeless print dress, white socks, and white Nike shoes, told them Mr. Ginderer was away on business.

They showed the warrant.  Millie protested and told them to come back when Mr. Ginderer returned, but Danny pushed open the door and the two men entered.

Guerevich tried to calm the woman. "I'm sorry, Mrs. Alverson, but we have to do this now."

They entered the living room and were struck by the neatness and arrangement of the furniture. The colors were muted browns and rusts, and fresh flowers sat in a vase on a runner on the dining room table. The scene looked like a model home ready to impress potential buyers.

Danny looked at the shelves of books. "This guy must be some neat freak."

"Yeah, well, he is an accountant. But it seems a bit much during the construction. No dust."

As they went from room to room, opening drawers and cabinets, Millie Alverson followed them with a dust cloth.

"Mr. Ginderer would be very upset if he came home and found things messy. He really likes everything in its place."

Although their warrant specified financial records, they also looked for any evidence related to the murder of Margason, thinking if they saw something suspicious, they could expand the warrant and return. They saw nothing. When they entered the bedroom and looked in the closet, they saw Ginderer's clothes arranged by color and style. Suits, sport jackets, and shirts were separated by about three inches on special devices.

In a small alcove which Ginderer used as an office, they found a file cabinet with the financial records they needed, plainly marked. They also confiscated Ginderer's lap-top computer, telling Mrs. Alverson it might contain other financial information. They planned to give the lap-top to Martín Velez.

Guerevich stopped at the door as he was about to leave. "Mrs. Alverson, why is the house being remodeled?"

"Mr. Ginderer is having the kitchen made larger. He loves to cook. It's one of his greatest pleasures." She lowered her voice. "He's been so frustrated. It's been torn up for almost a month."

The two men left the house and carried the material back to their car before Danny returned to look into the dumpster. "Maybe he threw some records away. Takes a lot of money for major remodeling. Doesn't hurt to have a look."

He pulled himself up the metal side and saw the partially burned remains of a woman's dressmaking dummy under some of the construction debris. He told Guerevich to have a look.

"What would he have been doing with a female form? You think he's a cross-dresser?" Danny laughed at his joke.

"Yeah, right. But why burn it before throwing it out? I remember Ann said she found cotton fiber on some of the glass fragments. That thing's covered in cotton fabric."

"And it's certainly capable of breaking a large window. What do you think?"

"Well, it's outside in public view, and it's in the trash. We have the right to take it as material evidence, even though it's not specified by the warrant."

Danny put on his gloves and climbed into the dumpster. He picked up the model, hoisted it up over the side, and handed it to Guerevich. Then he pawed through the debris and found the metal stand,.

"We'll just have to put it on the back seat." Danny climbed out of the dumpster. "We don't have any bags big enough."

"Wait a minute." Guerevich leaned the dummy against the side of the dumpster. He went back to the house and spoke to Mrs. Alverson. In a few minutes, he returned to the car with a large black plastic yard bag, big enough to hold the dummy and keep it from becoming more contaminated.

They drove back to the station and took the dummy to the lab. Ann carefully cut a small piece of unburned fabric from the form.

"Come back in an hour. I should have something for you."

They went downstairs, gave the financial records to Escobedo, and took the laptop to Martín, who said something to Danny in Spanish. They both laughed.

"What were you two laughing about?"

"I told him my thoughts about the dummy."

When they returned almost an hour later, Ann had the fabric under a microscope.

"Take a look at this."

Guerevich looked through the eyepieces. "Those two fibers look the same."

Danny looked and agreed. "What are we comparing it to?"

"The fiber on the left is the one I cut from the dress dummy. The one on the right is a fiber from the broken glass. They're identical. I also dusted the dummy and found Ginderer's finger and palm prints on the sides and on the center post which held it upright."

"How do we know they're his?"

"His prints are on record from when he was a teacher."

Guerevich nodded. "Even if he wasn't the shooter, he's involved in some way."

Within two hours, George Ginderer was arrested, brought to the station, and placed in interrogation room number four. After an hour of questioning by both Guerevich and Danny, he continued to maintain his innocence.

Danny's muscular body loomed over the slighter Ginderer. "Let's cut the crap, Mr. Ginderer, this is the same dressmaker's form that you threw through the window at Margason's to make it look like he broke through before he was shot. We know it belonged to Cathy Margason. And your fingerprints are on it. You threw it through the window after you shot Margason, didn't you?"

"I don't know what you're talking about. Of course I know it's Cathy's. A couple of weeks ago, we had dinner together, and she asked me to carry it from her storage room to the closet in the library. She planned to have some clothes made. How it got into my dumpster, I have no idea. The dumpster is out in the open. Anyone could have thrown it in there."

Guerevich put his face inches from Ginderer's. "Don't know how it got burned, either, do you? But you're looking at a long time in jail for your part in the murder. Help yourself out here. Tell us what happened."

Danny leaned against the wall. "You were having an affair with Cathy Margason and her husband found out. When she invited him for dinner, you saw an opportunity to cash in. Ten million and Cathy Margason. Pretty sweet."

"Sounds like you guys think you have it all figured out. But you have it all wrong."

Guerevich sat next to Ginderer and put his arm on the back of his chair. "Then you tell us what happened."

"I would if I could. You'll just have to believe me. I have no idea. I will tell you one thing. I didn't have an affair with Mrs. Margason. I'm gay."

"Gay or not, we know you had motive." Guerevich pulled back from Ginderer. "We're going to go back to your house and tear it apart. If you think those construction workers made a mess, they're amateurs compared to our guys.   Maybe we'll find those shoes with glass fragments from the broken window."

"You can examine anything you want.   You won't find anything.   And if you think threatening me with a mess will frighten me, you haven't met Juan."

"Who's Juan?"

"A dear friend.   And also my lawyer."   Ginderer smiled.   "And since you're intent on making me a part of Stan's killing, I suppose I will need to call him."

Danny stood up and walked around the table. "What do you have to hide, Ginderer?"

Ginderer looked at Danny and grinned.   "That's a line from a grade B movie. I have nothing more to say."

And after he uttered those words, no matter what Guerevich or Danny asked, Ginderer maintained silence. Within half an hour, his lawyer arrived.   Juan was about thirty, smooth face the color of coffee with a little cream, neatly trimmed black hair that hung to his neck.   He wore tight jeans and a fashion sweatshirt.   Sitting close to Ginderer, put his arm around the older man, and the two whispered.

Juan looked Danny up and down but avoided Guerevich. "My client has decided to maintain his silence."

The interrogation stopped.   Juan accompanied Ginderer to booking and arraignment, where he was charged with conspiracy in the death of Stanfield Margason.

From the moment he had stopped speaking in the interrogation room to the time he left the building, he had uttered only two words aloud.   "Not guilty."   He posted bail and they left the building in silence.

Guerevich and Sanchez sat in their office. The anger from the interrogation would not release its grip on them.   It was four o'clock on a Friday.   A thought insinuated itself around the edges of Guerevich's mind.   From years of experience, he knew that Orthodox Jews in the city were preparing for the Sabbath, and he felt a pang of guilt, or maybe it was just nostalgia, that he did not do the same. He decided he would buy a *chale*, the traditional braided egg bread, on his way to Ann's.

"Now we have two suspects," said Sanchez.

"Three. I still think Franklin is involved in some way. I don't know how just yet, but I intend to find out."

# CHAPTER TWELVE

Escobedo had hoped that Ginderer's arrest would break the case. When he refused to answer any questions, Guerevich and Danny believed he was withholding information about the shooting of Stanfield Margason.

The dressmaking dummy weighed nearly fifty pounds. Although Ginderer's fingerprints were on it, throwing it through the window would have taken strength he didn't possess. He had a reasonable explanation and any thought of an affair with Cathy dissolved like sugar in hot tea when they saw him and Juan Echevarría leave, the lawyer's arm draped suggestively over the older man's shoulder.

Thinking the casino sale was somehow an important piece of the puzzle, Guerevich followed through with his plan to fly to Las Vegas. Ann drove him to Sky Harbor for his morning flight.

"I hate Las Vegas," she complained. "It's so artificial, it doesn't even belong on this planet."

"That's exactly why I'm going."

She shot him a questioning look. "I have no idea what that means."

"The motives for Margason's shooting have to be based somewhere. I think maybe they have something to do with the casino purchase."

They said quick goodbyes and he walked into Terminal Four at seven o'clock. He had thought about going by car, but the dreary five hour drive would kill an entire day. As always, airport security made everything move in slow motion.

As a police officer, he had a license to carry his pistol on a plane. For this trip he decided to leave his weapon at home to maintain the appearance this was a pleasure trip to meet an old friend.  With his bag on the conveyer belt, his pockets emptied, and his shoes in the basket, he walked through the metal detector.  With an hour before his 9:10 flight, he had time for a bagel and coffee.  Of course, if things went the way they usually did, his flight would not leave the ground until 9:30 or 10:00, which would still get him into Las Vegas by noon.

The flight turned out to be smooth, quiet, and uneventful.  He deplaned, walked past a bank of clanging slot machines to the phones, and placed his call.  He spoke before Tony Gold could say hello.

"Tony, it's Aaron Guerevich."

"Son-of-a-bitch.  You in Vegas?"  Traces of a nasal Chicago dialect edged his rasping baritone.

"Just flew in.  I'm here on a combination of pleasure and business. Officially pleasure.  Mostly business."

"So this ain't a social call.  You shoulda let me know you was comin'.  But it don't matter.  Whatever I can help you with, just ask."

"I need some info, Tony.   It's not something I want to talk about on the phone.  Can we meet somewhere?"

"Of course. I got a condo on Flamingo.  You want me to pick you up?"

"No.  I'll take a taxi.  Give me the address."

In twenty minutes, Guerevich stood outside a walled condo complex.  He opened the unlocked gate and saw palm trees, each one neatly surrounded by a donut of dirt. The rest of the yard was manicured dichondra.  Against the building were several giant bird of paradise plants and next to Tony's door, in a shaded setback, grew a jade plant the size of a small tree.  He knocked and Tony opened the door. Guerevich extended his hand, but Tony pulled Guerevich in and embraced him.

Tony stood several inches shorter and was fifteen years older, but his hug had lost none of its strength. He wore shorts a slightly darker shade than his tanned legs and arms, and a navy blue sport shirt. His cheeks were a little fatter than Guerevich remembered, and his rounded nose had added a few more fine purple veins over the years, but his eyes had lost none of their glint. His hair still looked like a brillo pad, and it had become more white than brown. The circle of head skin had grown larger, although his arms still displayed enough hair to comb.

"Want something to drink?" Tony closed the door and walked toward his kitchen. "It's too early for a beer. You're not still drinking that diet shit, are you? You know, that stuff'll kill you."

"So I heard. Your memory still good, Tony?"

"Like a black hole. Things that get caught in it, stay in it. What. You think I'm an old man? I just turned sixty but I'm still in my prime. My golf game is improving and I can still hit a tennis ball pretty good. Zelda's gonna be sorry she missed you. You know what a crush she had on you."

Tony took a bottle of water from the refrigerator and popped open a diet cola, pouring it into a glass he had filled with ice. He motioned Guerevich to sit in the brown leather sofa, which felt cool in the air conditioned room and sat in a large matching chair across from Guerevich and crossed his legs.

"How is she? Let's see, she must be twenty by now."

"Twenty-two. Graduated from UNLV and works at Nevada State Bank as a loan officer. Imagine my daughter working in a bank. She's in California visiting her mother, Miriam. But you didn't come all the way from Phoenix to hear about her. What do you need to know?"

"I'm trying to get information on a casino purchase, or rather, a potential casino purchase. Does the name Stanfield Margason mean anything to you?"

"Is he that rich guy got killed by his wife in Phoenix? You workin' on that case?"

"Yes and yes."

"Talk at my club was he wanted to buy The Lucky Nugget, although why, no one could figure out. The place is a dump. Too far off the strip. No one goes there except some locals. And without tourist money, the place barely hangs on." He took a sip from the bottle.

"He was negotiating to buy it with money he hoped to inherit."

Tony leaned forward. "Inherit?"

"He stood to inherit about five hundred million next year when he turned forty-five if he could show the trustees of his late father's estate he had a career."

"Five hundred million? Lemme get this straight. He couldn't get the money for a year? Not a good idea in this town. People do not have much patience here. Sellers want cash right now. And let me tell you, patience is something I learned in the joint. If I don't do some things today, I'll do them tomorrow if I'm alive. And if I'm not, who gives a shit? I assume this guy Margason had to be alive to collect the dough, right?

"Of course."

"Who else can collect? His kids or his wife, right?"

"No. They're cut out."

"So what happens to the money?"

"Goes to a couple of hospitals. I haven't seen all the documents, but I'm sure his wife and his son'll try to get some of the money."

"So how can I help?"

"I want to know if anyone else is interested in The Lucky Nugget now Margason's out of the picture."

"No local would want that shit pile. The place has lost more money in the last year than K-mart. But I'll do some checking for you. Where you staying?"

"I booked a room at Harrah's. We get a deal through Harrah's Ak-Chin near Phoenix."

"You shoulda called me before you came. I coulda comped you into a suite at the MGM Grand. Bar, meals, everything. And anything else you might want."

"Thanks, Tony. I'm cool. Give me a call if you turn up anything."

"What do you mean if?" Tony stood up. "Unfortunately, I'm still working and I gotta get ready. I'll let you know what I find out tomorrow. How about a good steak dinner tonight? Six o"clock?"

"That sounds good."

"My private club doesn't have slot machines. It's a quiet place and I want the latest information from Phoenix. There are still some people there with long memories."

"Yeah, that's probably true."

"And stay away from the slots. You want to gamble, try single deck blackjack. The shoes are for suckers."

Back at Harrah's, Guerevich sat and watched people by the pool for an hour, playing a mental game of imagining lives for each of them. An overweight man could be a lawyer, but the young muscular man had to be a truck driver. At two o'clock, his stomach reminded him of the the bagel and coffee wolfed down at the Phoenix airport. In the coffee shop he ate a chicken salad sandwich and returned to his room.

Harrah's special was a single spartan room with a double bed, a table, and two chairs. A small TV hung on the wall over the formica dresser. The picture over the bed was bolted to the wall, and the only mirror was in the bathroom. The dark green commercial carpet showed signs of wear near the doors.   He sat at the table and opened his notebook.

He wondered if he were chasing a phantom.   He knew Cathy had lied about the broken window.  What else? Margason had become a rotten shit who needed her money until he could get his inheritance.  But shooting him in the chest as he lay dead or dying on the floor?   What a despicable thing to do.

A fatigue crept over him like an invisible fog, and his eyes began to close involuntarily. He fought it for a moment, and then gave in.  Stripping down to his shorts and tee shirt, he lay across the top of the bed for what he thought would be a fifteen minute nap.   He awoke at ten minutes before five, showered, dressed, and watched the news.   Then he went downstairs to wait for Tony.   Sitting at the bar, he ordered a diet coke and began munching on the pretzels as he watched a horse race on the TV above the bar.  When he had nearly emptied the bowl, the barman came to refill it.

"No thanks.  Didn't realize how hungry I was.  Don't want to ruin my appetite for a steak dinner."

The barman smiled politely and Guerevich picked up his drink and walked toward the clanging noise of the slot machines.  He took thirty dollars and sat down at a five-dollar blackjack table with a shoe, joining the two players who each had small stacks of five- and ten-dollar chips.  He handed his money to the dealer, a thin-faced woman whose dark hair had white streaks, giving her a zebra look.   Her name tag read Marie from Wyoming. She quickly pushed the bills through the slot and spread out six five dollar chips. Within fifteen minutes he had lost the thirty dollars.

"Maybe my friend's right about the shoe," he commented to the man to his right, who nodded without changing his blank expression. Guerevich walked back to the bar and ordered another diet cola. He had finished half of it when Tony walked in, saw Guerevich at the bar, and clapped his arm around the bigger man.

"Ready for a great dinner?"

"I'm starved."

"Then let's go. I can hardly wait to hear all the news. And I have a bit of news for you."

When they were seated at the private club, the waiter came to their table. Tony introduced Guerevich as the man who once saved his life. The waiter nodded and made a short practiced bow. Tony ordered two filets with all the trimmings and a bottle of Black Opal Merlot.

"Very good, Mr. Gold."

When he left, Guerevich leaned forward and asked what Tony had learned.

"There is someone interested in The Lucky Nugget. This interested person has already contacted the owners."

"Who are the owners?"

"A couple of Colombian brothers. I should be able to find out more tomorrow. But get this. When I heard the name of the potential buyer, I was blown away. This guy Margason, the one whose wife offed him, he's really dead?"

"What do you mean?"

"I mean really dead. Killed. No longer living."

Guerevich leaned back and crossed his arms. "Unless the Medical Examiner cut open a live one, he's as dead as he can be. What's this all about?"

"The interested buyer is also named Margason. Frank, no, Franklin Margason."

The waiter returned with their wine, and poured a small amount into Tony's glass. Tony lifted it and sniffed. He moved the goblet in a quick circle, making the wine spin against it. When the wine settled, he took a sip, held it in his mouth, sloshed it around, and swallowed. Then he took a breath through pursed lips.

"This is a keeper, Henry."

"Very good, Mr. Gold." Henry filled both glasses a little more than half full and left.

Guerevich, eager to hear Tony's news, wanted to move the conversation along. But he knew Tony from the old days. When Tony told a story, he told it in his own way. So Guerevich sat back and relaxed, telling himself he would hear everything Tony knew, just not all at once.

"You're becoming quite a wine connoisseur, Tony."

"Naw. I watch how the pros do it, and I copy. Makes these guys think I know what I'm doin', so they don't try to slip some shit past me. Believe me, if you look like you know what's what, people think you really do." He sipped his wine. "How's your father doing?"

"He's fine. As opinionated and stubborn as ever."

"He ever get over you becoming a cop?"

"We never talk about it. In fact, I haven't talked to him for a couple of months."

"You know, lots of people are too proud to admit when they make a mistake. Like I used to be. I used to think admitting a mistake was the same as being weak. Inside the joint, you show weakness, you're dead meat. It took me a long time to realize that on the outside, it means nothing. Your dad feels it in here." Tony pointed to his chest. "I'm sure he's proud of you. He ought to be."

A new waiter arrived and put their plates of food on the table. "*Bone apateet*, gentlemen. If you need anything else, just ask." He walked away.

"So who's this Franklin Margason?" Tony sliced a chunk off his two-inch-thick filet. Guerevich smiled, happy the conversation had returned to the case.

"He's Stan Margason's son. He's got no money of his own. Maybe he thinks he's going to inherit his grandfather's estate, but I don't see how."

"What I heard was Franklin had promised to put up ten million within ninety days to bind the deal, and come up with another fifteen million ninety days later. These Colombians have a reputation of being mean bastards. Like most casino owners in Vegas, they don't like being jerked around. When you make an offer, it better be good."

Guerevich bit into the first piece of his steak. "This is really good."

"It oughtta be. These steaks are flown in from Omaha every three days. The best corn-fed beef money can buy. So what's happening in your life? Have you met anyone yet? Last time I saw you, you were panting after some real estate saleswoman at Century 21."

"That ended happily, a relief for both of us."

For a few minutes, the two men ate in silence. Guerevich spoke only after finishing another mouthful of steak. He told Tony about meeting Ann Berendt when they worked on a few cases together.

"She a cop, too?" asked Tony.

"In a way. She works for the department. Forensic researcher."

"So you two make a good team? How serious is it?"

"I'd marry her tomorrow if she'd have me. She says it's too soon. Got divorced a few years ago, just before she started working at the department. Lived in Tahoe, on the California side. Her ex was a chef and part owner. One of the small resorts. She says she doesn't want to rush into anything, so we keep our own places. It's good. We need our own space sometimes."

"Let me give you some advice. I'm good at that. I don't take much, but I give it. If you love her, and she's good for you, hang on to her like a virus. Worst thing I ever did was let Miriam get away from me. Of course, the way I was livin' at the time, she didn't want no part of it. You remember Miriam?"

"Not well." Guerevich remembered the days when Tony was known as Sid Goldfarb. Miriam thought he worked for a car dealer and had no idea he was involved in the drug world. Those were days when he didn't have much time for law-and-order types like Guerevich.

Tony was silent for a moment and then shook his head slowly. "Well, that was another life." He put the last chunk of steak in his mouth. "Aaron, if I do say so myself, that was one hell of a steak dinner. Ready for dessert?"

"Tony, if I eat another thing, I'll be up all night."

"That's the idea in Vegas. No sleeping." He nodded to two big well-dressed men as they walked by and his expression changed from all smiles to bland seriousness. He lowered his voice. "I'll call you tomorrow as soon as I get more information about the situation you're interested in. C'mon. I'll drop you at your hotel."

"What about the dessert?"

"Have to put it on hold. I got to get over to my casino. Got to be on time for my late shift."

"You working nights, too?"

"Couple times a week. Casinos are a twenty-four hour-a-day business. I'm in the office. Human resources. A fancy way of saying I run the staff. And I need to make sure tomorrow's floor is fully covered."

"I thought with a felony conviction. . ."

"Not if you know the right people. Anyway, I got nothing to do with the money side."

Tony motioned Henry to come over. As he stood, he handed the young man a twenty dollar bill. "On my tab, Henry."

"Right, Mr. Gold."

As they walked toward the door, Tony put his hand on Guerevich's shoulder. "And call your old man. Don't wait until it's too late."

Late the next morning, when Guerevich came in from doing laps in the pool, there was a message from Tony to meet him at Denny's, six blocks from Harrah's. He walked from the hotel.

Tony arrived wearing ironed chinos and a green silk shirt.

"Why Denny's of all places?" Guerevich asked when they were seated and the waitress had brought two coffees.

"Because no one I know comes here and we can talk."

Guerevich strained to hear over the clatter of dishes and other voices.

"I didn't want to say anything last night. Too many ears. But there's something funny about the Lucky Nugget deal. It'll be hard to find out exactly what's going on. The information you want has dried up, which is strange. For money, it usually flows around here like water from a tap. Somehow, people here discovered you're a cop. One thing I did learn was the two Colombian brothers who bought the Nugget about three years ago didn't need to get much financing."

"They paid cash?"

"Mostly. These bozos come here from Colombia, and the next thing you know they're buying a fuckin' casino."

"Drug money?"

"Probably. But why a dying casino? Something's not kosher."

"You think they're selling drugs?"

"I don't think so.  The drug trade here is all bottled up, and the people who control it ain't gonna allow a new operation that could pop the cork.  Could be any one of a number of other things."

"You mean like skimming, or filing short reports?"

"You been doing your homework.  But if that was the case, why would they try to sell it?"

Guerevich took a sip of his coffee and looked for the waitress.  "You going to order some breakfast, Tony?"

"Are you crazy?  I wouldn't eat in this shit hole if they were paying me."  He looked at the gold Rolex watch nestled in the hair on his arm.  "I got to get going.  I'll try to have more information for you in a day or two."

Tony got up and touched Guerevich on the shoulder.  "See you."  He walked toward the door and then was gone into the crowds slow-marching to the electronic heartbeat along the sidewalk.  Guerevich ordered blueberry pancakes, ate, and walked back to his hotel.

He thought since he had nothing to lose, he might be able to get information on his own by calling the Nevada Corporation Commission.

After being on hold for a few minutes, he was greeted by a female voice with a nasal, New York accent. When he told her he was trying to get information on the purchase of The Lucky Nugget casino in Las Vegas, the voice had to transfer him to the correct department.

After being on hold for three more minutes and listening to tinny soft rock piano music, he got a human response.  Another transfer and several minutes later, he got to the Department of Commercial Real Estate Sales.

The manager of the department could tell him only The Lucky Nugget was on the market, and the realty company of record was Commercial Sales of Nevada. Guerevich thanked her for her help and called the realtor.

Pretending to be a well connected Arizona developer interested in commercial real estate, he was able to find out Stanfield Margason of Phoenix, Arizona, had made an offer to purchase the Lucky Nugget four months ago. According to their information, the offer was withdrawn on October twelfth and Margason suffered a thirty thousand dollar penalty. The Nugget was still on the market. The owners of record were two brothers, Carlos and Ruben Vasquez. There were other unnamed people who had an interest.

"Thank you. Is it common for someone to offer to buy a business and then back out?"

"It happens all the time in commercial offers. People get scared. Or they realize they don't have enough money. Or they examine the books of the business and find it isn't up to what they were told. Lots of reasons. Sometimes they have to pay a penalty, but not often. The Vasquez brothers insisted on keeping the earnest money because there wasn't a good reason for not following through with the sale. I assure you, the Lucky Nugget is an excellent investment. There are several other people who are currently in negotiations with the owners. Are you interested in owning part of a casino? There are several other casinos looking for partners."

He made an appointment to meet with the salesman the next afternoon, and made a note to cancel it the next morning. Why would Stanfield Margason pay a thirty thousand dollar penalty to withdraw his offer two weeks before he was killed.

Guerevich felt his thoughts about the casino purchase being nibbled around the edges by Tony's words. As he replaced the room phone, he thought about his father. For a moment he held the phone above its cradle. Then he replaced it, waited a moment, impulsively picked it up again, and called his father.

"Poppa, it's me."

"Aaron?  What are you calling me for?  Is something wrong?"

"No.  I just wanted to see how you were."

"I'm the same as I was the last time I talked to you three months ago.  Why do you want to know now?"

Guerevich was silent.  He could tell just how this conversation was going.  "I'm in Las Vegas working on a case.  I saw Harry Schneider the other day and he asked about you."

"I know.  He called me.  Said he saw you in *shul*.  I thought you worked on *shabbos*."

Guerevich stiffened at the accusation.  "I work when I have to.  Just like everyone else."

"No.  Not like everyone else."

"Pop, we've been over this a thousand times.  What I do is necessary."

"Really?  Tell me how looking for clues is like a doctor saving a life?"

"And what constitutes work?"  Guerevich clipped his words.  "When did pushing a button to make an electric spark become work?  If Uncle Asher, *olav ha'sholom,* had taken the elevator instead of walking up three flights of stairs, he wouldn't have had a stroke."  The instant he had spoken those words, he wanted to take them back.

There was no response for a minute.  "Well, thanks for calling.  Now we know we're both still alive."  The last word was followed by the crackle of static.

The old argument with his father put him in a dark mood.  The ancient rabbis had interpreted the admonition against working on the sabbath to include making a fire.  But it took modern Jewish bureaucrats to determine that pushing a button to turn on electricity was the equivalent of making a fire.

He picked up his notebook and walked to the pool, hoping the sun's warmth would ease some of his tension. Sitting at a sunny table, he ordered an iced tea and opened to a blank page. He wanted to list some reasons why Stanfield would withdraw his offer to buy the casino since the purchase would have virtually assured him of the inheritance. Half an hour later, the page was still blank.

After a late lunch and the loss of another thirty dollars at another blackjack table, Guerevich went back to his room. A few minutes after sunset, he heard a knock at his hotel room door, and he looked at his watch. 6:30. He was not expecting Tony. When he opened the door, two big men in their forties stood in the hall. They were not smiling. And their custom-made suits could not hide their six-foot-four, two-hundred-fifty-pound linebacker frames.

# CHAPTER THIRTEEN

The two men, clearly an aging muscle team, bulged a little around the middle. They walked into the room without being invited, pushing the door open wide to admit their bulk. As each one stepped forward, he filled the doorway. The first into the room had a bushy turned-down mustache which gave him a perpetual angry look. His eyes darted around the room, as if he wanted to make sure no one else was there. He had a neck wider than his shaved head. Guerevich could not tell if the man had tan or naturally dark skin. The other had slightly sunburned fair skin and combed-back, dark blond hair with sideburns out of the fifties. An intense expression was trapped in his pale blue eyes and his big hands showed faint purple scars on the knuckles. They looked vaguely familiar, like the hundreds of ex-pugs who used their size to intimidate their way through the streets of New York, Chicago, Los Angeles, or Phoenix. Guerevich knew them although he had never seen them before. He knew they were not cops. If they had been, they would have let him know before they bulled their way in. He looked closely for a slight bulge in their suit jackets, but he saw none. They were unarmed unless they had weapons strapped to their legs.

"Mr. Guerevich. I'm Tom and this is Jerry." The darker one spoke with a strong New Jersey accent and had a raspy tenor voice incongruous for someone his size. He smiled, showing very white teeth, perfectly straight suggesting veneers or implants.

Guerevich wondered if they had left all their other cartoon friends in the lobby but decided to keep the thought to himself.

"We need to talk." Jerry ran a hand over the top of his hair, showing a fat gold ring on his pinky with a large turquoise stone in it.

"We hear you're interested in learning about the sale of The Lucky Nugget." Tom crossed his arms over his large chest. "We represent the people interested in selling."

"Yeah," Jerry added with a nasal pitch like someone who had his nose broken too many times. "They asked us to be your tour guides." Jerry smiled like a crocodile about to grab an unsuspecting calf from the shore.

Tom furrowed his brow and shot Jerry a look which instantly caused the smile to drop from his face.

"Really? Did the Vasquez brothers send you? How are they?"

Jerry shrugged his shoulders and frowned a silent question at Tom. Then he turned back to Guerevich. "We've been asked to take you to the property so you can see this really is a straight-up business deal."

"That won't be necessary. I'm sure it's legitimate. But I don't understand why the Vasquez brothers would sell to someone who has no money."

"We don't know nothing about that," said Tom. "The people who sent us insist you see the property for yourself. We've been instructed to take you there."

"Couldn't this wait until morning?" The hair on the back of Guerevich's neck prickled as he sized them up. They were big, but probably slow. He felt he could hold his own against one of them with his quicker reflexes and police training. But this wasn't the movies. Taking both of them would be unlikely. His instincts told him to stay in the room. Going with these two thugs could be dangerous, but he also wanted to see how this would play out. He hoped this would add another piece to the puzzle of Stan Margason's murder. Now he wished he had brought his service revolver.

He took a light jacket, locked the room, and accompanied the two men to the lobby. He thought about just asking the desk clerk to call the police and refusing to go with them but that would defeat his purpose. The two men had done nothing and he would end up looking foolish. Dangerous as it might prove to be, he wanted the information that these two might provide. The three walked single file silently to the entrance of the hotel where an attendant brought their car, an older black four-door Mercedes. Tom tipped the attendant, said something to him quietly, and got in the driver's seat. Jerry pushed past Guerevich and quickly got in the back. Guerevich moved to walk around to the back of the car, but the attendant clearly had been told to hold the passenger door open for him. Not wanting to appear suspicious, he sat in the front seat.

"It's more comfortable," said Tom, as if he noticed Guerevich's apprehension. The attendant closed the door. The car glided quietly to the end of the driveway and stopped.

Half expecting Jerry to produce a gun from under his pant leg, Guerevich imagined the poke in the back of his head. He tried to turn around, but the seat belt prevented it. The tightness in his groin shuddered down his legs.

"You know, Mr. Guerevich, Stan Margason was a phony, a real playboy." Tom looked to his right as he pulled the car into traffic, heading east on Las Vegas Boulevard. "In all his life, he never accomplished nothin'. No education, not even a job. Nothin'."

"Yeah. He spent most of his life pretending to be a player. When all the time, he was just waiting for his old man's money."

*Apparently others couldn't wait either. They shortened their wait by fifteen or twenty years.*

"And he made a good faith offer to buy The Lucky Nugget," said Tom. "The owners was even going to carry him until he got his inheritance. And then he backed out without a good reason. The owners believe once you give your word, you ought to follow through."

"I'm sure they do," said Guerevich. *A lot they know about keeping promises.* He wondered why they kept talking about Stan Margason or if they were aware that he knew Franklin now hoped to buy the casino.

Guerevich listened patiently to the list of Stanfield Margason's shortcomings, thinking how many of them were probably shared by the driver and the passenger in the back seat. He said nothing. This was not a good time to voice his thoughts.

"Now he's been shot by his wife," said Jerry from the back seat. "We were told he slapped her around in public, something a real man should never do. The people we represent think his death was unfortunate but justifiable."

"Well, that's something the court will need to determine. Has Tony Gold been talking to you?"

"We don't know nobody named Tony Gold." Jerry leaned forward closer to Guerevich. "But when someone comes here looking for information, the news spreads pretty fast. The people we represent don't want their names to be part of a negative newspaper story."

"Well, the death of Stan Margason is a very high-profile case. The Margason name is extremely well known in Phoenix." Guerevich decided to play along with their game of ignorance.

"His death presented a problem for the owners. When Franklin came along, he smoothed things over a bit."

"So how does Franklin fit into all this?"

"He wants to make good on his father's offer."

Tom gave a sharp look in the rearview mirror. "If the case goes to court, the rags they call newspapers here will publish the owners' names, something they don't want. They're hoping they might be able to convince you to back off and let this unfortunate incident be considered either justifiable homicide or self defense, which it is."

"You know I can't do that. It's not my call. Besides, Stan Margason's dead, so his deal is off the table. They can sell the casino to anyone they want to, even to his son for all I care. Maybe for more money than Margason offered. Anyway, does it really make any difference?"

"It makes a difference to the owners." As Tom finished speaking, he took an envelope from his pocket and laid it on the armrest between them. Guerevich pushed the envelope back toward Tom and it slid to the seat.

"I'll assume there's a map in that envelope. Whatever it is, put it back in your pocket."

Now Guerevich began to get worried. The offer of a bribe meant Margason's death had become more than a wife-kills-husband event. Tom made a left turn, and the bright lights of the big casinos slipped behind them.

"How much longer until we get to The Lucky Nugget?"

"Just a few blocks more. We're almost there."

After another block, Guerevich noticed the sidewalks were almost empty of people. Instead of the crowded strip, or the well-swept residential streets, empty lots strewn with trash appeared between buildings. Even the street lights seemed dimmer. The red glow from the neon lights of the bars gave an eerie blood-like sheen to the sidewalk. The curbs were littered with old newspapers, bottles, discarded cola cups, plastic bags, and other debris.

"Where the hell are we?" Guerevich's fingers tightened into fists. His breathing became more rapid, and the adrenaline caused a classic fight or flight response.

"We're on Fairfield, right behind the Stratosphere. Tourists don't come here, mostly locals. It won't be long now."

Guerevich looked out and saw multistory apartment buildings, but no casinos. On nearly every corner several men stood, watching as the Mercedes went past. At Chicago Street, two women in short shorts and halter tops came out of a bar supporting a man who could barely walk. Guerevich clenched his fists, not in fear, but in anger at his stupidity.

Tom made a right turn into a street lined with wooden barricades along the sidewalk, and a chain-link fence surrounding a construction site. The pit of Guerevich's stomach tightened and he instinctively put his hand inside his jacket, reaching for the holstered gun. He swore under his breath when he remembered he had left it in Scottsdale. Looking at the darkened streets, he had no idea where they were. Times like this made him wish he had listened to his father and had become a doctor or a lawyer.

He quietly unsnapped his seat belt to open the door and roll from the moving car when Tom braked and made a quick right turn, throwing Guerevich forward and then left, his upper body bent over the seat divider. The car bumped down a dirt ramp into the construction area. Guerevich lunged at the steering wheel and shouted, when he felt a sharp pain just behind his right ear. Tom pushed him back into his seat.

"Sit down, tough guy. You ain't goin' nowheres."

Guerevich tried to reach up to touch the spot, but his arm refused to move, and his head seemed unattached to his neck. He slumped forward in the seat and saw strange colorful objects dancing in front him. And then, darkness.

# CHAPTER FOURTEEN

Guerevich opened his eyes. The bright lights made him squint and the plastic under-sheet on the hospital bed crinkled when he moved. His pain seemed constant and it came from everywhere in his body. His feet and his head were slightly elevated. A hammer beat a regular tattoo in the back of his head. He forced his head to roll to the left and saw the window.

Outside, a cloudless blue sky framed the graceful sway of a palm tree. He rolled his head back and heard the bones of his neck grinding like sand under a shoe. He looked to his right to the corner of the room and the wide partially open door. He thought about where he was. The throbbing had moved to just behind his eyes but the intensity increased, buzzing like a cheap amplifier. The pressure threatened to shatter his skull.

Pushing through the pain, he began to remember, but like looking through antique glass, he could not squinch it into sharp focus. He had been given morphine the year before when he took a bullet in his thigh during the drug shootout that killed his partner. He wanted some now to drift pleasantly away from the pain. Next to the open door he saw Ann sitting in a chair, sleeping. He could not imagine why she slept on a chair in this strange room.

Like a fire hydrant opening on a hot summer day, the memory flooded his mind. He had come to Las Vegas. Tom and Jerry had come to his room and he got in their car. The Lucky Nugget. A construction site. Pain.

He tried to reach the back of his head and grunted. Pain gripped his arm. His right side felt as if it were being ripped open. He knew broken rib pain. Playing tackle football at his yeshiva, he had reached up for a high spiral and felt the crunch of someone's shoulder in his side. The impact fractured three of his ribs and broke his clavicle.

Now he forced his hand to the back of his head behind his ear and felt a prickly shaved area and a ridge of rough skin under a bandage. Spiny plastic thread. Stitches. Slowly, he forced his arm back to his side, exhausted.

A petite thirty-something Asian woman with a very flat nose came into the room. The clean smell of soap mixed with antiseptic flowed in with her. The white jacket she wore over her wrinkled hospital blues covered her name tag. "Glad to see you're awake."

The sound of her voice woke Ann, who sat up in her chair, smiling and stretching. "I was getting worried about him. He hasn't moved for hours. Are you the duty nurse?"

She looked at Guerevich. "I'm Doctor Peng." Without saying another word, she walked to his bedside, pushed his eyelids up, and aimed a small light into his eyes.

"I want you to follow with your eyes." She moved her finger from left to right and back. She asked him to tell her his name and to count backwards from ten to one. She asked him to spell Mississippi and Wyoming. When he told her he had come in last in his sixth grade spelling bee, she

laughed.

Ann watched, afraid if she looked away, she would miss something important. "Is he going to be okay?"

"In a few days. The CT scan showed some badly bruised ribs. He also had a bad bruise on his head which probably caused a slight concussion, but I saw no evidence of brain damage." She looked at Guerevich. "Remember to breathe deeply to avoid complications from the rib injury. If you have pain, I can order something."

Guerevich smiled. "I'm fine as long as I don't move."

"Use the call button for the nurse if you need anything." She walked toward the door, stopped and smiled at Ann. "He needs to sleep. I'll check on him later and leave instructions for pain medication. Just in case. He'll have to take it easy for few weeks. No strenuous activity." Then she walked into the corridor.

Ann walked to the bed and touched Guerevich's face with the backs of her fingers. "You really gave me a scare, you big dummy. Thank goodness your injuries aren't too serious. You could have been killed."

"What hospital am I in?" Guerevich grimaced as he took a breath.

"Mountain View. Some construction workers found you and called 9-1-1. Lucky it wasn't the weekend. They thought you had fallen into the drain ditch at the site."

"Fallen?"

"They found you at the bottom of a ten-foot trench."

"How long have I been here?"

"Since yesterday morning. When Escobedo called me, I almost had a heart attack. I drove half the night to get here."

"How'd Escobedo know?"

"Tony Gold. You've been sedated to give your brain a chance to heal from the concussion. Someone rapped you good on the back of the head and dumped you there. Any idea who?"

"Yeah. Tom and Jerry."

"Really? Did they have Tweetie Bird with them?"

"That's what they called themselves. I guess it was their attempt at creativity. They looked like a couple of aging goons, but still able to do the job. One looked either dark-skinned or tanned and had a bushy down-turned mustache and neck wider than his head.   The other joker looked like ho spent too much time at the pool.  Sunburned, dingy blond hair, and sideburns out of the 60s."  Guerevich started to sit up, and the pain forced him back down.

"Sounds like my two silent escorts in Phoenix.  You look like you're in a lot of pain.

"Actually, it's not too bad.  Now.  Only hurts when I breathe.  And don't make me laugh."  He lay silent for a few minutes, then clamped his teeth and forced the effort to sit up, grabbing the side rails for leverage.  Grunting, he swung his feet over the side of the bed and punched the lever to release the rail which dropped with a clang.

"Can you lower the bed so my feet touch the floor?  I don't want to make the big leap just yet."

"Where are you going?"

"I have to pish."

"Do you want me to call someone?"

"I think I can go on my own.  But I want you to fill me in on everything when I come back."   He shuffled toward the narrow door and went in.  He gritted his teeth against anticipated agony, expecting it to be worse, and then wondered if Ann could hear the splashing.   When he shuffled back toward his bed, Ann had spread several papers and sat at the foot.  He opted for the gray plastic covered chair, his bare butt startled by the hard cold seat.

"Escobedo hasn't been able to come up with anything about my abduction.  She decided to put Sanchez on the case, since he's worked with you before."

"But Sanchez . . ."

"Don't even think about it.  You can't continue to work alone, and this incident proves it. After Tony Gold told us you were in the hospital, Sanchez insisted."

He smiled, his hard mask softening. "Good to have you here. I can tell you I was worried when I got in the car with those two thugs. I can only imagine what it must have been like for you getting that message."

"Well, I'm here now. Did Tony find out anything."

"Franklin had a couple of meetings with the owners of The Lucky Nugget. Apparently, he wants to take his father's place. In partnership with - guess who - Mrs. Stanfield Margason. But they don't have the money. Can they get anything from the estate?"

"Enough." Ann picked up her folder and flipped through a few pages as she sat on the bed. "A clause in the trust gives Franklin a one-time settlement of five per cent in the event of Stanfield's untimely death. He also gets the interest from the estate's investments for five years. That comes to about ten million up front and maybe another ten million a year. Cathy, on the other hand, only gets a one time acquittance of two and a half per cent, about five million."

"Franklin gets twenty million the first year? What if Stanfield had met the requirements of his father's trust and collected everything?"

"Then Franklin would have got nothing, unless Stanfield had a mind to share. But we know he wasn't the sharing kind, especially with his son. Regardless of what Cathy Margason said, the two didn't have a very good relationship." Ann shuffled through a few more of the pages. "When Franklin turned eighteen, Stanfield moved to legally disown him. Court documents show his son's life style upset him - steroids, speeding, assault. And other run-ins with the police. But each time Stanfield bailed him out. He dropped the disownment suit when Cathy appeared in court on the kid's behalf. The son had one up on his old man. Franklin had a career, if you can call being a bar bouncer a career.

He was also part owner of the bar where he assaulted that plumber."

"What about the e-mails on her laptop? Did Marty turn up anything?"

"Nothing we could connect directly to the shooting. Except she and Franklin Margason have had many - what can I call them? Get-togethers? At her house. At his apartment. At a couple of resorts."

"What do you mean?"

"Maybe you're not thinking clearly yet. It means they were having an affair. The son was shtupping his father's wife. And if you ask me, she saw a chance to get her hands on some of the twenty million and maybe part ownership in the casino."

"But if Stan Margason were alive, she could have had it all."

"Not if they were legally separated or divorced. They had a pre-nup. That's probably why he roughed her up and made those calls. He pushed her to get a restraining order and a legal separation, which she obligingly did. And the pre-nup also prevented her from claiming any share of the inheritance except for those explicitly stated in the trust."

"From what Tony told me, that casino is a money hole. The twenty million could be gone in less than a year." Guerevich stood slowly, using the chair arms to push himself erect, instinctively clutching the gown behind him. "And twenty million wouldn't even buy them full ownership. You know Stanfield backed out of the deal. A couple of weeks before he got killed, he withdrew his offer to buy the casino even though it cost him thirty thousand. That's when Franklin and Cathy seem to have stepped in."

"But why would he back out? And why would they want to buy in?"

134

"That's what we need to find out." He shuffled to the window and stared at the swaying palms.

"Maybe Ted Farkas can give us a little insight." She looked toward Guerevich and smiled.

"Who's Ted Farkas?" he asked turning around.

"You're not the only one with old friends. He's a Tahoe cop my ex and I were friendly with. He used to be a cop here in Vegas. I dated him once or twice after my divorce, before I moved to Phoenix. He always talked about having friends in Las Vegas."

A blue-uniformed nurse looked in the door. "You have a visitor. It's a few minutes past visiting hours, but I can let him in if you keep it short."

A few moments later, Tony Gold walked tentatively through the doorway, looking casual in sharply creased tan chinos and a white tee shirt emphasizing his hairy arms. "I stopped by the nurses station and they told me you were awake."

"You son of a bitch. You could have warned me."

"Warned you about what?"

"Those two mugs who cracked my skull."

"Hey, I didn't know. And what if I did and I told you. Would you have listened?"

"Probably not."

"Well, listen to this. I did some more checking about The Lucky Nugget. And what I found out about it ain't good."

"Hey, I don't think I introduced you two. Tony, this is

Ann. Ann, Tony."

"We already met, and the pleasure was all mine. Did this schmuck ever tell you how he saved my ass?"

"You mean about how he arrested you and you did time?"

"Yeah. Best thing ever happened to me. Not that I never did time before. Or since."

"Okay, okay, enough. What did you find out about The Lucky Nugget."

Guerevich shuffled back to the bed as Ann gathered up her papers. He turned around, faced away from the bed, and she held his hands as he sat down slowly. His grimace told them he needed pain medication. Ann lifted his legs and helped him lie back. Then she buzzed for the nurse as Guerevich waited for Tony to continue.

"What I heard is the current owners, the two Vasquez brothers, left Colombia with less drug money than everyone thought. Rumor has it these two *gonifs* bought The Nugget on a shoestring, and had to get a loan for about twenty million. They couldn't borrow from banks, so they went to the Miller family.

"Miller?" Ann pulled the light blanket over Guerevich's legs.

"Yeah, Miller. Used to be Müller. Austrian by way of Argentina." Tony pulled over a small chair and sat down facing Guerevich. "Here in Vegas we're not ethnically biased. Anyway, Max Miller didn't collect on the debt. He made a deal to own the building and lease it back to the Vasquez brothers."

"But if it's the dump you say it is, and it's losing money, why would anyone want any part of it?" asked Guerevich.

"Bad as the casino is, the land and the building's worth at least thirty million."

"It doesn't make sense. Miller now owns a building that cost him twenty million, and he leases it to a money-losing business. There's got to be more. And what about Stanfield? He offered to buy the Nugget from the Vasquez brothers and then he backed out.   And where do Franklin and Cathy come in?"

"Miller also loaned them money. Another ten million to own one-fourth of the business."

"My headache is coming back.  This problem is like one of those thousand-piece jigsaw puzzles, except there's no picture."

The nurse who had announced Tony Gold's arrival twenty minutes earlier walked into the room pushing a cart that held a tray filled with syringes and labeled cups with pills.  "Time for everyone to leave and for you to get some rest."

Ann shoved the papers into her briefcase. She moved next to the bed and kissed Guerevich on the cheek. He reached around her back with his left hand and pulled her down to him, grunting as the weight of her body pressed against his chest. "My mouth is still working," he whispered. "That wasn't much of a kiss."

She opened her mouth and planted her lips firmly on his.  Her tongue tickled his upper lip.  "Get better, you big dummy."

She and Tony walked to the door.  When Tony was in the hall, Ann turned around.  "I called your father."

"Why did you do that?"

"I told him you'd had a minor accident.  He seemed genuinely worried."

"I'm sure.  He probably thinks I deserved it."

"I don't get you two.  You're like little boys fighting over who's right."

"You don't understand.  My father doesn't even think Reform Jews are Jews.  He believes for Jews, the orthodox way is the only way.  His way is the right way."

"And what do you believe?"   She left the room on her way to dinner with Tony.

137

When the nurse asked Guerevich if he wanted a shot for the pain, he readily agreed. Why would Miller lend the Vasquez brothers twenty million on a business losing money, even for a building worth thirty million. Why would he lend Franklin and Cathy another ten million? Guerevich closed his eyes and saw puzzle-shaped hundred dollar bills imbedded in clouds and he knew they would fit in his puzzle if he could grasp them. He tried to float to them, holding a container under his arm, but when he touched the pieces, they popped like soap bubbles, and he couldn't gather them in. As he floated away, thoughts of The Lucky Nugget and the loans disappeared on the hazy cloud of morphine.

# CHAPTER FIFTEEN

Guerevich awoke Thursday morning in a sour mood. Deciding he had spent enough time in the hospital, he went into the bathroom and dressed. Mentally thanking Ann for plugging in his cell phone to keep it charged, he read the lengthy text message she had left. *Ted Farkas left Clark County Sheriff's department. Upset outside world assumed Vegas cops were paid off by casinos. Even cops in other cities think same. Big money. Sheriff's men distrust outsiders telling them how to do their job. You'll probably get no help, but check with a Captain Bill Tomasso.*

He made a quick stop at the nurses' station to tell them he was leaving. They advised against it, saying he needed to stay at least one more day in case he suffered the after affects of a concussion. He thanked them for their concern, insisted he felt fine, and walked out of the hospital. Although he felt a bit weak, he found a cab at the entrance and asked the driver to take him to the main branch of the Las Vegas police department.

Guerevich tried to put his preconceived notion aside as he walked into the building, wanting to believe the Clark County police were no different from cops in any other large city.

The sheriff's building looked more like an office complex than a police structure. The stucco front had palms and juniper bushes along the outside. Two dark-skinned men in large straw hats were mowing the lawn. Guerevich walked up the stone stairs, past the pillars, and through the front doors to a small receiving room. A female officer sat in a cubicle behind a thick glass window. She hunched over some paperwork. The plastic slide-in identification plate in the "Officer on Duty" holder in the window identified her as Officer Ralston.  She looked up from her paperwork as Guerevich approached.

"I'd like to file a report, Officer Ralston.  Name's Guerevich.  Detective Aaron Guerevich of the Scottsdale Police Department."

Pale and thin, with hair cut short enough to be called a buzz, she opened a large book.  "Scottsdale police?  You here on vacation?"

"I'm here trying to get information on a case involving a murder in Phoenix."

"Really?  Did you file the appropriate paperwork with the Clark County Sheriff?"

"No.  I didn't.  I'm here on my own."

"Of course."  She reached into a desk drawer and retrieved a sheet of paper.  Across the top, Guerevich could read the words INCIDENT REPORT FORM.  "What's the nature of the report?"

"Four days ago, two men hit me on the back of the head, knocked me unconscious, and dumped me at a construction site."

"Exactly when did it happen?" Her voice sounded like a recording.

"Four days ago." Guerevich spoke a little louder than the first time.  He gripped the shelf in front of the cubicle.

"Date?"

"October thirty."

"Time?"

"About nine PM."

"You're sure this wasn't some Halloween prank." She looked straight at Guerevich.  No smile on her face, no twinkle in eyes as flat as a dead cat's.

Guerevich gripped the ledge tighter to control his rising anger.  His voice took on the tone usually used for

140

mentally challenged offenders. "Of course it wasn't. I ended up in the hospital."

"Okay. Don't jump down my throat. Where did the alleged altercation take place."

"Alleged altercation? What altercation?. They hit me on the head and dumped me in a trench at a construction site." Guerevich raised his voice in exasperation, and his face flushed.

"What were you doing at the time?" Ralston's voice remained a detached monotone.

Guerevich gritted his teeth. His nostrils flared and he took a deep breath and let it out slowly, trying to calm himself. "I know you're just doing your job, Officer Ralston, but come on now. You have the police report, don't you?. I was sitting in the front seat of a car when someone hit me on the back of the head. Apparently two construction workers found me and called 9-1-1."

She reached behind her, hefted another large black book to the desk in front of her and opened it. "October 30." She ran her finger down the page. "There's no notation here about the incident."

"They found me the next morning." Icicles hung from each word.

She turned the page and slid her finger down several handwritten listings. She flipped through several more pages and then stopped, running her finger down another page. "Here it is. October 31, 5:45 AM." "Sergeant Leobardo Gonsalves handled the case. He was off duty but happened to be in the area when the call came in. He called for an ambulance and they transported you to the hospital. So what is the nature of your complaint?"

"This isn't a complaint. I want to file an official report."

"A report of the incident has already been filed."

"Then why is it no one bothered to find out if I had lived, or even to ask why I'd been sapped."

"Sapped?"

"It means knocked unconscious with a blackjack type weapon."

"According to this report abstract, Officer Gonsalves contacted the hospital around eleven o'clock, and they informed him your condition was not life threatening."

"Wasn't anyone interested in finding out why a Scottsdale police detective got clubbed and dumped?"

"No one knew you were a Scottsdale detective. You stated you didn't file a form 1202A. That's a request for cooperation. Did you have identification?"

The artery in Guerevich's neck began to throb, pulsing with each beat of his heart. The ubiquitous bureaucracy. For a moment he had the distinct impression that part of Ralston's job included frustrating people until they walked away.

"You would have known if you had asked the hospital. They knew."

"Well, the hospital apparently made no mention of your occupation. Maybe they felt it was not pertinent to our investigation."

Guerevich's voice rose. "What investigation? You just said Gonsalves only called the hospital."

"Mr. Guerevich, getting upset with me will not be to your advantage."

"Is it possible for me to talk to Sergeant Gonsalves?"

"Why would you want to talk to him?"

"To find out what happened. They found me unconscious. Isn't that what it says in the report?"

"I don't have the complete report here. It's been filed. All I know is Leo handled the case."

"Thank you. May I speak to him?"

"You'll need to get authorization from Captain Tomasso first. I'll call him. Would you have a seat over there by the door?"

Officer Ralston turned off her microphone, lifted the phone, and dialed. Guerevich recognized the name. Hoping Tomasso would be helpful, he walked away and sat in one of the three worn metal folding chair with padded seats whose stuffing stuck out at the edges like an old man's hair under a baseball cap. Guerevich folded his arms and crossed his legs and watched people wearing wrinkled suits punch numbers on a key code box next to a metal door. Each one bore the recognizable haggard look of someone who had worked too many hours without sleep.

He thought how police offices all seemed the same, even to the smell of sweat and disinfectant. He watched Officer Ralston on the other side of the bulletproof glass sorting through bundles of papers. So much police work involved bureaucracy, which required a slavish devotion to rules and procedures, tracking violations of trivial ordinances and logging complaints made by spiteful people.

The bureaucracy in Scottsdale was no different. He remembered one of his psychology profs had said the greater the depth of an organization, the more insulated those at the top became from the field.

After a fifteen minute wait, Guerevich saw a uniformed man stick his head out of a door marked NO ENTRANCE.

"Detective Guerevich. Sorry to keep you waiting. I'm Captain Bill Tomasso. Would you follow me, please?"

Guerevich got up and walked through the doorway, following Tomasso up a short flight of stairs to an office where a secretary sat at one of the two desks. She stared at a monitor and tapped on a keyboard. The other desk had

Tomasso's nameplate.  Through an open door behind the desks, Guerevich could see into a small conference room with a long table and several chairs on both sides.

"Why don't you go into the conference room.  I'll be there in a minute."

Guerevich walked into the gray room and sat down, while Tomasso spoke quietly to the secretary, who immediately got up and left.

Tomasso stepped into the conference room.  "Now what can I help you with?"

"I really wanted to speak with Sergeant Gonsalves."

Tomasso moved a chair to the opposite side of the table.  He sat down, folded his hands, and placed them on the table.  "And why do you want to speak to him?"

"He's the one who came to the scene when the construction workers found me unconscious and he's the one who filed the report."

"Well, I can get the report for you.  I'll have it brought to me here."

"Captain, I don't want to see the report.  I'm sure it was filed correctly, but it's a police report.  I want to talk to Gonsalves.  Often things that never get into the report are as significant as the things that do."

"You're not suggesting my men don't know how to

file a proper report, are you?"

"Of course not.  But I'd like to get his impressions, his opinions.  Opinions usually don't get into reports."

Tomasso looked grim, his demeanor professional.  "Right.  Just so we understand each other.  I wouldn't want you to think my men aren't up to standard.  If you wait here, I'll check the duty roster."

Tomasso walked back to his desk and picked up the phone.  In a minute he returned.  "You're in luck.  He's on duty today in the building. I've sent word to have Gonsalves meet you here in about fifteen minutes. You know, you're fortunate Gonsalves was close by when the construction workers called 9-1-1. The area isn't part of his regular routine. Now, if you'll excuse me, I have a mountain of paperwork to attend to. I'm sure you understand."

"No problem. Paperwork is a large part of my job, too."

Left alone in the conference room, Guerevich looked at his watch. A little after one. He had been at the police station almost two hours, and so far had accomplished nothing. Ten minutes after Tomasso left, a young Hispanic man walked quietly into the room, dressed in a lightweight cotton summer uniform, with two sharp creases down the chest of his light blue shirt and a knife-edge down his darker blue trousers. He moved lightly on his feet, and carried a thin file folder. His hair was cropped short, almost shaved on the sides and cut flat on top, and his mirrored aviator glasses reflected the inside of the room. Sitting in a the chair across the table from Guerevich, he placed the closed folder on the table, removed his glasses, and set them down carefully.

"So, you want to know what happened?"

Guerevich thought his behavior odd. No greeting, no glad-to-see-you're-up-and-around, no smile, no handshake.

"Yes, and I'd like to get your impressions as well."

Gonsalves opened the folder, shuffled through a few pages, and started reading. He did not lift his eyes from the words on the folder.

"Wednesday, October 31. White male, age approximately thirty-seven, discovered unconscious by two construction workers on the New Binion Casino construction site, approximately 5:45 AM."

"Sergeant, I'm forty-two and I'm not interested in what the report says. I'm sure it's accurate. What I want from you is what isn't in the report. Your opinion."

Gonsalves was brusque. He looked directly at Guerevich and grinned. "My opinion? You shouldn't have been there at all."

"And?"

"I think you were mugged. The two men weren't trying to kill you. If they were, the workers would have found a dead body. I think it was probably a clumsy attempt at a robbery. They hit you and when they looked in your wallet and found out you were a cop, they dumped you and took off. You're lucky you were found so soon."

"So you knew I was a cop?"

Gonsalves shifted in his seat. "The hospital told me when I called."

Guerevich scooted to the edge of his chair. "Are you aware these two goons who called themselves Tom and Jerry came to my hotel room? They not only knew who I was, but why I came here."

"Did they, now? And called themselves Tom and Jerry? Not very original for Las Vegas."

"So it's your opinion they came and picked me up at my hotel, drove me to the construction site, and knocked me on the head just to rob me. Then when they discovered my occupation, which somehow they already knew, they threw me in the ditch. I had over two hundred dollars in my wallet. It was still there when they found me. It doesn't sound like a mugging to me."

Gonsalves looked directly at Guerevich. "In that case they knew more about you than we did, didn't they? So what does it sound like to you? Why'd you even get in their car, anyway?"

"I got into their car because they were going to take me to see The Lucky Nugget."

"Why would you want to see it?"

"Because the man who planned to buy it got killed in Scottsdale, allegedly shot by his wife, before he could inherit five hundred million dollars."

Gonsalves listened with a disinterested stare and nodded from time to time as Guerevich explained the shooting of Stanfield Margason. Several times during the explanation, the officer surreptitiously glanced at his watch. Guerevich had the distinct feeling Gonsalves was anxious for this meeting to end.

When Guerevich mentioned Margason's son and widow were now attempting to purchase the casino, Gonsalves showed an interest. "Seems like his wife made a big mistake, not waiting for the money."

"The two guys who dumped me knew all about the murder. They were willing to bribe me to drop the investigation and treat it as a shooting by the victim during a home invasion. A justifiable homicide."

"But you're not going to do that, are you?"

"I came here from Scottsdale to get information about the potential purchase, because it might be related to the murder, and I wound up in a hospital."

"Well, there's not much we can do about that now. This isn't Scottsdale, is it?"

"Didn't you find anything? What about tire tracks?"

"Tire tracks?" Gonsalves sat up straight and leaned toward Guerevich. "Did you ever examine a construction site? Have you been back there? Of course there were tire tracks. From about a hundred vehicles -- the cars and pickups of the workers, the site managers, the engineers, the architects. Not counting the dump trucks, earth movers, back hoes, cats, you name it. Should I go on?"

"No. You made your point."

"Fortunately for you, I happened to be driving home when the 9-1-1 call came in. You do have a problem, however." Gonsalves leaned closer to Guerevich. "You should have told us who you were and why you were here. We might have been able to help you. But clearly you didn't trust us because we're here in sin city. You probably think we're all on the take because you mistakenly assume the casinos pay our salaries. But we get paid by tax money, same as you. Only our citizens aren't bled to death to pay their taxes." Gonsalves warmed to his topic and his voice rose slightly. "And let me tell you we run a clean city. At least as clean as most others. We don't have to waste our time busting guys for playing a nickel and dime game of cards, or hustling johns and hookers. Everything's out in the open."

Guerevich sat back in his chair and put his hands on the table. He had not expected this harangue. He became a backboard, letting the words rebound, although he wanted to push the table and Gonsalves through the opposite wall. He wanted to reach across the table and knock the grin off the younger man's face, but he said nothing.

Gonsalves pointed his finger at Guerevich and continued. "You're a detective. You should have known better than to get into their car or even to come here without telling us."

Gonsalves relaxed back into his seat and folded his arms, clearly finished with his lecture, apparently waiting for

Guerevich to respond.

When Gonsalves heard only silence, he stood up, pushing his chair back with his legs. "Now with what little we have, we'll try to follow up. From what you just told me, it sounds like these guys may have set you up. But there's only so much we can do at the moment, so we'll put it aside and get on with the rest of our work. Just like in Scottsdale, we keep open cases on file. We don't put them aside and forget about them."

"Isn't there a mug book I can look at to identify them?"

"They don't sound like locals. Locals wouldn't call themselves Tom and Jerry. Probably a waste of time, but I'll bring the books up if you want."

"I appreciate it. But wouldn't it be easier for me to go down to the offices?" Guerevich now felt somehow guilty for imposing on Gonsalves' time, but he didn't know why.

"No, I'll bring the books up." Gonsalves disappeared through the doorway of the conference room and returned a few minutes later with two books of photographs. With Gonsalves looking over his shoulder, Guerevich turned the pages slowly, but didn't recognize any of the pictures.

"Like I said, they didn't sound like locals."

Gonsalves picked up the mug books and walked toward the open doorway. "What you ought to do now is go home. Work the case from Phoenix, and if anything turns up here, we'll call you. Now, unless there's something else, I have to get back on duty. Pleasure to meet you, Detective." With those words echoing in the room, Gonsalves left.

Guerevich's jaw muscles tightened as he clamped his teeth together. Guerevich shook his head and mentally thanked Gonsalves for nothing. Then he stood, shoved his chair back under the conference table with a thump, and took a deep breath, letting it out slowly, trying to assuage his anger. He walked down the stairs and pushed hard on the door to the outside. The automatic closer resisted, which intensified his resentment.

In the bright sunshine, he saw people walking slowly, pointing at the buildings and staring, as if in a trance. He stopped outside the doorway, took several deep breaths and tried to calm himself from the frustration that had built during his meeting with Gonsalves.

*One day these people will wake up and realize they had been played for suckers. Then casino winners will be attacked and killed instead of applauded.* The thought of death jerked him back to Margason.

*What was going on? Everyone called The Lucky Nugget a losing business. Why had it suddenly become such a hot enough property for Margason to get himself killed?*

Pain shot through Guerevich's head. He had not yet regained all his strength, and his frustration had started to give him a headache. He called for a taxi to take him to back to his room at Harrah's where he took a hot shower to relax.

He called Ann at her hotel and left a message telling her he had left the hospital. When she called back moments later, he told her he was good and asked her what she wanted to do about dinner. She said she would come to his hotel but he insisted that he needed the exercise and time to think so he would meet her at hers about seven o'clock.

"I left an extra key card in your pants pocket. Do you have it?"

"Yes, I found it. See you at seven."

After a short nap, the edge of his anger and his disappointment with Gonsalves and with the Clark County Sheriff's Department dissipated. He was thankful that his clean clothes were still in the small closet. He dressed in navy trousers, a pale blue collarless shirt, and a tan jacket. Then he hiked the eight blocks to her hotel. As he walked, he reviewed questions in the talmudic fashion. *Why was*

*Gonsalves conveniently in the area of the construction site at that time of the morning? Why did I have to ask Gonsalves to look at the mug books? That should have been standard procedure in a case like this. How did Gonsalves know there were two men? That information couldn't have been in his report.* "The best defense is a good offense," Guerevich said aloud as he walked into the MGM Grand. His suspicions crowded out all thoughts except one. *I wonder what else Gonsalves knows?*

# CHAPTER SIXTEEN

Using the key card Ann had given him, Guerevich walked into her hotel room and threw his suit jacket down on a chair. "That was some of the worst bullshit I've ever been through," he announced with palpable frustration in his voice. The door to the bathroom was partly open and he raised his voice. "Gonsalves must think I'm some idiot who just stepped off the boat."

"What did you expect?"

"Better treatment. At least that."

Ann walked out of the bathroom. Her black spaghetti-strap dress clung to her hourglass shape and hinted at cleavage without revealing too much. Although Guerevich had seen her clothed and naked, he was always surprised by the way she looked in evening clothes. He stopped for a moment and looked at her, his angry attitude softening.

"I had an idea about dinner," she remarked as she walked toward him.

At a loss for words, he could only ask her where she wanted to eat.

"The last time I came here, about five years ago, my friend Joanne took me to the buffet at Circus Circus. One old man looked frenzied enough to stab me with a fork. He was after a steak that looked like a shoe sole drowned in greasy water. People acted like sharks with the scent of blood." She walked over to him, took his hands in hers, and looked up into his eyes. "I'd like to have a quiet meal with the man I love. Sit and relax while I finish putting on my face."

"Nothing wrong with the one you have on now."

She smiled and kissed him. Then she went back into the bathroom and closed the door.

He straightened his tie, tucked in his shirt, sat in a chair, and thumbed through a magazine while he waited. When she emerged from the bathroom, he mouthed the word "Wow," reached his arms out toward her, and watched her smile grow.

For a moment, he wanted to suggest they stay in and order room service, but he remembered her comment about not wanting to be taken for granted. Besides, they were now both dressed for an evening out.

"Tony told me about The Top of the World at the Stratosphere." Ann picked up a small black beaded purse and walked toward the door. "If it's as good as he said, we can sit and view the sunset and have one of the best dinners in Las Vegas."

Guerevich took out his small pad and thumbed through the pages. "He told me, too. Look, here it is in my notes. He said it's rated the best place for a dinner date in Vegas."

"Hoping to get lucky, mister?" She spoke over her shoulder as she opened the door.

He smiled. "One never knows. One can only hope."

As they rode the elevator to the main floor, he held her hand and told her more about his treatment by the Clark County Sheriff's Department. "Why do you think they don't want me here?"

Guerevich knew the police turf-control attitude that occurred in movies and on television dramas did not often happen in real life. He remembered one instance when he and his partner were called to a shooting death that took place in Phoenix less than half a block from the Tempe city boundary. His partner suggested only half jokingly that they drag the victim across the city line to Tempe and call the Tempe police.

Guerevich felt he understood some animosity from Tomasso, in charge of the department. His mountain of paperwork increased with Guerevich's presence and the unfortunate incident. But Gonsalves had nothing to lose by treating him in a friendly and respectful manner. In fact, just the opposite. He had been off duty and yet still responded to the call. Gonsalves could have played the hero. Instead, he acted as if he had more important things to do than follow up on an incident where an Arizona cop stupidly got into a car with two thugs. But more than impatience, something seemed terribly wrong with Gonsalves' attitude. It indicated either disdain or just lack of concern. Or perhaps something more sinister.

"We probably need a reservation." Ann's comment punctured his thought. She took out a small compact and applied lip gloss while they waited for the elevator.

They had the concierge call the Stratosphere and got a reservation for an hour later. Then they waited for a taxi.

As they waited, Guerevich told her more about his meeting with Gonsalves.

Ann took his hand. "Maybe we've worn out our welcome here. Could be it's time to pack up and go back to Scottsdale to pursue other leads. The Clark County cops feel you're tromping on their toes. You'd probably feel the same way if the conditions were reversed."

"Maybe, but that's not the feeling I got. I think it's something else. No one should have known I was here, much less what I came here for."

"What about Tony? He knew what you wanted."

"I can't believe Tony'd do that to me. Unless he got himself jammed up and saw me as the way out. But there were no signs, no nervousness.   Besides, he didn't even know I was coming until I got here."

"Did you make the hotel reservation from Scottsdale using the department discount through Harrah's?

"Well, yes."

"Then people knew you were coming."

"I should have thought of that."

They arrived at the Stratosphere and the elevator whisked them to the top, where they found the bar, ordered glasses of house red, and sat back to watch the people while they waited for their names to be called.   After a short wait they were seated near a window overlooking the city.

Ann smiled. "What a zoo.   It's hard to believe so many people all come here with the thought of winning money."

Guerevich reached across the table and touched her hand.   "Did I thank you properly for coming out here and sitting by my bed for two days?"

"You did.   But you can certainly do it again tonight. And again and again."

"Do you mean I'm going to get lucky?"   Guerevich's smile split his face.

"One can only hope.   Isn't that what you said?"

"It is, indeed."

A waiter came by with menus and water, and they ordered a bottle of Mondavi Chenin Blanc and two racks of lamb.

"It's good to see you ordering meat in a restaurant."

"Why shouldn't I?   The lamb's probably kosher anyway.   I remember an Italian butcher near U of I campus in Chicago who told me he always went to the Jewish section of the market to buy kosher lamb because it was cleaner. The dietary rules I follow aren't the ones set up by some ancient rabbis, who tried to encompass every imaginable circumstance. I suppose it would be easier if I became a vegetarian, but I like the taste of meat."

"Hey, don't preach to me. You know where I stand. I work in a lab in the rational pursuit of facts. Give me humanistic Reform Judaism, not old men in swaying back and forth in prayer shawls and women sitting in the back behind a curtain."

Ann's statement jogged his memory. His father had often said there was no difference between *goyim* and Reform Jews. He took a deep breath, not wanting to let his father ruin what could turn out to be his first pleasant evening since he had come to Las Vegas. He smiled, sipped his water, and leaned back in his seat. "This is the first time since I arrived that I feel like I can relax. How about you?"

"Well I do have some news. I was waiting for the right time to tell you, and this seems to as good a time as any. While you were visiting Vegas' finest, I checked back with the lab. And you'll never guess what. Those hundred dollar bills Margason had on him when he was killed were counterfeit."

He put his glass down. "Why'd it take so long to find out?"

"Because they were so good." She put her elbows on the table and folded her hands under her chin. "The lab tested the paper. It was legitimate government rag content paper. But when they were bagging Margason's personals, one of the techs noticed they were new bills with a 1969 date. She used to work at the Federal Reserve Bank in San Francisco, so she did some further checking."

"What's so odd about 1969?"

"That was the first year of the newly designed treasury seal. When she looked at the bills under a microscope, she discovered some of the concentric fine lines behind Franklin's portrait showed minute gaps. She took one of the bills to an expert at the FBI, who speculated it could have been part of a batch that came from Iran in the 70s. He sent them on to the Bureau of Engraving and Printing."

"How would Margason get his hands on those bills? It doesn't make sense. There's got to be some connection between the money and the Lucky Nugget." He chuckled. "I suppose I could ask Carlos and Ruben Vasquez. Tony told me they bought the place a few years ago and paid their share in cash. Ten million."

"In cash? Where would two Colombians get that kind of cash? Wait, don't tell me. They worked hard picking coffee beans with Juan Valdez and saved their money until they had ten million."

"No. Tony said they had to borrow the rest of the money."

She smiled. "You think they went to a bank for a small business loan?"

"No. They had to borrow about twenty million from a private lender named Miller. You're not suggesting a drug connection, are you?" Guerevich emitted a forced laugh.

"I wouldn't dream of it. Why not just call them and set up an appointment. You could ask them, oh, let's see, 'What's the connection between a murdered man in Scottsdale, the sale of your casino in Las Vegas, and counterfeit money.' And of course, they'll tell you, won't they?"

"But then they'd have to kill me, wouldn't they?"

They both forced laughter. The counterfeit money added a new dimension to the already confusing puzzle. The waiter appeared, interrupting their conversation.

As soon as the waiter left, Guerevich shook his head. "We need to come up with a way to ask them. We need someone on the inside, right? Someone who can get in without arousing suspicion."

"Maybe you can pose as someone looking for a job." Ann sipped her wine.

Their salads arrived and Guerevich took a mouthful of salad, waited for the waiter to get a few feet away, and put down his fork.

"You're right. It's perfect. Someone looking for a job."

"What can you do in a casino?"

"Not me. Marty. The Vasquez brothers are Colombian, aren't they? I'll bet they'd hire another Colombian, especially an illegal, who's looking for a job in the kitchen. He could get in, wear a wire, and maybe get the information we need."

"Wait a minute, Aaron. Marty's not a cop like you are. He's a computer professional. What does he know about cooking?"

"Are you kidding? When it comes to Colombian food, I don't think there's anything he doesn't know. He and his family owned a restaurant in - I don't remember the name of the town - in Colombia before he came to the states."

Before Guerevich could ask Martín to go undercover as an undocumented alien, his participation would have to be cleared through Escobedo and the Scottsdale Police Superintendent. Guerevich was certain Martín would agree. Because the Vasquez brothers had paid ten million in cash, it meant drug money, and drug money meant they were involved with the anti-government FARC. And Martín hated the FARC.

Guerevich had to explain the FARC to Ann, although he could not remember exactly what the acronym stood for. He called them the revolutionary guerrilla army of

Colombia, which had been fighting for thirty years to overthrow the legitimate Colombian government and distribute the wealth of Colombia to the poor people.

"Is that so bad? Giving the poor people a share of the wealth?"

"It would be a wonderful idea, but the FARC is backed by some powerful drug lords. For the FARC, distribute the wealth is a clever way of saying take money and property away from the educated, the wealthy, and the middle class people and give it to the poor illiterate peasants, with the government as custodian. Sort of like what Castro tried to do in Cuba. Marty's parents were middle class restaurant owners who sided with the government and opposed the FARC. That's why they were assassinated."

Because of the late hour, Guerevich decided to call Martín and Escobedo the next morning. After dinner, Guerevich and Ann rode the elevator down and walked out into the mild night. Looking up, they could see only a few of the brightest stars. Guerevich put his arm around Ann's shoulder. "It seems a shame we have two different hotels. Come over to mine."

"I don't think that would be a good idea."

Guerevich's happy expression turned upside down and his eyes squinted in a quizzical look. He didn't know why she said that, and he didn't want to ruin the close feeling by fretting. "If you really don't think so, it's okay. You're probably safer at your own hotel."

"It's not that, you big dummy. You need to check out of your hotel. Whoever bopped you knows where you're staying. So go to your hotel, get your things, and tell the clerk you're going back to Phoenix. Then you can come to my room at The Sands."

"Great idea."

"Now you won't have to pout all night."

"I wasn't pouting. I was concerned for your welfare."

"To say nothing of your own."

They took separate taxis back to their respective hotels. Ann got in her car and drove to Harrah's, where she parked in the free lot and waited as Guerevich went in to pack his few things and check out.

As he walked through the hotel lobby, Guerevich noticed a man seated at one of the bench seats, reading a newspaper. He was middle aged and needed a shave, a bit overweight, and dressed in faded khakis and a shirt that had been washed so many times the red flowers were a pale pink. The man lowered the newspaper, but when Guerevich looked at him, he raised it again. Guerevich walked over to the concierge desk.

"I'll be checking out after I pack my things." Guerevich spoke louder than he had to. "Just keep everything on my credit card. And I'll need a taxi to the airport."

"Of course, sir. Hope your stay here has been a pleasant one." She sounded like a recorded message.

Fifteen minutes later, Guerevich came down to the lobby, walked outside to the curved driveway and got into a waiting cab. As the taxi drove away from the door, Guerevich watched the man inside put down his newspaper and take out a cell phone.

As the taxi left the hotel, Guerevich turned and saw Ann's car leave the parking lot and follow. Once at McCarren Airport, he paid the driver and walked into the terminal. Twenty minutes later, he emerged from the southeast door.

Ann drove up and he got into her car. "You see the guy in the lobby reading the newspaper?"

"Hard to miss him. It's after nine o'clock at night, everyone has checked in or is in the casino. Except for one seemingly homeless, overweight man reading a newspaper. What a joke. Let's hope he's a snitch. There's less chance of the cops trying to kill you."

"Maybe, but I'm not so sure."

Ann parked in the side lot and they entered the hotel separately, Ann through the lobby carrying his bag, and Guerevich through the casino, where he blended in with the crowds sauntering past the blackjack tables and slot machines.

Once upstairs, Guerevich removed his shirt and trousers and sat up in the bed, with pillows propped behind his head. As Ann walked by him, he reached out, grabbed her hand, and tugged her across his legs.

She drew her hand away and stood up, saying she didn't think she could get back in the mood. "I'm a bit thrown off by all that has happened."

Guerevich pulled her softly toward him again. She knelt by the side of the bed and he kissed her. She moved away with less insistence than a moment earlier. Another kiss and she kissed him back forcefully, as he put his hand against her back. As she bent toward him, he felt the zipper at the back of her dress, gripped it, and slid it down.

With a little help, the dress fell to the floor, and she collapsed on top of him, her body going limp. "You're crazy, you know that."

"Crazy to be with you."

She stood up, unsnapped her bra, slipped out of her panties, and crawled under the covers. Guerevich finished undressing and joined her. Putting her head in the fold of his neck, she whispered, "When I got that call from Tony that you were in the hospital, I was scared."

"That makes two of us. We need to be careful."

He felt her breasts pressed against his chest, and her leg hitched across his left thigh. He felt rather than heard her soft breathing. He was aroused by her face pressed against his neck and her hand rubbing across his chest.

After making love, they rested quietly, letting the warmth carry them away. Then he heard the soft, regular breaths and felt the heat of her exhalation on his neck. He stroked her back slowly, and felt the softness of her hips. After a moment, she took a deep breath and let it out slowly in a sigh. Then she rolled over to her other side, and fell asleep.

Guerevich stared at the ceiling for a few moments before he sat up. "In the morning, we need to call Marty and see if he'd be willing to help us."

Then he closed his eyes, and had his childhood dream of flying over rooftops and through walls unhurt. But somewhere in the deepest recesses of his mind, he knew it wasn't true.

The next morning after a room service breakfast, Ann called Captain Escobedo in Scottsdale while Guerevich showered. She purposely used the land line and asked for Guerevich, since whoever might be listening believed he was now in Scottsdale. When he emerged from the bathroom wearing a white terrycloth robe, Ann was sitting in

a chair, looking out the window.

"So when's Marty getting here?"

"He's not. Escobedo said *no way*. Marty isn't a street cop. He's a lab tech. Putting him in a dangerous situation wouldn't be right. Escobedo won't jeopardize one of the best computer techs - make that her only computer tech - on such a hit or miss operation.

"Hit or miss? Is she crazy? Did you talk to Marty?"

"Why should I. Once Escobedo said no, I dropped it. She told me we should use Danny Sanchez. He speaks Spanish and he's a street cop, so he's used to dangerous situations."

"But he can't cook. And he's too big. And he's not Colombian, he's Dominican."

"What's the difference. He knows the language."

"It's not the same Spanish. And the difference is we need someone inside. Can you imagine Danny as a bell boy? He'd intimidate the men and have the women inviting him to their rooms. We need someone the Vasquez brothers would feel more relaxed with. Another Colombian. They'd feel a kinship. Something to tie them together. I'm going to call Marty. Let it be his decision."

"Not really. Not when his boss says no."

"Escobedo said no to you, not to Marty. I think if Marty asks, the answer might be yes." Guerevich picked up the phone. "What's the lab's extension?"

"You can't call. You're not here, remember. And keep your voice down. I'm supposed to be here alone."

"Then you call. You know as well as I do we need Marty."

"Damn you. I know you're right."

She picked up the phone, dialed the direct number of the computer lab, and spoke to Marty. Guerevich could hear only her end of the conversation, and she kept saying

"Right."

When she hung up, Guerevich sat next to her on the bed.

"Well, what'd he say?"

"Marty agreed and said he'd talk to Escobedo. Didn't even hesitate. Said he'd do it even if it meant quitting his job."

163

Half an hour later, Martín called and Ann answered, said a few words and hung up. "Marty'll would be there late this afternoon. He's bringing Danny Sanchez with him.

"What's the point of bringing Danny? How can he help?"

"Marty said he had an idea but he didn't want to explain over the phone. I guess we'll have to wait until he gets here to find out, won't we."

# CHAPTER SEVENTEEN

Martín and Danny arrived at the hotel a little after six in the evening. Danny wore his usual gray tweed sport jacket over a black tee shirt, the fabric stretched across his buffed chest. Martín carried a briefcase and wore chinos and a brown plaid sport shirt. His chunky five foot four inch frame, coupled with his scraggly black hair, made him look like an overstuffed scarecrow. They called up to Ann's room, and waited in the lobby for her. Ann exited the elevator wearing tan designer sweats, jogged across the lobby, threw her arms around Danny's neck and lifted her feet off the ground.

"I'm so glad you made it, Danny," she exclaimed loud enough for people close by to hear, but without overdoing it. Then she let go of his neck, took his hand, and looked at Martín. "And you must be Martín. Danny has told me so much about you. Let's go on up to the room."

"That's quite a greeting for someone who hardly knows me." Danny spoke quietly unable to force the smile from his face as they entered the elevator.

Ann waited for the doors to shut. "I just didn't want anyone wondering why you were here. Now, anyone who saw us knows. Or thinks they know, which is just as good."

A smiling Danny looked down at her. "Aren't you afraid you'll be made?"

"No one here knows me except those two goons who took me for a ride and they're probably somewhere in California by now."

In the room, Martín put his briefcase down by the door and walked straight to the small bar. He took a soda and then joined Ann, Guerevich, and Danny who were seated at the small round dining table.

"How was the trip," asked Ann.

"Boring, as usual," remarked Danny. "The section of Highway 93 from Kingman might as well be on Mars. Martín told me to wait until we got here so he could explain his plan to everyone at the same time." He removed his jacket and hung it over the back of the chair. His stretched black tee shirt showed every muscle in his chest and arms.

"Aaron, I think I know what you have in mind," announced Martín, taking a sip from the can of cola. "I'm about to get a new job. *Verdad, jefe*?"

"How did you know?" asked Guerevich.

"Danny filled me in a little. As I understand, the owners of the casino are Colombian, and they have money, which probably means they have ties to the FARC."

Ann looked at Martín. "What is this FARC? Aaron told me a little but I still don't understand."

"It's the *Fuerzas Armada Revolutionarias de Colombia*. A military group that has been trying to overthrow the elected government. I just hope the Vasquez brothers left Colombia on good terms with them. If not, we may be in bigger trouble than you can imagine."

Guerevich shrugged his shoulders. "That doesn't matter. My thought is for you to get a job in the kitchen at The Lucky Nugget."

"What makes you think they'd hire me?"

"Because they're Colombians. They might have a little sympathy for an undocumented Colombian alien who fled the civil war in Colombia, which is exactly what you did."

"Undocumented is good," declared Danny. "He won't have to have any ID."

"And they'll trust him because he has something to hide," added Guerevich.

Ann leaned into the conversation. "They'll think they have something to hold over his head. Maybe Martín should tell them his family had been killed by the FARC to gain their sympathy.

Martín rejected the idea. "If they bought The Nugget with Medellín drug money, telling them would be dangerous. The Medellín and the FARC work together. If the Vasquez brothers are FARC, they won't hire me. I'd be happy to do whatever I can to get back at them for the death of my family, even without telling anyone my past."

Martín reached in his pocket and withdrew a cook's thermometer and a small plastic tube which he placed on the table. Then from the tube he slid a chip the size of the tip of a ball point pen and flatter than a dime.

"Are those for pencil mics?" asked Guerevich.

"Normally, they are," asserted Martín. "But kitchen workers don't usually carry pencils. Especially undocumented aliens. These are mini-microphones. They're pretty expensive, but I'm under budget for this year, and I don't want to lose any money for next year. You know how it works in the agency. I can insert one into my chef's thermometer and have one in reserve. These will pick up sound up to thirty feet away. Unfortunately, the thermometer won't work any more, but that's a minor problem."

Martín retrieved his briefcase, opened it and pulled out what appeared to be a small cell phone. "The sounds picked up by the microphone will be relayed to this receiver, which can be up to half a mile away.

"I guess I don't have to tell you about technology," declared Guerevich. "Let's just hope once you're inside, the

Vasquez brothers will say something about the sale of The Nugget."

"If I get the job.    And if they even come into the kitchen."

The four people sat around the table like Brutus and Cassius plotting the death of Julius Caesar.  Guerevich knew, like those ancient conspirators, deception would be just as necessary to bring their plan to fruition.

"I'm getting hungry," complained Martín.  What are we going to do about dinner?"

"Always hungry," joked Danny.    "Maybe that's why. . ."

"Don't even go there," responded Martín.  "I haven't eaten since lunch." He looked at Ann. "I brought Danny so he could insult me."

"And I can do it in three languages."    Danny chuckled quietly and smiled at Martín, who grimaced.

By the time they had finished discussing the plan, it was a little after eight o'clock and everyone felt hungry.  Ann went to dinner with Danny at the hotel restaurant where they would be seen.   They ate in the main dining room, ordering large steak dinners which they knew they would never finish.

While they ate, Danny explained that he came with Martín because was a certified translator, helping at the courthouse during trials and interrogations.  "I just came to assist, since Martín will be speaking only Spanish to everyone.  I can record the conversations, and translate for you and Aaron."

When they scooped everything on the table into take-out containers and returned to the room, it was almost ten o'clock.  Martín nearly inhaled the food.  Guerevich ate only the potatoes and vegetables.

The next morning, Ann called room service for two breakfasts. After the food arrived, she and Danny went to eat at a small restaurant nearby. Later in the morning, they rented a small SUV. Ann planned to leave her car in the back lot of The Lucky Nugget with the relay device inside. She needed something to drive and thought an SUV would attract little attention. When they returned to the hotel, Ann noticed a man in one of the large chairs reading a newspaper and surreptitiously looking at them. She suspected he was the same man who had watched Guerevich check out of his hotel. She reached to take Danny's hand and smiled at him.

"I think we're being watched," Danny spoke barely moving his lips, smiling at Ann.

"You're right," she whispered. Then she observed loudly, "Let's go back to the room. I think we need a replay of last night." A grin split her face, and Danny nodded his head in agreement.

After Martín and Guerevich had finished the room service breakfasts, Martín opened his suitcase on the bed and took out a small digital voice recorder and two sets of earphones. He carefully placed them on the bed and looked at Guerevich. "There they are." He passed his hand palm up over the array of electronic devices, as if inviting Guerevich to examine them.

Guerevich looked at the material and frowned. "This is dangerous, Marty, maybe more than you realize," he contended. "If these guys discover what you're up to, they won't wait for explanations. They'll kill you on the spot."

"You think I don't know. Those FARC bastards didn't give my family any explanations. Or any second chances, either."

The mention of second chances reminded Guerevich of his father whose teaching at the university was characterized by his belief that everyone deserved more than one opportunity to get things right. *Everyone except me.*

A few minutes after Ann and Danny came back to the room, Martín took his chef's thermometer and walked into the bathroom where there was more light and a smooth formica counter. In a few minutes, he returned.

"Well, it's done. I inserted the mic and mini-battery into the head of the thermometer. The thermometer is useless now, but it doesn't matter. I never used one when I cooked in my parents' restaurant, and I got along perfectly well. Half the time these things aren't much use, anyway."

Martín picked up the articles spread out on the bed and placed the items on the table. He clipped the thermometer to his shirt pocket and walked into the hallway. Looking up and down the hall and seeing no one, he asked, "Can you hear me, Aaron? I'm speaking in a normal voice."

"Loud and clear," Guerevich half whispered to Danny.

"It's perfect," said Ann.

"But he's only on the other side of the wall," responded Danny. "What if he's working in the kitchen and we're a few blocks away?"

Martín returned to the room and closed the door. "Could you hear me?"

"Perfectly," replied Guerevich.

Ann picked up the cigar-box instrument. "What's this?"

"It's a relay. The microphone will pick up whatever anyone says. Then it's broadcast to the relay device to boost the signal. We can set up the relay outside the casino in the trunk of your car. It will send the signals to the room here and you'll be able to hear and record everything." He shrugged his shoulders. "But I don't have the job yet."

Martín took out a large paper bag from his opened suitcase and carried it into the bathroom. He came out dressed in faded jeans, a red and gray checked flannel shirt with a small tear at the shoulder seam, and well-worn work shoes.

A laugh erupted from Danny. "*Ai, amigo.*" You look like one of those *obreros* who stand outside Sunset Trailer Park waiting for someone to come by and give him some work."

"The only problem, Marty," remarked Ann, "is we can listen to you, but we can't talk to you."

"That's right," added Guerevich. "Can't we set up a two-way communication? I'd feel safer if we could communicate with you in case of an emergency."

Danny shook his head. "Too dangerous. With stings like this, he can't afford to have anyone hear him talking to us. All we need to do is to hear them talking."

Ann put her arm around Martín's shoulder. "You ready to go looking for work, Marty?"

"I'm as ready as I will ever be. I even worked to regain my old Colombian accent. "*Mi inglés no es barry good.*"

"Not too heavy, Marty," said Guerevich. "All the time you spent losing your accent might come back to haunt you. Besides, you'll be speaking Spanish most of the time, especially to the Vasquez brothers. And look a little scared. Remember, you're undocumented. You're a Colombian who sneaked into the US from Mexico."

"*Sí, señor.*" Martín intoned in a sing-song voice. He reached up, grabbed an imaginary straw hat, and held it with both hands in front of his stomach as a sign of respect for someone important. He nodded his head, looked at his shoes, and lowered his voice. *"Lo siento mucho, señor,"* he repeated.

Danny laughed. "You sound good, mister. You even sound like an *obrero*."

They discussed the plan and worst case scenarios. Guerevich remembered his *Yeshiva* training and the endless *what if* questions. What if he wasn't offered a job? What if he was offered a job, but not in the kitchen? What if they discovered he was educated? What if they found out who he really was. But even after all the questions, there was no decent alternative. After an hour of *what ifs* Danny didn't want to discuss it any more.

Ann, Danny, and Martín went downstairs to the casino for dinner. They looked around for the newspaper reader but he was nowhere to be seen. They made a conspicuous show about losing a hundred dollars at a blackjack table. Guerevich stayed in the room with the NO HOUSEKEEPING sign on the door. He dared not turn on the TV, knowing the hotel staff expected the room to be unoccupied. Ann had bought his favorite book, *Abraham's Children*, by John Entine which traced the DNA of the Chosen People. Guerevich had read the book several times but found it fascinating enough to read it again. About seven in the evening, the three returned with food.

"We need to get some sleep," declared Ann. "Tomorrow we have a huge amount of work ahead of us."

Ann and Aaron slept in the bed. Danny opted for the sofa and Martín slept in the chair. The next morning, Danny and Martín went to the coffee shop for breakfast and brought bagels and coffee back to the room. Guerevich again told Martín he could back out before he got in too deep. Martín insisted on going through with it.

After their bagel breakfast, the four walked down the seldom used back stairwell. They exited through the rear door which opened onto the overflow parking lot in the back of the hotel where Ann had left her car. The rented SUV had been parked at the casino restaurant. Martín carried the paper bag with the relay.

Just after Martín and Danny walked out of the building, Ann pulled Guerevich aside. "Do you think you ought to go with us? What if you're seen?"

"No one's looking for me now. Wait a minute. You still have my old baseball cap in your car?"

Ann walked to her car, got the crumpled baseball cap and a pair of sun glasses while Martín and Danny set up the relay in the trunk. Guerevich put on the cap, pulled it low over his face, and tried on the sunglasses.

He looked at his reflection in the glass door. "Amazing how a cap and sunglasses can change a person's appearance, isn't it?"

"Don't be too sure," she admonished. "If they're looking for you, they'll find you. Maybe you ought to quit this investigation and turn it over to the Las Vegas police."

"Not now. Besides, I want to find out who knew I came here and set me up. Even Tony knew something here wasn't kosher.

"You're the boss on this one. I just hope we still have jobs when we get back."

Ann and Guerevich returned to her car. Martín and Danny were seated in the back.

"Danny needs to listen to everything," Martín insisted as Guerevich entered through the passenger door. "It's good to have someone who knows Spanish."

"If you run into a problem, speak English." Ann started the engine.

"Then they'd know for sure and I'd be dead."

"Then how about a code word or phrase?" asked Danny.

"I don't like the taste of yellow maracuja."

"What's that got to do with anything?" Danny voiced the question that puzzled Guerevich and Ann as well.

"No. It will be my code phrase. I don't like the taste of yellow maracuja. I'll say it in Spanish. *No me gusta el sabor del maracuja amarillo.* It's perfect. It won't arouse any suspicion. But if I say it in English, it means I am in serious trouble."

"What's maracuja?" asked Ann.

"It's a Colombian passion fruit. There are two kinds. Purple and yellow. Yellow maracuja fruit is very bitter."

"I don't like yellow maracuja." Ann took out her notebook and started writing.

"No. It's 'I don't like the taste of yellow maracuja.' Make sure you get it exactly. I don't expect any trouble, but I want to be prepared."

"There's an alley about two blocks from The Nugget," observed Guerevich as he exited Ann's car. "When you get there, pull in and let Marty out. I'll take the SUV and wait for you at The Nugget's back lot."

"What about the valets?" asked Danny.

"The Nugget doesn't have valet parking in their back lot," said Ann. Guerevich walked to the SUV in the front parking lot. Ten minutes later, he entered The Nugget's back parking area and saw Ann's car. Only Ann and Danny were in it. This early in the day, the lot had few cars. Guerevich parked the SUV next to Ann's car. Danny got out of Ann's car and entered the passenger side of the SUV. Ann wandered into the casino.

Danny saw Martín's relay device between them on the seat. Both men were still surprised by its small size. About half an hour later, Ann walked out of the casino. She approached the SUV and opened the rear door.

"Well, I think they hired him. He went into an office and didn't come out. Is the relay ready?"

"I think so." Danny picked it up and got out of the SUV.

Guerevich did not leave his place behind the wheel. "Let's hope it works the way Marty believes it should. The recorder at the hotel won't be much use without it. And we can't sit here all day."

"Put the relay in the trunk of my car where it won't be seen and let's go back to the hotel. I'll come back here every day to move my car."

"Good idea."

After Danny put the relay in the trunk of Ann's car, they drove back to the hotel. No one spoke.

Guerevich entered through a side door directly into the crowded casino, while Ann and Danny used the valet service and went in through the front. When they were all back in the room, Guerevich opened the cover of the small recorder and looked for a switch of some kind. He pushed the small red reset button and slipped the earphones on. "I don't hear anything."

Danny sat down next to him. "Maybe they aren't talking." Danny put on the second set of earphones, keeping the adjustment bar at the back of his neck.

After a few moments, they heard a whirring sound and then voices speaking Spanish.

"I don't like this. I'd feel a whole lot better if I

understood what they were saying."

"Relax. Why do you think I came along? I'll do instantaneous translation."

"But what about when you're sleeping?"

"I'll only sleep when Martín is here. And if there's trouble, remember, Martín will say his code phrase in Spanish. And if he is in real trouble, he will say it in English."

The first day, listening intently, they heard loud talking and laughing in the kitchen of a restaurant where all the workers spoke Spanish. True to their culture, the workers sang as they worked. Everything seemed to happen in double time. Danny knew that most of the kitchen workers, like most illegals, were unhappy with their lives but still made jokes about *la migra* - immigration police.

When he returned the first night, Martín reported that nothing suspicious seemed to be happening. He never met or even saw either of the Vasquez brothers.

The second morning, about 7:45, the kitchen became quiet. A man who seemed to know everyone came into the kitchen, and they treated him with what sounded like respect, even fear. No one mentioned his name. They called him *patrón*.

When Martin returned that night, Ann asked him who had come into the kitchen and what had happened.

"A Mexican cop who helps the *jefes,* the bosses. The workers told me he takes money from the Vasquez brothers so everyone gets to work. And he gives money to the INS so they will protect the Mexican workers. And we have it all recorded."

"Cozy scheme," said Guerevich. "What's his name?"

"Leobardo Gonsalves."

176

## CHAPTER EIGHTEEN

The minute Guerevich heard the name Gonsalves, he looked at the ceiling, closed his hands into fists, shook his head, and growled. "That son-of-a-bitch. He knew who I was all the time. Whatever's going on at The Lucky Nugget, he's in on it. Tomasso may be in on it, too. Maybe even running it."

Ann switched on the table lamp. "Someone at your hotel must have tipped them off. But it doesn't get us any closer to learning why it was worth killing Stanfield Margason and putting you in the hospital. We need to find the connection between the Nugget and the murder."

That night, Guerevich tossed and dreamed of bashing in Gonsalves' face.

At five the next morning, Ann drove Martín to work in the rented SUV as usual. The traffic was light and there were few cars in the parking lot. Her car was still where she had parked it the day before.

By 5:30, she and Guerevich were at the digital recorder listening to Danny's translations of kitchen workers preparing orders and complaining about their situations.

Danny summarized the workers' conversations. "The workers all want to make more money. They all want green cards so they can work at one of the big hotels and send more to their families." Danny held up his hand. "Hold on. Someone just told Martín he didn't need to worry if the people from *la migra* came because this is a safe kitchen."

Guerevich smiled. "No bus ride back to Mexicali."

Danny continued. "They say the bosses have everything under control. No Mexicans will be deported from here. Everyone laughed when Martín told them he was Colombian, not Mexican. They told him INS agents didn't care where he came from. They think everyone who speaks Spanish is Mexican."

When Martín returned each evening, he reiterated what Danny had translated earlier. No one in the kitchen had a concern about immigration. Someone at INS had been paid off, but either no one knew or dared to name the official. All they knew was Gonsalves had taken care of everything. Although Martín talked to everyone while he worked in the kitchen, he couldn't ask too many questions without arousing suspicion. "Everyone there just wants to work and keep low profiles. Most of them live in a section they call the Barrio. It's a rough area, east of The Strip, where tourists seldom venture.

"I know it only too well," commented Guerevich.

The next morning, about an hour after Martín left for work, Danny awakened Guerevich, shaking him by the shoulder.

Guerevich sat up and slipped a pair of Bermudas over his briefs. "What time is it?"

"A little past 6. Martín and the breakfast staff are all in the kitchen. We may get something. One of the Vasquez brothers just walked in."

Danny put the earphones back on to listen. Guerevich put on the second set of earphones although he did not understand a single word of what was said. The two men huddled around the small box. Ann sat up in bed and watched them.

Danny commented as he translated. "Everyone calls him *jefe*, boss. Martín's clever. He made a point of calling him Señor Vasquez.    Now Vasquez is asking Martín about his life in Colombia."

"Can you tell which brother?"

"No.  Martín didn't mention a first name.

Danny looked at Guerevich and translated Vasquez's words exactly.    "Velez.    You have a very famous name. Where did you learn to cook?"

Ann slipped on a robe, her hair tousled from a night's sleep.  She yawned and rubbed her eyes.  She went into the kitchenette, started the coffee, and returned to the table to sit next to Guerevich.

For several minutes, Danny said nothing.    He squinted as if trying to hear better. Then he continued with an account of what was happening.    "Martín is explaining. He said his father and mother ran a cafe in Baranquilla, and he worked there from the age of ten.  The cafe was owned by a wealthy family."

Guerevich grimaced. "But Marty told me he's from Sincelejo."

Danny held up his hand for quiet.    Suddenly shouting battered their ears through the earphones.

Guerevich leaned forward, his expression worried. "What's Vasquez yelling about?  Is Marty in trouble?"

"It's nothing.  He's yelling at one of the kitchen staff for not wearing gloves.  Food inspectors are coming."

Ann silently motioned a request to see who wanted coffee.  Danny shook his head no, but Guerevich nodded. Ann got two cups and poured one for him and one for herself.

Danny continued. "Martín is still talking.    He says he always loved cooking, and the rich owners treated him well, but when he got older, he wanted more, a life away from the civil war."  Danny paused again.    "Vasquez asked Martín if he's related to Manuel Marulanda Velez."  Danny shrugged his shoulders as he translated. "Martín said he heard of that name in connection with the revolution, but he has many cousins he has never met. He asked who Manuel Marulanda Velez is."

"Do you know who he is?"

Danny just shrugged his shoulders again and held up his hand for quiet.

"Now Vasquez is explaining that Velez was a hero of the revolution, and turned the peasants into the revolutionary army." Danny paused. "Martín asked if Vasquez means the FARC? Damn. I hope he's not going to let his anger mess things up."

Danny leaned toward the recorder and adjusted the earphones. "Vasquez told Martín the FARC fights for equal opportunity and distribution of wealth. He said the United States calls them communists and drug dealers and pays the government of Colombia to fight them and prevent progress. Vasquez said if the FARC had been in charge, Martín's family could have owned the restaurant, not just worked for some wealthy *terratenientes*. Oh, Shit. Vasquez sounds upset."

"Shit is what Marty'll be in if he continues." Guerevich leaned back and gripped his forehead with his hand. "What the hell is he doing?"

Ann leaned forward and put her elbows on her knees, her head in her hands. "He's going to get himself killed. I knew we shouldn't have asked him to do this."

"Wait," said Danny. "Martín just told Vasquez he's

right. A revolution is necessary for Colombia to change."

The three at the table all exhaled simultaneously, as if they had been holding their breath.

Danny smiled. "He's really clever. Saying something that's true without telling the truth."

When Ann poured another cup of coffee for herself, her hand shook and she spilled some on the table. The sun peered over the tops of the tall buildings, illuminating the hotel room through streaked windows, the vertical blinds creating a prison bar effect in light and shadow.

"Vasquez just called Martín a very intelligent man and asked very quietly if he would he like to make some extra money. Maybe even a thousand dollars. Martín said yes. Then he could send some to his parents and maybe bring his two sisters here from Bogotá."

"Does he have any sisters? He told me his whole family had been killed."

Danny waved his hand for quiet. "Vasquez just told Martín to come to his office after work and he will tell him how it could be done."

Ann carried her cup back toward the kitchen. "Why would he single out Marty? I have a bad feeling about this."

Guerevich removed his headphones and looked at Ann. "Marty is a Colombian. Maybe Vasquez feels he can trust another Colombian."

Danny raised his voice. "Wait. Something's wrong. Another cook asked Martín for his thermometer for a roast. Vasquez told Martín to give the cook his thermometer."

"I knew this whole plan was crazy." Ann poured coffee into her cup and walked back to the table.

Danny said nothing for several seconds. "Vasquez is talking to other workers. He must have walked away, because the sound is a bit weaker. *Mierda*. Things are getting worse. The other cook is yelling the fucking thermometer Martín gave him doesn't work. Vasquez told the cook to throw it away and borrow one from someone else."

"No, no, no." Guerevich stood and shook his head. He put one of the phones to his ear. "That's all we need."

"Now it sounds like Vasquez is leaving the kitchen. It's hard to hear, but I think Martín is telling him goodbye and will meet him in his office after work."

"Now there's nothing," Guerevich threw his earphones toward the sofa. The short cord kept them from hitting anything. "What the hell's going on?"

Danny removed his headset. "I think the cook who took the thermometer threw it in the trash. In a few minutes, it'll probably be covered with all kinds of kitchen garbage. What do you want to do?"

"What can we do? We'll have to wait until Marty gets back."

Ann jumped up and headed for the bedroom. "You mean we're going to sit here like we're deaf? No way. I'm getting dressed and going over there. The situation's way too dangerous for him. We need to extract him."

Danny stood and pretended to do a fast draw. He aimed his pencil at Ann. "We could barge in there like they do in the movies. Only none of us would come out alive. Aaron's right. There's nothing we can do, even if there is a problem." He threw his pencil down on the table. "*Mierda!*"

"Maybe Ann's right. We need to get Marty out of there." He walked to the window, looked out, took a deep breath, and let it out slowly. "On the other hand, nothing has happened so far, so let's not panic. Martín is smart. He won't do anything foolish."

"Dammit. I hate it but you're both right." She sat back on the chair and folded her arms, as if her action

would protect both her and Martín.

Guerevich smiled at Ann. "Yeah. Remember *Julius Caesar*? Just before they go into battle, Brutus says to Cassius, *O, that a man might know the end of this day's business ere it come! But it sufficeth that the day will end, and then the end is known."*

"I majored in Poly-Sci, not Lit, Aaron. I really don't give a shit what Brutus said. Marty could be in trouble. He may end up dead, and all we can do is wait? It sucks."

Time moved like a snail on dry pavement. Guerevich looked at his watch. 10:10. Half an hour later, he looked again. 10:15. He tried to keep an outwardly relaxed and upbeat attitude, but imagined Vasquez had somehow found out Martín was an undercover cop and called him to the casino office to kill him. The remainder of the day dragged. They all went through the motions of living but remembered none of them.

"Maybe I should call my father," Guerevich said aloud. "I could ask him if there is a Halachic passage related to this dilemma. Or maybe have him quote me some prophet about how we're suffering for our iniquity."

"Sarcasm doesn't help, Aaron. We're all just as worried as you are."

"At least when Joshua sent spies into Jericho, they had Rahab to shelter them. Martín has no one. He's completely on his own."

Danny agreed with Ann. "Nothing we can do but wait. Martín's a very clever man. He can look after himself."

"It's like holding my breath under water." Guerevich gave up his pretense of being relaxed and unconcerned. He paced the floor drinking one cup of coffee after another. For an hour before Danny left to get Martín, Ann sat immobilized on the sofa, looking at the TV news but unable to concentrate on the broadcast.

Danny drove into The Lucky Nugget's parking lot at two o'clock. He prayed Martín would come walking out as usual. It had been nearly five hours since the microphone had ended up in the trash and he had heard the last voice contact with Martín.

Danny sat in the parking lot drumming on the steering wheel. Would he discover the Colombian had disappeared? Would he be told no one named Martín ever worked there. Martín had told him that government informers against FARC had been found with their tongues cut out and fingers chopped off. Danny wondered if they would find Martín's mutilated body in a shallow grave after a rain in the desert.

# CHAPTER NINETEEN

Danny thought about his cover story, if anyone asked. He worked in heavy maintenance at Harrah's casino and lived there with his girlfriend. They shared a room with Martín and several others, relying on the commonly held belief that illegals crowded as many people as possible into a single living space to save money.

Waiting back in the hotel room, Ann and Guerevich stared at the recorder, as if they expected it to start broadcasting miraculously. Another hour passed, the sixth. Every few minutes, Guerevich walked over and moved the vertical blinds aside so he could look out the window.

"What if Danny doesn't find him?" Ann's anxiety forced tears to her eyes. "He can't just walk into the casino looking for him. How long can he sit outside in the parking lot and wait for Marty to come out of work?"

"He can go in if he has to. His cover story is a good one. Logical."

"Danny doesn't look or act like a man working for

minimum wages."

"He'll know how to act if he has to go inside. Marty went to meet with Vasquez, nothing more. Why would Vasquez have even mentioned the money unless he wanted Marty to do some kind of a job for him?"

Ann got up and walked toward the bed when her cell phone buzzed. The sound caused her to bolt for the phone. As she put the phone to her ear, she eyed her service pistol on the table near the doorway.

Her assistant at the lab had heard from the BEP. The hundred dollar bills were definitely counterfeit, but no one at BEP would say anything about their source.  Counterfeit bills could usually be traced to a source based on the paper or ink, but these bills had caused the CIA to become involved. Ann stood next to the bed and told Guerevich, whose eyes opened wide in surprise.

"The CIA?  Why would the CIA be interested in a counterfeiting operation?"

Before she could answer, they heard the key card snap open the door lock.  Guerevich momentarily froze, his head turned toward the door.  Ann, moved to the small table, picked up her semiautomatic Smith and Wesson and held it in both hands.  The door opened fully and Danny walked in followed by Martín, who carried a black briefcase.

Danny saw Ann holding her pistol in the ready position. *"Madre de Dios.  Who were you expecting?"*

"You two, but we wanted to be prepared, just in case."

Martín set the briefcase down on the floor just inside the door.

"Marty, what the hell happened?"  Guerevich walked toward the two surprised men and hugged Martín. "It's almost four.  We've been going crazy here.  Thank God you're both safe.

Ann lowered her weapon and returned it to her holster on the table before she walked back to the living room area. "We've been going nuts since we lost contact with you this morning."

"You are not the only ones who worried," said Danny.  "I sat outside so long, someone asked if I was a limo service."

"Can you believe my *pinche de suerte*?"

Danny laughed. "You really are starting to sound like a Mexican."

Martín flopped in the sofa, his arms gesturing in the air. "César borrowed my thermometer and threw it in the trash because it didn't work. I wanted to strangle him."

Guerevich exhaled loudly and gave an embarrassed laugh. "We figured he threw it away. Ann wanted to go over there to pull you out." He stepped back. " What happened at the meeting?"

"I have been given a very important assignment. I told Danny about it on the ride back. Look what I brought."

Martín picked up the briefcase and opened it on the coffee table. He turned it toward Guerevich and Ann who had seated themselves on the sofa. They both stared.

Ann leaned forward to get a closer look. "I don't get it, Marty. It's an empty briefcase."

"Empty now. Tomorrow morning it will be filled with hundred dollar bills."

Ann's face brightened and she whistled. "You mean counterfeit hundred dollar bills."

Guerevich rubbed his hand on the green felt that lined the case, examining it for a false bottom. "What're you talking about, Marty?"

Martín got up, walked into the kitchenette and took a cola from the refrigerator. "I'm starving. What are we doing for dinner?"

Guerevich scowled. "I thought you worked in a kitchen."

"I do. We work. But we can't take time to eat."

Guerevich lowered his head and stared, the bottoms of his eyes almost glowing white. His eyebrows met in furrowed wrinkles on his reddening forehead as he glared at Martín. "Dammit, Marty."

"Okay, okay. No suspense. I'm meeting Carlos Vasquez in the morning." Martín walked back, pulled up a chair and put his feet up on the low coffee table. He took a sip of his cola, put the can down and stared at the recorder in the middle of the table. "Now that thing is useless."

The light from the late afternoon sun gave an orange glow to the room. Guerevich and Ann looked at him anxiously, waiting for him to continue. Guerevich's anger seethed just below the surface. "You going to tell us or do we have to beat it out of you?"

"I didn't tell you because it took a while to put the pieces together to understand."

Guerevich shouted. "Understand what?"

"A couple of days ago, I helped unload a delivery of large cardboard boxes. We carried them down to a lower level and put them with a stack of others. All the boxes were all old and dirty and marked in English and another language I don't know. All squiggles and dots. It could have been Arabic. Anyway, it took two of us to carry each one. They weighed about a hundred pounds each and were about four feet square and two feet high. As César and I carried one box, he lost his grip and dropped his end, breaking the box and exposing the contents. It was filled with large sheets of paper. Carlos screamed at César for dropping his end."

Ann nodded. "What's the big deal about paper?"

"There is only one kind of paper like that. It had red and blue threads woven through it. When I helped put the sheets back into the box, I felt like I was touching money. Casinos do not use that type of paper. And before I went back to work, I saw a large machine in the basement covered with tarps. I lifted one end and saw the name. Whelan Intaglio."

"Intaglio? Of course," Ann laughed. "They're printing money. And what better place than a casino? This gets crazier by the second."

She walked into the small kitchenette, took a block of cheese from the refrigerator and started slicing it on the counter. She grinned when everyone stared at her. "I have to munch when I get upset. It calms my stomach."

Martín nodded. "Slice some for me, too. And bring some crackers."

Guerevich shrugged his shoulders and raised his hands, palms up.

Danny, seated on the sofa, agreed. "It doesn't make sense."

Ann carried a plate of cheese and a box of crackers toward the table where the three men sat. "Yes, it does. That paper with the thread in it is BEP money-quality paper."

Martín nodded at Ann. "If the Vasquez brothers are running a counterfeiting operation, they must be using the old Iran hundred-dollar plates. They'll be able to print bills that are undetectable."

Ann looked at him. "Not exactly. But like the hundred dollar bills Margason had on him, it took a microscopic examination by the BEP to detect them. If you're right, Marty, I know why the CIA is involved."

Guerevich sounded irritated. "Will you two tell me what the hell you're talking about? You seem to know something Danny and I don't."

Martín took two slices of cheese and popped them into his mouth. "Don't you remember the Iran-Contra scandal? Only part of it involved the Nicaraguan Contras."

"I read about that when I was a teen-ager in Monte Plata," said Danny. "I belonged to the Central American and Caribbean Bodybuilding and Fitness Federation. Back then I wanted to become a world-class body builder. When I competed in Santo Domingo, I was one of the top ten in the heavyweight division."

Ann broke a slice of cheese to fit a cracker and smiled. "What happened? People still stare the way you fill out a tee shirt."

"Too time consuming. I didn't want to work out six or seven hours a day. But that's not important. What about the Contras?"

"Right. I had a prof who was a Reagan supporter for one of my graduate Poly-Sci courses," said Ann. So naturally I did my major research project on the Iran-Contra scandal. In the early seventies, the CIA secretly gave the Shah of Iran a set of hundred dollar printing plates, along with ink and banknote quality paper. Reagan couldn't give the Shah money directly without the consent of Congress because of the Boland Act. The Shah was a nasty son-of-a-bitch, but he was our ally. It became quite a scandal that eventually involved Reagan and George Bush who was Vice President at the time. Bush had been head of the CIA but he maintained he had been kept in the dark. Reagan said he had been out of the loop and didn't know what was going on, which was probably true. When Ayatollah Khomeni returned to Iran from exile in France and the Shah escaped to the United States for cancer treatments, he left everything behind in Teheran. Plates, press, ink, paper, and billions in hundred dollar bills."

"That's how Khomeni got the plates," added Martín. "I learned about Manuel Noriega's involvement when I worked for Miguel Santiago at the bank in Panama."

"But wasn't Noriega convicted of drug smuggling?" Guerevich added to his question with arm gestures and a shoulder shrug. "How does he fit in with counterfeiting?"

"It was a bit complicated," said Martín. "There had to be some kind of a deal between Bush, Noriega, and the Iranians. Noriega was the unfortunate head of the military government in Panama when eight billion in newly printed

U. S. currency was deposited at the Banco Nacional de Panama. Santiago told me it went into the account of Pablo Escobar, the Colombian cocaine king, as some sort of a payoff. Then four billion of that deposit was taken to Iran where it was exchanged at the Tehran mint, one legitimate bill for every two counterfeits. The other four billion was given to Bush. He called it funds from an arms transaction with Iran part of which was used to support the Contras."

"What happened to the rest?" asked Guerevich.

Ann became animated, her hands flying. "It disappeared down the ultra-black hole of covert finances. But the BEP told my techs the Teheran plates had an intentional flaw. A minute imperfection to make them detectible as counterfeit. There's a minute white space between some of the lines around Franklin's portrait. They can only be seen under a microscope."

Guerevich looked at Ann. "You mean exactly like the bills they found on Margason's body."

Danny looked confused. "Why would the CIA buy counterfeit money? And why would Iran give it up? They could have done real economic damage and they hated the America."

Ann smiled and put another slice of cheese on a cracker. "You don't understand world power politics. Iran needed military equipment for their war with Iraq. They wanted arms, ammunition and replacement parts for weapon systems. The exchange of equipment and money was arranged by Colonel Oliver North on behalf of the CIA's William Casey who hoped Iran would also free their American hostages."

Martín took the last slice of cheese. "Santiago told me he watched the money off-loaded from a cargo plane on two shrink-wrapped pallets, guarded by the Panamanian military. Can you imagine? Eight billion in counterfeit from

Iran at Howard/Albrook Air Force base. The money was deposited in Escobar's name, but the CIA knew it could never leave the bank vault. I am sure Noriega knew about the ruse, but Escobar didn't. Not so strangely, he died in a police shoot-out. Unarmed. A British TV documentary crew filmed the entire incident."

"Noriega was luckier than Escobar," said Danny. "He ended up in a federal resort prison."

Martín sat back and waited for a response, like a cat who had discovered a hidden mouse hole. "And that seemed to be the end of the story of the Iran plates and paper. Until now."

Danny began packing away the the electronic equipment on the table. "But what happened to the other four billion? They only sent four billion to Iran."

"That was the part of my research that really rankled my prof. The money went to Nana DeBusia of Guyana. He laundered it through various banks, including the Vatican's. For his trouble, DeBusia took a commission of $200 million. The remaining $3.8 billion was then secreted in private numbered accounts around the globe controlled by George Bush and William Casey." She looked at Martín. "You think the plates and paper somehow ended up in Colombia?"

"Had to. Maybe sent to Escobar along with the eight billion. I don't know how the Vasquez brothers got them. My guess is they stole them when they discovered what they were."

Guerevich brightened. "So that's why the CIA is interested. If the plates are traced back to them, it'll be worse than egg on their faces."

"That is ancient history. Tomorrow morning, Carlos Vasquez is going to give me one hundred thousand in counterfeit hundred dollar bills printed on real government paper, probably with those plates." He smiled, took out a small note pad, and flipped through several pages. "Of course, I can't know that. I am to take the money to Yuma where I meet someone at the Best Western at Avenue 2E and the Interstate. My guess is he will take the money into California and then across the border to Algodones."

Ann looked at Martín. "Why Algodones? Why not Tijuana? Or Nogales?

"Too big and watched too carefully," declared Danny. "Algodones is very small, and a common crossing place for people who spend the winter in Yuma. Hundreds of American and Canadian tourists go across every day to shop and to get cheap medicine. You crossed into the US there, didn't you Marty?"

Guerevich cut off Martín's response. "You're not going across the border to Algodones, are you?"

"No, no. Once I deliver the money, my part of the job is done."

"They trusted you to go alone?"

"No way. They're sending that cop, Gonsalves, with me. He is going along to guard me, I suppose. More likely to watch me."

"He'll do more than watch you. How are you supposed to get back?"

"Gonsalves. He won't carry the money himself so he

goes along as an escort."

Guerevich cut him off. "Don't underestimate him, Marty. If something goes wrong, the illegal gets blamed. After he's dead, of course. There's miles of empty desert between Yuma and Gila Bend. Even if nothing goes wrong, you'll wind up in a shallow grave. In twenty years or so, your bones will show up after a hard rain."

"You're probably right. Safer to find another mule than to trust me to keep my mouth shut."

Ann closed up the box of crackers. "Do you know who you're supposed to meet in Yuma?"

Martín nodded and smiled. "Frank Margason."

Guerevich stood up. "I'll be damned. I knew it, that fucking son-of-a-bitch."

"We could have the Yuma police arrest him when he meets Martín," said Danny.

Ann shook her head. "No. If we have him arrested with counterfeit money, it'll look like entrapment. Even if he pleads guilty, he'd probably get probation. But he'd know we're on to him. And so would the Vasquez brothers."

Martín looked puzzled. "So what should I do about the money?"

"Take it to Yuma and make the transfer," said Guerevich. "And make sure you give Margason the briefcase in a public place, like the lobby where there are other people. He probably has a room under an assumed name. Don't go there. If there's time, find out whatever you can from him. Ask him about his father. Make it seem you're asking to practice your English."

"I could tell him about my father being killed, too. That might get things rolling."

Ann interrupted. "No, no. There's no way you could know about his father's death. Ask him as if you think his father is alive."

"Then what?"

"Once you've made the transfer, get the hell out of there," said Guerevich. "Disappear. Go to the bathroom. Hide. Anything. Just don't go back to Las Vegas with Gonsalves. Remember, you're the only outsider who knows about the money transfer. If you're dead, you're just another undocumented alien. Gonsalves could even say you tried to rob him."

"Without a gun?"

"After you're dead, Gonsalves'll find a gun in your possession. He'll be the Vegas cop who followed you after a robbery and shot you in self defense. Don't trust him. As soon as you can, get back to Scottsdale and report to Escobedo."

"What do I use for money?"

Guerevich handed him a twenty-dollar bill. "Put it in your pocket. I'd give you more but you can't carry much without suspicion. And you sure can't use any of the counterfeit. We'll let the Las Vegas police know about the counterfeiting operation. I'd bet they'll want to button it up before the CIA comes nosing around. I just hope Tomasso isn't part of it."

Martín smiled and shook Guerevich's hand. "Thank you."

"Why are you thanking me? You're the one who might get killed."

"True. But this feels right. When I signed on for police work, I never thought I'd be able to avenge my family's death as well."

Guerevich put his hand on Martín's shoulder. "This is something you don't have to do, Marty. "You work with computers, not chasing dangerous people."

"Aaron, you must be joking. I'd go back there right now with a gun and blow those *chingadores* away if I

thought it would do any good."

"Now you do sound like a Mexican," said Danny.

"Having a gun might not be a bad idea. Ann has an extra one. A .38 Colt snub nose in her cosmetic bag. It's small, but it can do the job if necessary. Especially with hydroshock slugs."

"I'm supposed to be an illegal worker. Do you think an illegal would carry? It would be better if I went unarmed in case they search me." He closed the briefcase and left it on the coffee table. He got a small bag of potato chips and another cola, and returned to the dining area where Guerevich, Ann, and Danny stood next to the sofa.

Danny patted Martín on the back. "You are one gutsy *hombre, amigo.* I don't know if I would go without a gun. If they find you out, you're a dead man."

Ann scowled. "How are they going to find out? As far as they know, he's just another undocumented alien looking to make some money to send home to his family."

Martín put the last of the chips in his mouth and drained the cola. "Now, let's get some dinner before I pass out."

The three of them went to the hotel dining room and ate, leaving Guerevich alone in the room.

The next morning, Danny dropped Martín at The Nugget. There would be no communication with him. Once again, there was nothing they could do but trust to Martín's cleverness.

# CHAPTER TWENTY

Danny returned to the hotel room. "He's on his own now."

Ann walked toward the bed and put her suitcase on it. "So are we. It's time to get out of sin city. What are we going to do about the counterfeiting?"

There was silence for a moment until Danny spoke. "If we report it to the Las Vegas Police Department, we could risk Martín's life."

"Only if Tomasso's in it with Gonsalves," said Guerevich. "I talked to Tomasso. My gut instincts tell me he's not involved."

Danny grimaced. "Do you think we can take that chance?"

Ann spoke as she started throwing her clothes in the travel bag without folding them. "Maybe we ought to wait until the money transfer's completed and then call the FBI. That way, Marty'd be in the clear. Counterfeiting's federal. And if Marty's right, the CIA's going to be involved."

Danny agreed. "Even if Tomasso isn't part of it, he could cause us all a pack of trouble. What if he says he knew about the counterfeiting and we interfered with his ongoing investigation. Ann's right. We need to wait and call the feds once we're out of Nevada."

Guerevich shook his head. "I know we don't have any jurisdiction here. But we need to let someone know about Gonsalves. Especially if Marty has any trouble. Better if someone here knows."

Ann and Danny nodded their agreement as Ann continued to stuff her suitcase.

Guerevich picked up his briefcase and walked to the door. "My bag's packed. I put all the recordings and other evidence here in my briefcase. I 'm going to take it to Tomasso while you two finish."

Danny nodded. "I'm packed, too. I'll come with you. Just in case there's a problem. I can wait in the car." He parked in the visitor's lot as Guerevich trudged into the Clark County Sheriff's building for the second time, hoping this meeting would not prove as frustrating as his first one. Once through the metal detector, he presented his credentials to a different receptionist and asked him to call Lieutenant Tomasso. After a ten minute wait, a uniform escorted him directly up the staff-only stairs to the lieutenant's office. Their footsteps echoed as their shoes clicked on the steel-capped steps. The stale smell of old dust and sweat still permeated the stairwell.

Tomasso acted surprised to see him, but Guerevich thought it could be pretense. "Well, Detective, I had a report you went back to Phoenix last week."

"From Gonsalves, no doubt."

"That's right. You won't be able to speak to him again. He's away on a special assignment."

"Guarding illegals on a bus back to Mexicali?"

Tomasso leaned back in his swivel chair and smiled more cordially than at their last meeting. "No. As a matter of fact, he's on loan to Laughlin for the summer motorcycle rally. It's something he does every year. Have a seat. What can we do for you this time?"

"I hate to be the one to bring bad news, Lieutenant. This time, it's what I can do for you. I have evidence Gonsalves is being paid to turn his back on the illegals working at The Lucky Nugget."

Tomasso looked at the ceiling, and gave a breathy whistle. He put his hand on his chest in mock surprise.

"Wow. That's astonishing." He sat up and looked directly at Guerevich. "You think that only happens here in Nevada? Arizona has the same problems, doesn't it?"

"That's not what I meant."

Tomasso cut him off. "We're short handed and I got more important things to do than to chase some illegals. Besides, it's an INS responsibility."

"They wouldn't be here if no one hired them. But if that's all it was, I wouldn't have bothered you. It's something bigger. The Vasquez brothers are operating a counterfeiting ring from The Lucky Nugget."

Tomasso leaned forward across the desk. "What? You have any hard evidence?"

Guerevich put his briefcase on his lap and clicked open the locks. He took out a manila envelope stuffed so full it wouldn't close and pushed it across the desk toward Tomasso. "Here are the recordings and written documents implicating Gonsalves in both the bribery and counterfeiting operation. He's not in Laughlin. Right now, he's accompanying a mule with $100,000 in counterfeit bills to Yuma, Arizona. The mule is an undocumented Colombian, which is probably why the Vasquez brothers trusted him."

"Undocumented?"

"Not really. He is a Colombian, but he's one of my men. The money is going to be given to my murder suspect, Franklin Margason. Then he'll probably transport most of it across the border to Algodones, Mexico."

Tomasso leaned back and folded his arms. A look of interest spread across his face. "That's a hell of a story, Detective. Wouldn't be the first time Gonsalves crossed the line. You say you have recordings?"

"They're all there in the envelope. No doubt the funny money will find its way back to the United States in the possession of some unsuspecting tourists. And the bills are almost perfect.    Hard to detect.    It's a sweet setup. Tourists come from all over the United States and Canada, so there's no pattern to the movement of the bills.   Of course, the money could also become part of the black market in Colombia and Guatemala, where they use U. S. currency."

"Just how the hell did you get all that information?" Tomasso now leaned across the desk and spoke softly, his expression of interest deepening in his eyes.

"My man, Martín Velez, posed as an undocumented alien and got a job in the casino kitchen. Because he was Colombian, the Vasquez brothers trusted him and we were able to record conversations.  It's all in this envelope.  By the way, there's also an Intaglio press in the basement of the casino, along with all the material for printing money."

Tomasso folded his hands and bounced his thumb against his chin.   "Dammit.  Too bad the feds won't be able to use the recordings.  You got them without a warrant."

"I know.   I was just trying to get information about my murder suspect."

"Yeah.     But I think they'll be glad to get them, anyway. You won't mind if I turn over all your information to the CIA, will you?"

Guerevich's head popped back.   "The CIA?  That was fast. When the hell did the CIA get involved?"

"Beats me.    Someone must have tipped them off." Tomasso stood up and leaned across his desk.   "You're not CIA, are you?"

"You kidding?"

"Two days ago, a couple of guys from the CIA came to see me.  Said they'd been watching the Vasquez brothers and wanted to make sure we didn't do anything to mess up their investigation. They didn't say anything about counterfeiting."

"They're lying about an investigation, but I think I know why they're interested."

"Doesn't matter. Believe me, if they want the Vasquez boys, they can have them. I got enough to do."

Guerevich stood. "It's your game now. Or should I say it's the CIA's. You've got all the information I gathered. Do what you want with it. My involvement never has to be mentioned."

"Oh, I'm sure they'll keep your name out of the media. Bunch of glory hounds."

Guerevich laughed. "I'm sure they will." He shook hands with Tomasso. "I'm heading back to Phoenix. For real, this time. If there's anything I can do, please let me know."

"Will do. And if ever we chase bad guys to Phoenix, you'd be the first one I'll call."

Guerevich and Danny drove silently back to the hotel to get Ann.

Danny broke the silence. "Hard to believe that a young man could be involved in the shooting of his own father. Makes me want to visit my father back in Santo Domingo. I haven't seen him for over a year. I think I'll take some vacation time when this is over and go home for a couple weeks."

"Yeah. I ought to give my father a call. Maybe someday I can convince him that what I do is an important public service. We don't always see eye to eye. We always argue when we talk."

"Hey, man, he's the only father you have. Just bite your tongue and tell him you love him."

"Right. Let's get our bags, and head back to Scottsdale.

When they clicked open the door to their room, Guerevich's thoughts about his father evaporated like soap bubbles in the air.  Two beefy men sat on the sofa with Ann scrunched between them.    The one with the shaved head and dark skin held a Glock 19 pointed at Ann's head.  The one with dark blond hair and sideburns waved a forty-five caliber semiautomatic in greeting.

# CHAPTER TWENTY-ONE

Guerevich entered the room first and froze. "Shit."

The familiar man with the blond hair grinned, his feet on the coffee table. "That's what you're in. Carlos didn't believe it when Gonsalves told him you might still be here. He told me and Gary to check it out."

"Hey, Walt. We ain't supposed to use our real names."

"Won't matter now. These three ain't gonna live long enough to tell anyone." He grinned at Ann. "Are you, sweetie?"

Guerevich glared at the two men on the sofa. "Tom and Jerry suited you two rats better."

Walter laughed. "Get smart while you can, funny boy. You won't be laughing with a new hole in the back of your head."

Ann looked down and spoke quietly, almost without moving her lips. "Aaron, these are the two men who. . ." Her voice trailed off into an unintelligible mumble.

"Yeah. I know who they are."

Walter kept his eyes on Danny whose muscular arms were evident through his jacket. "Looks like you brought your own muscle. Too bad you guys can't take a hint. Put your guns on the floor. Slowly. Even the leg hardware."

Guerevich opened his jacket and removed his service pistol. "You mean the thump on my head? That was your idea of a hint?"

Danny took off his jacket and took his service revolver from his shoulder holster and slowly placed it in front of him on the floor.  He raised his pant legs to show he had no leg holster.

"And giving your sexy girlfriend here a ride home. We should have helped her into her apartment."  Gary grinned and reached his arm around Ann's shoulder. His gun drooped in front of her, touching her breast.

Walter gave Gary a stern glare that knocked the grin from his face as if he had been slapped.  "Cool it, Gary. You'll have your fun soon enough."  He turned toward Guerevich. "You people must be stupid.  A wife shoots her abusive husband and you can't let well enough alone.  None of this was any of your business."

Danny's hands formed into fists.  "Gonsalves made it our business.  And the counterfeiting was really brilliant.  It's bringing in the feds."

Walter scowled.  "That fuckin' Gonsalves is an idiot. Always bragging to his Mexican friends about what he can do."

Walter and Gary stood up in front of the sofa, the coffee table almost touching their shins.  Gary pulled Ann up by her arm. Walter walked over and kicked the two floored guns several feet from Guerevich and Danny.  Using their own guns to point, Walter and Gary motioned the two detectives toward the door.

Guerevich looked at Walter.  "Well, suppose we all just walk out the door and head on back to Scottsdale.  We have no authority here, anyway."

Walter forced a laugh.  "Not so easy.  A thump and a short ride won't do.  Pick up the gun, Mac, uh, Gary."

Gary smiled broadly at Ann, as he bent to retrieve the guns on the floor. Danny took a step toward him.

Walter sneered, one side of his lip raised.  "Back up, muscle man, before I put a window in your chest .  Turn around and let's go."

Ann gave a pleading look at Walter. "I need to go to the bathroom first."

"Better than peeing your panties later. Leave the door open. And your purse stays here on the table."

She trudged to the bathroom, opened the door and pushed it part way closed.

Gary took a step toward the bathroom. "Maybe the lady needs some help with her clothes."

Walter pushed him back and glanced at the ceiling as if he were dealing with a child. "Later."

Guerevich smiled when he heard the toilet flush. He remembered the snub-nosed .38 with hydroshock bullets in her cosmetic bag on the bathroom counter. Walter and Gary held the grips of their guns lightly, keeping their fingers near the triggers, men accustomed to firearms. They moved around the coffee table continuing to aim at the two detectives. After a few moments, Ann opened the bathroom door and stood for a moment in the doorway, her right arm hidden by the door frame.

Gary leered at her again. "Let's get going, sweetie. You and I are gonna have some fun later."

Guerevich and Danny turned and walked toward the door as Walter and Gary dropped their arms to their sides and pointed their guns toward the floor.

Ann stepped to the center of the doorway, braced her right hand with her left, and fired once at Gary, blowing a chunk from his left shoulder, shattering his collarbone, and splattering his flesh and pieces of his jacket on the wall and the sofa. The impact spun him around and he fell to his knees. Blood mushroomed from the wound. He instinctively brought the Glock up and fired in the wrong direction. Ann fired again almost instantly, missing both men but shattering a lamp and putting a large hole in the wall. She slammed the bathroom door shut as Walter fired several times in her direction. The door splintered with a cracking noise, the sound reverberating through the room, stinging their ears. Then a moment of silence, as if the bullets had imbedded the sound in the door with them. Blue smoke and the smell of cordite hung in the air.

Walter looked at Gary, still on his knees. He trained his gun on Guerevich and shouted. "Jesus Christ. Gary."

Gary got to his feet, his knees wobbly. He dropped the Glock and grabbed his shoulder with his right hand, his left arm hanging loosely like a piece of rope from a post. He looked at Walter, a his mouth twisted in a grimace of pain. "Son of a bitch."

Seeing their opportunity, Danny and Guerevich dived at the two thugs, surprising them and knocking them back, overturning the sofa. Gary's head banged against the wooden window ledge. His gun bounced across the carpeted floor to the wall behind him. Guerevich landed on top of the wounded gunman but the impact knocked the wind from the detective's lungs. Blood pulsing from Gary's shoulder splattered on Guerevich's shirt and jacket. Shaking his head, Gary rolled Guerevich off him. Scrambling to his knees and crawling the few feet with his good arm, he grabbed his gun and whacked Guerevich on the top of his head. The blow split open his scalp and

knocked him over on his back.

Danny jumped from the back of the upturned sofa and kicked the surprised Walter in his side, cracking ribs and driving out his breath. He rolled to the floor and lay silent on his side, knees drawn up to his chest.

Gary got to his feet, gun in hand, his left arm still dangling useless. He fired, grazing Danny's side. Danny went down but the shot had gone through the soft flesh, punching another hole in the wall. Gary shouted for Walter to get up.

The dazed Guerevich rolled to his knees between the overturned sofa and the window, blood running down his forehead into his eyes. He blinked at the floor unable to focus as he wiped the blood away with his hand, smearing it over his face. The ringing in his ears echoed through his head, slowly diminishing into a high pitched whine. When he looked up, everything spun, like a one-note carousel.

The bathroom door burst open and Ann fired twice, one shot taking a large piece of Walter's ear, the other slamming into a picture on the wall. Instinctively, both thugs dropped to drop to the floor. But fearful of hitting Danny or Guerevich, she could not shoot again and slammed the door closed.

Blood now soaked the front of Gary's shirt and jacket. He staggered to the bathroom door and tried to bump it open with his good shoulder. When it did not open, he fired two more shots through the lower part of the door. Walter grunted as he rose to his knees, aiming his gun at the wounded Danny on the floor. He held his left side with his hand, his breath short and strained. He kicked Danny in the side and screamed at him. "Get up, God damn you. I'm going to turn your face into hamburger, muscle-man. Get the fuck up."

Danny struggled to his feet. Gary walked behind him and hit Danny on the top of the head with the butt of his gun. Danny's legs buckled. As he slumped, Gary wrapped his good arm around Danny's neck, choking him, wrenching him up to his feet. As Gary held him, Walter gut-punched Danny, who uffed, but made no other sound.

Walter stood back, legs spread, and raised the gun over his shoulder. "Pretty tough, ain't you. Let's see how tough you are after I beat your fuckin' face in."

A siren wailed its warning in the distance, getting louder as it neared.

"We ain't got time," shouted Gary. "We got to get the fuck out of here."

Using Gary's choke-hold to support him, Danny kicked Walter in the groin, dropping him to his knees with a howl. As Walter went down, his gun fell to the carpet. Guerevich shook his head, lunged for the gun, and aimed it at Gary, who still held Danny.

"Drop the gun, or I'll choke the life out of him."

"Only if you want to die."

Sensing a momentary lull, Danny bent at his waist, lifting Gary off his feet. Then Danny lurched forward as he dropped to his knees. The surprised Gary went flying on his back across the room. He rolled to his one good hand and his knees but didn't loose the grip on his gun.
Danny dived toward Gary, who fired as Danny reached him. The force of the bullet stunned Danny who stepped back several feet. Before his body hit the floor, Guerevich fired at Gary, hitting him in the side of the mouth, shattering teeth and snapping his head back. Danny lay on the floor, blood spurting from a large hole in his chest.

Guerevich, the dried blood staining his face, screamed in anguish and scrambled to his friend's side. He heard the gurgling blood and saw bubbles pumping from his chest.

Danny tried to speak. "Tell ...father ..." Then he was silent.

Walter, down on his knees and one hand, held his genitals and tried to catch his breath. Guerevich screamed and ran toward him. As if his head were a football on a kicking tee, he booted him full in the face, smashing his nose, shredding his lips against his teeth, and flipping him onto his back.

Kneeling astride the downed man, Guerevich screamed again as he used his gun to beat the unconscious Walter's face back and forth, ripping pieces of his cheeks and exposing bloody bone.

Holding the gun at his side, Guerevich staggered to the bathroom door and tried the handle. Locked. He raised his foot and slammed it against the bullet-riddled door. The door lock gave way and splintered open. Guerevich shouted. "Ann, It's me."

Blood covered parts of the floor and trailed to the tub, where he saw Ann lying on her back, knees up. Her pant leg was saturated with blood, but her snub nose .38 special was aimed at his chest.

"Ann," he said again. "It's me." He kneeled next to the tub. After putting his gun on the tile floor, he gently took the gun from her hand and placed it next to his.

She exhaled from pursed lips when she saw the dried blood on his face. "Are you all right?"

"What about you?" He leaned over the tub and pulled her to him. "Where are you hit?"

"One of their shots got me in my calf, but I don't think it's very bad. I'm glad this hotel has old-fashioned cast iron tubs."

"Danny wasn't so lucky. Shot in the chest. He's in a bad way. But so's the asshole who shot him."

She closed her eyes, made her hands into fists, and

pounded on the sides of the tub. "Damn! Damn! Damn!"

Guerevich helped her hop from the tub, drops of blood falling onto her shoes. As she sat on the edge of the tub, he grabbed a towel. With a small pocket knife, he slit her jeans up to her knee. As he started to wrap her leg, two uniformed officers kicked open the hotel door and stormed in, guns drawn.

"Police," shouted the first one through the doorway. "Everybody down on the floor." He aimed his sidearm at Guerevich and Ann in the bathroom. "Now."

"Face down," bellowed his partner. Moving his pistol from one to another of the motionless bodies on the floor, he shouted to his partner "Holy shit, there's blood and bullet holes everywhere." Using his shoulder radio, he called for an ambulance.

# CHAPTER TWENTY-TWO

"We're police officers." Guerevich shouted from inside the bathroom. He stood and indicated himself and Ann. "My partner's hurt bad and this officer needs medical attention."

"I don't care. The ambulance is on its way." The first officer on the scene aimed his service forty-five at Guerevich. "Put your guns down and get on the floor. Face on the carpet."

Guerevich entered the room and dropped to his knees. "My name's Detective Aaron Guerevich. What's yours?"

"I'm Steve Casey and my partner's Al Grondin. Now face the carpet and let's see some ID."

Guerevich looked up. "My ID's in my wallet. Back pocket. We're with the Scottsdale Police. Here on a case. Tomasso knows us. The woman in the bathroom's been shot and needs help. She's my fiancée Ann Berendt. She's a forensic officer and she's been shot. She needs help."

Guerevich stretched out facing the carpet, arms above his head, palms down. "C'mon. Ann needs help."

Al Grondin, inched toward the bathroom, his pistol gripped in both hands. Guerevich swore into the carpet, but knew he would have done the same had the situation been reversed.

Casey bent down and felt Danny's neck for a pulse. When he stood up, he shook his head. "Sorry. What about them?" He nodded toward the other men sprawled on the floor, but kept Guerevich in his gun sight as his partner, Al Grondin, entered the bathroom.

"They're wanted for kidnapping in Arizona, and assaulting a police officer here in Nevada." He paused. "One's got some broken ribs and face bruises. I think the other one's dead."

Casey side-stepped over to Gary. "Holy shit. Half his face is blown off, but I recognize him." He looked back at Guerevich. "Take your wallet out. Slowly. Keep the other hand flat on the floor."

Guerevich rolled slightly to his right side and did as Casey told him, retrieving his wallet from his back pants pocket with the fingers and thumb of his left hand. He threw the wallet across the floor toward the officer, who nodded when he opened it and saw the shield.

"Can I get up?"

"Yeah. Slowly. But no gun."

"The guns are on the floor in the bathroom."

Johnson groaned and Casey looked at him closely for the first time. "I'll be damned." He shouted to his partner in the bathroom. "Hey, Al, guess who we got here. Walter Johnson, minus part of his ear and a few of his prison teeth. And the other ugly mutt with half a face is Gary MacMillan."

"You know them?" Guerevich rose to his hands and knees.

"Couple of hired goons. Nothing but trouble. They been in and out of Lovelock for years. You done the state a favor with MacMillan." He closed Guerevich's wallet and tossed it back to him. Grabbing Johnson by the collar of his shirt, Casey raised him into a sitting position, pulled his arms behind his back to cuff him as he shouted in pain. Casey routinely Mirandized him and pushed him back down to the floor. Johnson shouted in pain again

Grondin emerged from the bathroom with Ann's arm around his shoulder, helping her hop to a chair.

Guerevich looked at her. "You all right?"

"I don't know. I've never been shot before."

Grondin unwrapped the towel around her leg where the bullet had ripped across the side of her leg. The blood had started to clot around the wound.

"Looks like the bullet just grazed your calf. You call for the CSI team, Steve?"

Steve nodded. He walked into the bathroom and retrieved the two weapons. Guerevich told the officers the Glock and the .45 were the guns MacMillan and Johnson had used and the snub-nose was Ann's.

"You guys shot up the place pretty good," said Grondin. What the hell did you use? A cannon? Who shot MacMillan?"

"I fired hydroshocks," said Ann. "But when they started shooting at me through the door, I dived for the tub."

"Good thinking," said Grondin. "The CSI'll be able to get some slugs from the wall. Self defense?"

"They wanted to take us somewhere to kill us. She hit Jerry, I mean, MacMillan, in the shoulder. I'm the one who finished him."

"Almost took his shoulder off. Don't wash the blood off your face until the CSI team photographs you."

The blood on Guerevich's face had left dark brown smears on his forehead and cheeks.

Ann bent down to look at the wound and blood on her leg.

"Damn, that's starting to hurt." She grimaced as tears welled in the corners of her eyes. "And it's going to leave a big scar."

"No, no." Steve rewrapped the towel. "Looks clean. Just nicked the surface."

In less than five minutes, the elevator door in the hallway pinged and the paramedics charged into the room. They rushed to Danny and Johnson, kneeled at their sides for a moment, then rose slowly and frowned. "Nothing we can do for these two."

Guerevich collapsed in a chair, took a deep breath, and allowed his shoulders to slump. The adrenaline that had pumped through his body began to dissipate.

The first paramedic put a fresh bandage on Ann's leg. "That's probably going to need a couple of stitches."

"I'm going to end up with a nasty scar."

The paramedic wrapped tape around Ann's leg. "I don't think so. Won't leave much of a mark. Maybe you'll have a little dimple."

Casey and Grondin stood next to Guerevich. "What the hell are detectives from Arizona doing here in Las Vegas?" asked Casey.

While the paramedics finished bandaging Ann's leg, Guerevich told the Casey and Grondin why the murder of Stanfield Margason had led the three of them to Las Vegas. But he said nothing about the Lucky Nugget, counterfeiting, or Martín.

The Las Vegas CSI team and a gloved assistant from the medical examiner's office entered the room, followed by two uniformed officers, who stood in the doorway.

"Too many live people walking around here," said one CSI member. "You guys'll contaminate the scene before

we even get a chance to process it."

"Be happy you got here after the shit hit the fan," Grondin said as he pulled MacMillan to his feet and dragged him, staggering and limping to the doorway and handed him to the two officers, who pushed him into the hall.

"We'll take him to Desert Springs Hospital over on Flamingo," said the first. "They got a prison section."

"Good," said Grondin. "He don't need the ambulance."

The second officer laughed.   "Right. We got the wagon."

Grondin looked at Guerevich and Ann.  "I'll go with you and fill out the paperwork."

After the CSI photographer had taken pictures of Guerevich's face and Ann's wound, the paramedics took them to the trauma section of the University Medical Center. Steve Casey followed the ambulance to the hospital.  The bodies of Danny and Johnson were left to be taken by the Medical Examiner's team for autopsy.

While a nurse shaved and bandaged Guerevich's head, Ann lay face down on a gurney as a doctor put five stitches in her leg. When he stood up, he smiled at her.  "In ten years you'll never see it."

Steve Casey helped them complete the official paperwork at the hospital.  Then they were interviewed by other Las Vegas detectives.

Three hours after they had arrived at the hospital, Guerevich and Ann accompanied Steve Casey to the police station where Tomasso questioned them again and took their depositions.   They agreed to return and testify when MacMillan's case came to trial.

Tomasso took them to the medical examiner's office. Ann had worked with autopsies for many years, but she could not hold back tears when she read the ME's notes.

Danny had not died instantly, but had bled out through a punctured aorta.  When she told Guerevich, he turned away, put his arm across his forehead, and leaned against the wall.

After a few moments, he turned to Tomasso, tears glistening in his eyes.  "We'll make arrangements to have Danny's body sent back to Scottsdale for a full honors funeral and burial."

Later in the afternoon, they went back to their hotel.

"I can't believe this happened in my hotel," the Harrah's manager kept repeating. I can't let you back into your room, but I have a suite you can use. No charge, of course. If there are things in the room, I'll try to get them to you." He expressed his condolences as he comped them into the small suite.

Guerevich went back to their original room, although it was still sealed off as a crime scene. He ducked under the tape, and opened the door. The CSI team had completed their investigation, and left white powder everywhere. Seeing Danny's blood soaked into the carpet, the finality of his friend's death grabbed him like giant hand squeezing his chest and stomach. A wave of sadness flowed down from his head, washing over him, as if his head had become a fountain of melancholy. His legs weakened and he sat on the floor, tears welling in his eyes as the sadness then turned to anger at the needless death and Ann's getting shot, even though the wound was not serious.

Danny, the big man who had spent hours translating, and without whose help they never could have succeeded. The man who once aspired to become a world-class bodybuilder, his scratchy alto voice now silenced forever.

He knew Danny's father still lived in the Dominican Republic. Yet he was struck by how little he really knew about Danny's personal life. Other than Danny was a Dominican, he knew little about Danny's life before he became a Las Vegas detective. The task of calling Danny's father and relaying the appalling news of his son's death would fall to one of the Spanish-speaking grief counselors.

"I wonder how would my father take the news of my death," Guerevich mused, as he exited the room. "And how would I react to his?"

Guerevich had attended many *Kaddish* memorial services. He had seen children torn by grief, wives and husbands ravaged by the pain of permanent separation from their spouses. He knew the memorial liturgy by heart. It made no mention of death but spoke instead about extolling the honor of God. The prayer asked for the blessing of peace. Judaism referred to life as a journey and death as one stage along the way.

*But how can a just God allow this to happen?* he mused.

He had not seen his father for several months, and the last time they spoke, they had argued. But the thought of never seeing him again caused a swelling in his throat which he could not dislodge by swallowing. Although they differed in the approach to their religion, they had both led ethical lives, helping others as Judaism required.

*We really need to end our foolish conflict. He may not agree with my religious views, but I need to go see him when we get back."*

In the small closet, Guerevich found the three packed suitcases, which he placed outside in the hall. Before he ducked under the tape again, he looked back into the room, staring again at the shattered bathroom door, the blood on the floor, and overturned sofa.

*Danny died to save my life*. Guerevich made a silent promise to say *kaddish* for his friend.

The next morning Guerevich and Ann checked out of their hotel and headed down Highway 93 toward Kingman and home. Ann sat in the back seat with her leg propped up.

From Boulder City to Hoover Dam, they remained silent, listening to a country/western station but not paying attention to any of the lyrics. Then a song by Reba MacIntyre erupted into their consciousness. *The Greatest Man I Never Knew* brought tears to their eyes when they heard the words.

Guerevich had to pull off the road until his eyes cleared. When he pulled back onto the highway, he voiced his concern about their other missing colleague. "I know you're thinking about Marty, Ann. He'll make it. What was is that Danny called him? *Hombre de verdad.* He's tough. Shit. He walked from Colombia to Mexico, dammit. I only wish there was a way for him to contact us."

"Or for us to contact him." Ann shifted her position, putting the pillow under her knee.

"I intend to have Danny listed at the synagogue as a *Chasiday Umot Ha-Olom*, a Righteous Gentile."

"Isn't that reserved for Christians who saved Jews during the Holocaust?"

"It doesn't have to be limited to the Holocaust. He died saving my life."

"You know more about that stuff than I do. But there are lots of other ways to honor his memory. I intend to recommend him for the Medal for Valor." She wiped her eyes again and leaned forward. "Maybe the rest of the state is okay, but Las Vegas is like a whole different planet."

Guerevich looked at her in the rear view mirror. "Well, don't relax too soon. Marty told me some stories about the FARC that make the Russian Mafia seem like volleyball players at the seashore. If they can wipe out a family because of politics, imagine their anger toward us. These are people who make their own rules. Let's hope the CIA catches up with Carlos and Ruben."

"Yeah. But I'm afraid we haven't heard the last of them."

They fell silent again until they crossed Boulder Dam and into Arizona. They both gave a little cheer, happy to be out of Nevada.

# CHAPTER TWENTY-THREE

"I'm getting hungry. How do you feel about stopping here in Kingman for lunch." Guerevich slowed the car as they approached the first Kingman exit.

Ann readily agreed. "Good idea. As if I have a choice. Besides, my back is killing me, sitting like this. And once we get on I-40, there's nothing until we get to Ash Fork. Do you see that sign advertising Stromboli's over on Beale Street? Just past the interstate. You can probably get a vegetarian pizza or lasagne. Maybe they even have Chicago style the way you like." She smiled at her suggestion.

He laughed. "Not likely. We're in Arizona. They put artichoke and pineapple on pizzas."

The roar of semi trucks rumbled by as they turned off the interstate at the Beale Street exit.

They found the small restaurant and walked in, Ann hobbling on her crutches. At eleven thirty, the restaurant had just opened and waiters were setting tables for lunch but the smell of garlic was unmistakable.

After they ordered a vegetarian pizza and sodas, Guerevich started to talk about his strategy for pursuing the Margason case. He reviewed the facts, keeping his voice low. "We know Franklin and Cathy are having an affair."

"Even though she was married to his father, Stanfield. The problem is we don't know when the affair started. It could be important. My guess is the affair started before he was killed."

Guerevich picked up one of the pencil-thin bread sticks, scooped some butter up with it, and popped it in his mouth. As he chewed, the crunch of bread caused a scene from his childhood to jump into his mind. *He was sitting at the kitchen table listening to voices from the dining room. He looked through the open sliding doors and heard his father's after-dinner Talmudic discussions with other Bible scholars. The taste of his mother's challah bread with raisins lingered in his mouth and mixed with the rigid form of logical reasoning that Talmudic scholars used.* Over and over he heard the phrase in Hebrew, *"Yes, but what if. . ."*

The same speech pattern came from his own mouth as he spoke to Ann. "You know, everything is significant. As much for what is as for what isn't. It's a bit like psychoanalysis. At the Yeshiva, we used to call it hypothetico-deductive method of interpretation. The need to raise a series of *what if* questions before we can be satisfied that we fully understand the meaning of anything. Any analysis requires both accurate information and good judgment. Basically, it's the scientific method."

"The scientific method? That's what I've been trained to do. That's also the forensic method."

"Exactly. And things apparently contradictory to each other can be reconciled if we can discover some subtle underlying connection. Even things that seem irrelevant to each other can become compatible."

"You're starting to sound like one of my old science teachers. But okay. Let's examine what we have and set up a hypothesis. If we believe Stanfield made an offer to buy the Las Vegas casino, he did it to give himself a career."

"That's obvious."

"Right. Because in doing so he could cash in on his father's millions. So then we have to ask another question. Why did he back out?"

"What if he found out about the counterfeiting and got scared, not wanting to be involved in an illegal activity with a couple of Colombians."

"Perhaps. Or maybe he found out about the affair. Or both."

Guerevich drained his water glass and signaled to the waitress for another one.

Ann propped her leg up on the chair next to her. "We know from her phone records Cathy called him the day Stanfield went to the house and was shot. The autopsy analysis of his stomach contents showed he had eaten a substantial meal about half an hour before he died. Which means either she invited him for dinner or he had eaten before he got to the house."

"What if she offered him something to get him there."

"You and your *what ifs*."

"The *what if* is important. So, let's think about that. He needed maintenance until he inherited the estate. If we assume she told him she was ready to give him everything he wanted, he would have had a good reason to breach the order of protection. On the other hand, if he found out about the affair, then his reason for going would have been to confront her."

"If he had eaten before he arrived at the house and went there to confront her, she could have shot him during the altercation. She admits the shooting but says he crashed in through the window, which we know is physically impossible. The odd thing is she waited three hours before calling the police."

"And that she called the police instead of 9-1-1."

They stopped talking when the waitress brought their drinks and told them the pizzas would be up in ten minutes.

Ann sipped her diet cola. "What about Ginderer? We know he's gay so where does he fit in? His prints were on the dressmaker's dummy. We know the dummy was thrown through the window because we found particles of the fabric on the glass."

"Ginderer stands to make a bundle of money from the estate whatever the outcome.     I don't believe for a second Ginderer threw it through the window.  He doesn't have the strength.  Who does have the strength?  Franklin. He's the only one with that kind of muscle.  And he has motive as well."

"But how'd Ginderer's prints get on the dummy we found in his dumpster?"

"Let's say Ginderer is telling the truth.  Let's say he handled the dummy at some time to help Cathy out. Franklin must have known that.  How much trouble would it have been for Franklin to carry the dummy to Ginderer's house?   He's having some remodeling done and there's a large construction dumpster in front of the house.  Franklin burns parts of the dummy, being careful to preserve areas where he knows the prints would be.  Then he puts it where he knows we'd find it.  If that's true, then Cathy and Franklin conspired to set him up."

"That's also just a theory.  Back up a minute," said Ann.  "We know Cathy shot Margason.  Let's say she shot him three times.  He falls backward and lands on his back. But he isn't dead.  So she takes the gun and puts one into his

chest and through his heart."

"That's possible.  Cold but possible. Here's another theory.   What if Franklin shot him the first three times. When Cathy shot him, she did it to put her prints on the gun and get powder residue on her hands and clothes."

Their pizza arrived and they were silent for several minutes, eating and savoring the tomato sauce, olives, and onions.

Guerevich picked up a slice and took a bite. "It's not hard to believe that a certain type of man would kill his own father for inheritance. Five hundred million is a huge motivator. Even though my father hates my profession and we don't always get along, the thought of killing him would never enter my mind."

"Five hundred million is more money than I can even imagine." She took a small bite of her slice. "So what are you going to do when we get back?"

"About what?"

"About your father."

"I'm thinking I'll call him when we get back. I'll take him out to a kosher restaurant for dinner and maybe we can resolve some of our differences."

Guerevich thought about his father's rejection of restaurant food, except for the two kosher restaurants in Phoenix. The idea of restaurants caused Guerevich to think about Martín and his love for food. He looked at Ann and smiled at her as she ate, but said nothing. He secretly worried that Martín had been found out, and Franklin or Gonsalves had taken him out in the desert to shoot and bury him. Over the years, hikers periodically discovered remains after a heavy rain, unidentified bodies buried ten or even twenty years earlier, fathers or mothers or brothers or sisters whose families had not forgotten but had long since ceased mourning. He did not want Martín to become one of those

murder victims.

Guerevich held the last piece of the vegetarian pizza near his mouth and waved it like a pointer. "All this talk about Franklin and Kathy has given me an idea. When we get back, I'm going to question them again. Separately. If we do it right, we might be able to flip her. Based on the evidence, we can charge her with homicide. She admitted the shooting."

"But the ME's report only stated the potential cause of death was the shot through Margason's heart. He had lost so much blood the conclusion was moot."

"She doesn't know that." He took a bite and fell into his Talmudic analysis mode. "But what if, when she fired the bullet into his chest, he was still alive. Even barely. The bullet shatters his heart and he dies instantly. If we assume that, it's murder and not self defense."

They left the restaurant and debated the plan further as they drove east on I-40. Over Ann's weak objections, Guerevich determined to follow through with the arrest of Cathy Margason for the murder of her husband.

The sun was high overhead when they made the turn on I-17 from Flagstaff. After they arrived in Scottsdale, Guerevich called Escobedo, who was making preparations for Danny's burial, but had heard nothing from Martín.

As they arrived at Guerevich's apartment, the sun was setting. The windows reflected white clouds turning to red and orange fringed with gold. But they were unable to appreciate the beauty of the sunset. Now that they were home, a sadness descended on them like a heavy blanket as they remembered Danny and worried about Martín.

# CHAPTER TWENTY-FOUR

Late the next morning, as Guerevich sat at his desk staring at the pile of paperwork from the events in Las Vegas, his phone rang. He grinned and did a fist pump as he recognized the voice of Martín.

Martín spoke slowly. "I just got to my apartment and you are my first call." His voice sounded tired and had a hint of his Colombian accent. "I need to get some sleep. Can you meet me in the computer lab about two this afternoon?"

"Of course. Take as much time as you need. I am just happy you are here in one piece."

"So am I, my friend. So am I."

Guerevich immediately called Ann to tell her the news. Then he persuaded assistant DA Mark Benopolis to find Judge Farnham and get him to issue a warrant for Cathy Margason on the new charge of homicide.

"Farnhan isn't going to be happy. Are you sure you want to do this?"

"Damned right I do. I don't think even her fancy lawyer will be able to get her out of this one.

The warrant was delivered at fifteen minutes before two in the afternoon. Before he went to serve it, he left his pile of notes and paperwork on his desk, and walked up the stairs to the computer lab.

When he entered an empty lab, disappointment masked his face. As he turned to leave, Martín opened the door, shuffled in, and hugged the taller man. "Thank you, my friend."

"Why are you thanking me? You took all the risk. Without you this whole operation would never have happened."

"Perhaps. But what you have done is to give me the opportunity to make a small retaliation for the deaths of my parents."

"What you did took a lot of guts. I thank God you were able to get back here safely. How'd you get away?"

"After I delivered the money, I took your advice and went into the men's bathroom." Martín smiled. "Fortunately, the bathroom in the lobby of the hotel has a supply room with an outside door for deliveries. Once I got out, I was able to blend into the crowd. There are many Mexicans in Yuma, and most of them look like me. I only wish I could have seen the expression on Margason's face when he discovered I was not coming back. Franklin and Gonsalves probably figured my disappearance was caused by my fear of *la migra*. He threatened to turn me in a few times."

"You'll get the chance to see Frank Margason's face again. And this time he'll be more than surprised. Tomasso called Escobedo and told her the Vasquez brothers have vanished."

"Who's Tomasso?"

"I forgot you never met him. He's a police captain in Las Vegas. Anyway, the CIA hauled away the paper and the press, which closes a not too brilliant chapter in their history. And the Lucky Nugget is no longer for sale, unless the INS puts it on the block. Franklin has no idea about any of this, but it doesn't matter. He and Cathy Margason won't be buying any casinos."

"Where's Danielo? I want to tell him about my great escape."

The smile dropped from Guerevich's face like a steel wrecking ball. He looked away as tears filled his eyes and he wiped them away with his forefingers. He turned to face Martín. "I have bad news about Danny. When we went back to our room, the two men who had kidnapped Ann were waiting for us. There was a fight and Danny was killed."

Martín's mouth opened to say something, but no words came out. He began breathing heavily and then sat in a chair. "That's not true. That can't be true. *Mierda!*"

"It's not something I would joke about."

"Of course. It's just so hard to believe. How did it happen?

"They were going to kill us. Ann shot one of them by surprise and during the fight, one of them shot him. If it makes any difference, the man who shot Danny is dead."

Martín looked at Guerevich, a question in his eyes, a frown on his face.

"I shot Danny's killer."

"Danielo was someone I trusted with my life. He was a man I could confide in. I will miss him terribly, Aaron.

"So will I, Marty. So will I.

The two men hugged before they trudged down the stairs to Escobedo's office, where Ann met them. She ran to Martín, threw her arms around his neck as tears of happiness smeared her mascara. After they both hugged and cried for a few moments, they started laughing. The tension released, she asked how he got back.

"I was very fortunate. I hitched a ride from Yuma with some Mexican farm workers who were going to Casa Grande to harvest broccoli. They invited me to spent the night in a farm cabin. I never told them who I was or what I had been doing. They never would have believed me. When I told them I was an illegal from Colombia with a job waiting for me as a cook in Phoenix, they scraped together sixty dollars and told me about the airport shuttle bus from Francisco Grande Hotel to the Sky Harbor Airport in Phoenix. From there, it was easy to find a Mexican gypsy taxi to take me home and wait while I got some money. I always keep a small stash of money in a shoe in my closet."

Ann and Guerevich left. Martín began the tedious task of starting the paperwork about his undercover experiences in Las Vegas and Yuma.

Later that afternoon, Escobedo assigned a uniformed officer, Ralph Johnstone, to accompany Guerevich when he served the arrest warrant on Cathy Margason. As they got in the car, Guerevich looked at the young African-American, probably less than a year out of the academy, his uniform as fresh as he was. When he spoke, Guerevich missed Danny's gravelly voice.

As Guerevich and Officer Johnstone drove to the Aster Street address, he told the young man about Cathy Margason's money. "If she gets away with this, she may inherit her late husband's five hundred million."

"That's a truck-load of cash. Think she'll be able to buy her way out?"

"I don't think so. In fact the money may be detrimental this time. I hope the DA would ask for no bail because of it."

Arriving at the house, they saw Franklin Margason's car in the driveway. They walked up to the house and rang the bell. Cathy answered, wearing a thick white terrycloth robe, her hair rumpled as if she had just got out of bed. She smiled at the two men and invited them in.

"Mrs. Margason," said Guerevich. "This is official. You're under arrest for the shooting of your late husband, Stanfield Margason. If you just step outside and come with me quietly, I won't need to cuff you."

"Cuff me? Lieutenant, this seems so silly. I'm not even dressed. I don't understand. I've already confessed to shooting him."

"You're being arrested on a charge of homicide."

Cathy Margason's mouth opened and closed, but her voice had stopped working. She turned and looked into the house, as if she expected someone to rescue her, but no one appeared.

"We'll wait while you get dressed. Judge Farnham doesn't want partially dressed women in his courtroom."

She slipped into a pair of clogs conveniently at the door and walked back into the house. Johnstone waited by the door while Guerevich accompanied Cathy and waited outside her bedroom while she dressed. He escorted her outside to the unmarked car, holding her elbow and automatically stating her rights.

She looked up at him. "You're making a big mistake."

"That may be. Do you understand your rights?"

"I'm not stupid. Yes, I understand them."

Johnstone helped her into the rear seat, making sure she didn't bump her head on the door frame. She folded her arms as she sat behind the lexan screen that separated the front seats from the back. As he walked around the car to the driver's seat, Guerevich saw her look back toward the house. He turned in time to see the curtains in the foyer

window move slightly.

When they got to the station, Assistant DA Benopolis officially charged Cathy Margason with first degree homicide and she was escorted to a cell to await arraignment. Her lawyer arrived within an hour, and three hours after that, the two were standing before Judge Farnham, pleading not guilty. ADA Benopolis requested remand because of her wealth, but Judge Farnham mentioned her position in the community and said he did not consider her a flight risk. He set bail at one million dollars which she posted using her house as collateral. Before noon, Guerevich and Benopolis stood in the marble and tile entry room and watched through the huge windows of the Maricopa County Building as Cathy and her attorney walked toward the parking lot.

"Well, that sure as hell didn't go according to plan." Benopolis turned away from Guerevich and strode toward the stairway that would take him down to his office.

"You think?" Guerevich muttered as he caught up with him. "But it's not over yet. The Vasquez brothers are out there somewhere, and by now they believe Franklin took the hundred thou and ratted them out. She or Franklin might be hearing from someone very soon."

His words were prophetic. A little after ten the next morning, Cathy Margason called. Her voice was tremulous and high pitched. "I need you to come over to my house, Detective. I have some new information that will help your investigation."

"Are you positive you want me to come? You know you can't speak to me without your lawyer present. And I won't do anything that will jeopardize this case."

"No. I won't need my lawyer for this. You have to come right away. Please."

Guerevich heard the pleading in her voice but still was suspicious. The Vasquez brothers had not been

apprehended. They might be involved.

He asked Escobedo to accompany him. The captain took two squad cars as back up. When they arrived and drove past the house, they saw a car they didn't recognize in the driveway, a black Mercedes with Nevada plates. Franklin's car was not in sight. Guerevich and Escobedo, along with the two black-and-whites, parked around the block.

Guerevich planned to walk up to the house as if he were merely responding to her call, but he touched his service revolver under his jacket as he approached. To avoid arousing attention, Escobedo waited from a position behind some bushes where she could see the front door of the house but not be seen. They had arranged a signal. If Guerevich suspected trouble, he would scratch his head as he entered the house and keep his radio open. Everything said could be heard.

The moment the door opened, Guerevich knew a problem existed. Cathy's normally serene face looked startled, her eyes white and round as overcoat buttons. Guerevich immediately scratched his head before he entered the foyer. Walking into the dining area, he saw three men whom he didn't recognize seated at the table. Two were big, heavy-set, muscular Hispanics. Their size and features suggested Indian blood. The third, a slender man with fair skin, wore dark glasses. He stood up as Guerevich entered the room behind Cathy.

"You must be Detective Guerevich." He offered his hand. His English had an unusual Spanish accent with a hint of German. "My name iss Max Miller. So you are the Jewish detective." He spoke his first name as *mocks*.

His words caused Guerevich to frown and stand more erect. "Miller?"

"It was Müller but I use Miller now. You and I have something in common, Detective. My grandmother was married to a Jewish man many years ago in Berlin. Her married name was Blaufarb. He was a printer. She and my grandfather helped many Jews escape with false papers before they were both caught and sent to Auschwitz. However, their story must be saved for another time. Today I have a problem. You see, I have a very large financial interest in the Lucky Nugget." Miller smiled showing both upper and lower white, even teeth. "Please excuse my choice of words. English is not my first language. I have come to -- how can I say it politely? Ah yes. To execute my claim."

## CHAPTER TWENTY-FIVE

Max Miller wore a navy blue business suit obviously tailored to his slim build. Although the temperature hovered in the mid eighties, his white cotton Henley shirt was buttoned to the neck. Almost as tall as Guerevich, he stood with his back straight, an air of arrogance issuing from him. He moved to stand behind a chair at the head of the table with almost insolent slowness, giving the impression the world moved on his orders. He removed his dark glasses and motioned for Guerevich to take a seat.

"These are my associates." He moved his hand toward the two hatless men with shoulder-length black hair.

One glance told Guerevich they were bodyguards. One had a dark pockmarked face and the other, smooth brown skin slightly lighter. Their faces were expressionless, their eyes unblinking. Round-faced and barrel-chested, they reminded Guerevich of drawings he had seen of ancient Aztecs, except they had no elaborate headbands. Wearing identical gray tweed sport jackets that did not quite cover their barrel chests, they nodded their heads once when Miller pointed toward them. They did not rise, but sat rigidly at attention with their hands folded on the table.

Miller moved to stand beside the seated Cathy and Guerevich looked at her. She had her elbows on the table, her hands on her cheeks, and stared down at her empty coffee cup. Her shoulders slumped. Guerevich had never seen her look so defeated.

He pulled back a chair and sat down, his right arm on the edge of the table, his hand next to his suit jacket where he could quickly retrieve his service pistol if it were necessary.   He saw Miller's eyes follow the position of his hand.

"Please.   Do not do anything to arouse the anger of my associates."   Miller placed one hand on the back of Cathy's chair.   "Let me assure you, they have nothing to lose. They are from a part of the world with prisons not so nice as the country clubs here in the United States."

Guerevich looked at the two bodyguards.   "Are they armed?"

The question drew a smile from Miller.   "It is quite legal for them to carry guns in Arizona."

Seated across the table from Guerevich, Cathy's face looked ashen.   When she raised her head, her eyes darted to the two associates and back to Miller again.

Miller continued.   "Cathy and I have been discussing the unfortunate events in Las Vegas. The killing of your friend. The disappearance of the Vasquez brothers.   I believe they will face charges of counterfeiting and hiring illegal aliens."

"If they are apprehended.   Have you intimidated her?"   Guerevich looked at Cathy.   "Have you been threatened?"

The smile dropped from Miller's face.   His eyes widened, the pupils ice blue.   "Mr. Guerevich.   Please. I do not threaten people. I am a businessman."

Guerevich looked at Cathy, who shook her head slowly.   He couldn't tell if she made her negative response to his question or to Miller's statement.   She looked up at Miller, her brows furrowed.   Her hands had not moved from the sides of her face.

Guerevich knew Escobedo and the other officers were watching the house, listening to the entire conversation, awaiting some signal from inside.

"So what is it you want from me, Mrs. Margason?" Guerevich leaned back in his chair and placed both hands on the table edge. "You said you had important information for me."

Max put up his hand to prevent Cathy from speaking. "Mrs. Margason and I were discussing our mutual financial affairs. You see, I loaned her and Franklin a large sum of money. Five million dollars to be exact."

"I'm sure the interest was sufficient to make it worth your investment. But why did you lend them so much money?"

"So they could invest in The Lucky Nugget. I thought the casino a poor investment, but I never give financial advice. Now the casino is out of their hands because of the greed and stupidity of the Vasquez brothers." Miller shook his head and sat next to Cathy. "The INS has confiscated the property and closed the casino. Temporarily. I understand the CIA has taken the presses, plates, and paper to the Treasury."

Guerevich looked at Miller. "Is that the new information? What does it have to do with me?"

"As I said , Mr. Guerevich, I'm a businessman. I came here to protect my investments. Officially, I own the building. But now the Vasquez brothers' legal difficulties have created a slight problem for me."

"Since you own the building, the US Attorney will probably want to indict you for the counterfeiting along with them."

"Quite unlikely, Mr. Guerevich. I love the laws of this country. I leased the building to the brothers. I had no knowledge of any illegal activities. In fact, they signed an explicit provision which prohibited illegal activities. However, it may take some time for me to pursue my claim with the proper authorities." Miller paused. "But speaking of legal issues, I need to know what is going to happen in the murder case against Mrs. Margason."

"What makes you think we have a case against Cathy Margason?"

Cathy Margason's voice rose slightly above a whisper and she didn't raise her head. "I shot my husband in self-defense."

"Mr. Guerevich, I am an intelligent man and I have many sources of information. Planting an undercover Colombian in the kitchen was very clever."

"I don't know how you learned that. But as an intelligent man, Mr. Miller, you know I can't discuss an ongoing investigation. All I can tell you is what is already public knowledge. If she is found guilty, her prison sentence may be a long one."

Miller smiled. "Is it also true her stepson Franklin is involved in the counterfeiting?"

"I can't comment."

"It doesn't matter. I am aware of his involvement with the Vasquez brothers." Miller looked at Cathy. "You are quite fortunate, Mrs. Margason."

"Fortunate?" She raised her head and glared at Miller. "I'm accused of murder and counterfeiting and I may be going to prison? You call that fortunate? What are you talking about?"

"Raul and Carlos Vasquez are vindictive people. They have not yet been apprehended." Miller addressed Guerevich. "For her, prison may be a better alternative than the Vasquez brothers no doubt have in mind. And since Mrs. Margason and her stepson are no longer capable of inheriting the estate, I find it necessary to take steps to recoup my investment." He turned to Cathy. "But I am not like the Colombians. I do not want your blood. Just sign this form and I shall not trouble you any more."

He held his hand out toward the dark associate who reached down, opened a briefcase at his feet, and pulled out a sheaf of papers and a pen.  He handed
them both to Miller, who pushed the papers and pen in front of Cathy.  She stared at the papers and her hand trembled as she picked them up.  Then she looked up at Miller.

"What is this?" she asked.

"This is a bill of sale for your property and its contents."

"If I sign this document, I'm giving you my house and everything in it?" she asked, her voice quivering.

"No, no.  Not giving.  Selling.  I believe the proper phrase is deeding it over to satisfy the lien. Although the house is not worth more than three million, there is artwork and jewelry.  Under the circumstances, I am willing to take the temporary loss.  At today's rising market, I believe everything soon will be worth more and I will recoup my money."

Guerevich frowned.  "Let me understand.  You're taking her house and contents in repayment for the loan?"

"Quite so, Mr. Guerevich.  The house was the collateral.  Now, I would appreciate it if you would be kind enough to witness this transaction.  Everything is quite legal."

Cathy, her face frozen with fear, looked at Miller.

He grinned, the smile of a crocodile before devouring a victim.  "You and your stepson assumed you would inherit a sufficient amount to pay me back.  With interest, of course.  Unfortunately, you didn't. Signing this contract will free you from your financial obligation."

"But where will I live?"

Miller's smile slipped from his face, the steely look in his eyes grew intense, his words clipped.  "Where you live is not my concern.  And you may soon have no need of this or any other house."

Guerevich stood.  "You came here to kill her, didn't you.  And you coerced her into selling you her house."

"Of course not.  As I said earlier, I never threaten people."

"You know, this house is surrounded by police.  We could arrest you and your so-called associates for complicity in the counterfeiting.  As the owner of the property, you have an obligation to see nothing illegal occurs there."

"True.  But what would be the point?  I invest in commercial property.  The casino was inspected by the Nevada Gaming Commission. They found nothing wrong." He turned to Cathy.  "Please press hard, Mrs. Margason. There are several copies."

Cathy looked at Guerevich as if she expected him to do something.  He was almost amused by her dilemma.  If she signed, she lost her house.  If she didn't, her body might be found in a dumpster if it were found at all. And then Miller would still own the house.

She signed quickly and threw the pen to the table when she had finished.

"Thank you, Mrs. Margason.  And to show you my generosity, there is no hurry to move out.  You are welcome to stay here until your trial has concluded.  Rent free." He turned to Guerevich.  "Will you please

sign here as witness?"

"I can't do that. As a detective working on this case, it would represent a conflict of interest.

"Ah, yes. A conflict of interest. I do understand. However, I believe one of my associates is able sign as a witness to the transaction."

Miller pushed the papers toward the lighter skinned man who signed the contract. To everyone's surprise, the dark skinned man took a notary stamp from the briefcase, stamped the document, and signed it. Miller removed the notarized copy and placed it in front of Cathy. Then he stood, motioned his men to do the same, and the three walked toward the front door.

"Mr. Guerevich. Would you please accompany us to my car. I do not wish to create a disturbance in this pleasant neighborhood."

Guerevich had never been confronted by such a scene before. As he walked with them to the door, he tried to consider where Franklin might be hiding. Guerevich opened the door and walked out first, signaling everyone to back down. Miller and his men got into the Mercedes and drove away.

Escobedo came running up to Guerevich. "What the hell happened in there? If I heard right, Cathy Margason just sold her house."

"It was the strangest real estate transaction I ever witnessed. But that's exactly what happened. She owed Miller a lot of money and he didn't make any overt threats."

"Shit. His very presence was a threat. But we can't arrest him for that."

"Any word about Franklin?"

"Nothing yet."

Guerevich squinted in the bright day and tightened his jaw. His voice became coarse with tension. "Well, we need to find him before the Vasquez brothers do. At least in our custody, he'll stay alive."

# CHAPTER TWENTY-SIX

After Miller and his men drove away, Escobedo sent one of the patrol cars back to the station, but told the other car to remain. She and Guerevich walked back to the Margason house where the door was still open. As soon as they entered the dining room, Cathy looked at them and began crying. Her mascara streaked down her cheeks and her eyes were ringed in black, making her face look like a Halloween mask. She pushed her cell phone aside.

"Can the act." Guerevich flopped in one of the padded chairs at the table. "We know way too much about you. But can you explain what I just witnessed with Miller?" Guerevich glared at Cathy, his palms on the table.

Cathy, sitting down across from him, took several tissues from a box on the table and wiped her eyes and face.

Escobedo remained standing, arms across her chest, accentuating the start of a belly.

Elbows on the table, Cathy propped her head in her hands, and stared at her cup of cold coffee. "That quiet son of a bitch Miller came here to kill me and take my house." Tears formed again and slid down her cheeks. "I got so scared I didn't know what to do. That's why I called you."

Escobedo rolled her eyes and sighed. "And Miller just insisted you call the police?"

"I told him about the new charge against me. That the DA changed it to homicide, but he didn't believe me. He wanted to hear it from you."

Guerevich sat back in the chair. "So you made up that stuff about having new information on the case?"

"I had to say something . Would either of you have come if I'd said Max Miller was visiting and wanted to meet you?"

"Probably not," said Guerevich.

"Damn right, not" added Escobedo. "We're not in the habit of wasting police resources."

"We never should have borrowed all that money from him to buy into the Nugget, but we planned on the inheritance. We were going to turn it into a small version of the Bellagio. We thought once the estate was settled, I would get at least twenty million, and Frank'd probably get as much or more. We would have paid Miller back, even with all his interest. But then everything turned sour."

Guerevich nodded. "You're right about one thing. You shouldn't have borrowed the money from him. He's not the kind who'd sit by quietly and wait for his money. So he got the house. You're still alive. You said 'we borrowed money.' I assume you mean you and Franklin. So where is he?"

"He had to go out of town on business."

"You mean he went down to Yuma," said Escobedo.

Cathy sat back and frowned at the them. "Yuma? Why would he go there?"

Guerevich laughed. "To pick up a hundred thousand dollars in counterfeit money to take across the border."

She sat up straight, pulled her chin back, and squinted her eyes. Her questioning dark look told them she had no idea what they were talking about. After they questioned her further about the counterfeiting, they believed she knew nothing about it. She maintained she had only visited the casino once, when Stanfield was alive and took her there.

"Franklin didn't go to Yuma," she insisted. "He drove to Flagstaff to meet with an attorney who specializes in difficult estate cases. I have his name and number. He thinks he can get us more than ten per cent of the money.

"We'll be sure to check it out." Guerevich spoke to Escobedo as if Cathy weren't present. "I guess twenty million just wasn't enough."

"Not when ten times that amount or more was at stake." Escobedo continued the pretense. "And Ginderer? He'll walk away with ten million he didn't earn."

Cathy looked from one to the other, her fists clenched on the table, her face growing redder as they spoke.

"Well, he apparently earned his salary when Stanfield was alive. Look at how his investments paid off for poor old Stan." Guerevich turned to Cathy. "I'm surprised he had the strength to throw your dressmaker's dummy through the window. He'll be remodeling his house while you're sitting in prison for the rest of your life. We know about his role in the shooting. How much more did you promise him?"

"Is that what the old fag told you? He wasn't even there. He could have had twice as much if he'd done. . . ." The second those words jumped from her mouth, she

clapped her hand over her lips, her eyes wide open.

Guerevich nodded at Escobedo.

Escobedo took Cathy by the arm and helped her to stand. "I think it's time for you to come down to the station. We have a lot more questions, and we need some truthful answers."

Guerevich pushed her cell phone toward her. "You better call your lawyer and have her meet us at interrogation."

Cathy smiled at Escobedo. "Are you going to cuff me?"

The tremor of her voice made Escobedo step back in surprise and speak almost apologetically. "I'm afraid I have no choice."

They escorted her to their car, put her in the back seat behind a bullet-proof mesh partition, and drove toward the central Scottsdale Police Station followed by the patrol car. For the first five minutes of the drive, she sat silently, her teeth clamped, her arms pinned behind her.

She spoke finally. "Did you mean what you said about me going to prison for life?"

"Every word," said Escobedo, as Guerevich maneuvered the car through traffic. "You're in the real world now. This isn't a parking ticket where you pay a fine and walk away. Murder has serious consequences."

For the rest of the trip, no one spoke. Cathy sat sullenly and looked out the window. When they got out of the car in the underground garage, Escobedo took her immediately to one of the lower level interrogation rooms, removed the cuffs, and told her to go in and have a seat.

Before Cathy sat down, she asked if her lawyer had arrived. "I've seen those police shows on television," she said to Escobedo. "You'll be watching me through that one way mirror and listening to everything I say."

Guerevich entered and sat across from her. "Absolutely true. Before your lawyer gets here, there are some things you need to know. You've been charged with first degree murder. Do you know what that means? It means premeditated. It means you planned the whole thing. And this isn't TV."

Tears, which Guerevich began to think were a staple of her depository, began their messy journey down her cheeks. She wiped her eyes with a tissue from the box on the table.

He raised his voice slightly. "If you're found guilty, you could be executed by lethal injection. They strap you to a table and everyone gets to see your body twitch as you die."

Cathy hung her head and stared at the table.

"Then your body gets shut in a drawer in the morgue until someone claims you. You really think Franklin will stop partying long enough to come for you? And if he doesn't, you'll be dumped in a desert grave with a number for your marker."

Guerevich walked around the table to where Cathy sat. He put his hand on the back of her chair and leaned toward her, speaking softly. "We know you invited Stanfield to the house. We requisitioned the phone records from Qwest." Guerevich almost shouted in her ear. "You shot him and watched bleed to death on the floor of the library."

"No. No. I didn't," she stammered through her tears.

"But that wasn't enough. You walked next to him and fired one final bullet. And that's where you screwed up. Because he was alive when your bullet shredded his heart."

The door to the interrogation room opened and Judith Westerly walked in, briefcase in hand. "Have you been badgering my client? You know better, Aaron."

"Not badgering, counselor, just acquainting her with the consequences of the charge."

"I could hear you even without the microphone. You were harassing my client. Now, I need some time with her. Alone, if you don't mind. And turn off the damned microphone."

Guerevich got up and walked toward the door. "Take all the time you need. She's not going anywhere."

Escobedo stood outside, looking through the one-way mirror. "Once Westerly gets through with her, we'll get nothing."

"I don't agree. Once they see the Medical Examiner's report, and read the part that indicates Margason was probably alive when she shot him, I think she'll tell us everything."

"But the report on mechanism of death wasn't conclusive. The report only indicated Margason could have been alive when the bullet entered his heart. He had lost so much blood his death was imminent and the examiner couldn't determine definitively if he was still alive when the bullet pierced his heart. Unless the ME re-examines the evidence."

Guerevich snapped his fingers. "We won't need the ME to re-examine anything. There's another way."

"I hope you know what you're doing."

Guerevich called Martín and asked him to come to the interrogation area.

When he arrived, Guerevich took him aside and quietly asked him if he could call up a copy of the Medical Examiner's summary report.

Martín sat at the computer terminal. "That's easy to do. Why do you want it?"

"I want you to change the wording."

"Is that legal?"

"I want Cathy and her lawyer to think it's a true copy, and I want the altered copy to state the mechanism of Margason's death was a lacerated heart muscle."

Martín nodded and agreed to the ruse. "I can do that. The change doesn't alter the fact Cathy has admitted to shooting her husband."

Using his access code, Martín called up a copy of the ME's summary from the archives, and with a few key strokes, made the changes and printed the altered copy.

With the altered copy in his hand, Guerevich called Ann and asked her to come to the interrogation area. He hoped her position as head of the forensic department would be intimidating.

"I want you to take this report into the room and put it on the table. Then I want you to leave as if you just remembered an important meeting. Make sure you tell them they are not to read it unless you're there to explain it."

"They just brought Franklin in," said Escobedo, walking into the corridor outside the room where Cathy Margason sat with her attorney. "He's in room four."

"Time to put the plan into high gear," said Guerevich. "Ann, once you put the report on the table, you leave. Martín, I want you to come over to room four and wait outside until I call you. Now you'll get a chance to see Franklin's look of surprise when he sees you. And once he gets a look at your face, I'd bet a hundred thousand dollars he'll remember you."

# CHAPTER TWENTY-SEVEN

Martín smiled, slipped his bulk from the chair, and followed Guerevich down the narrow hall to Interrogation Room number four. They stopped outside the room where they and Escobedo could watch through the one-way glass.

"He's asked for his lawyer," said Escobedo, who had waited for them. "All he would say is he knows nothing about his father's death other than what his stepmother told him. He doesn't know she's here. I hope you're right about her."

They waited for fifteen minutes until Franklin's lawyer, Jack Peterson, arrived, briefcase in hand.

"Good morning, gentlemen. Have you questioned my client?"

"Not a chance, counselor," said Escobedo. "We were waiting for you."

Peterson entered the room alone and closed the door.

Escobedo glared at Guerevich. "I think we'd better get whatever information we can from Franklin. We can't hold him for more than a couple of hours unless we charge him with something. And you're sure we'll be able to pressure Cathy into telling everything?"

"In exchange for pleading to a lesser charge than murder one? She might act tough, but she won't choose life in prison while Franklin walks away with more than twenty million."

"I hope you know what you're doing, Aaron. Just exactly what do we know about this guy?"

"We know Franklin is somehow involved in the counterfeiting operation. I believe he probably wanted to buy into the casino because of it. He met Marty in Yuma to deliver the bogus money. He hated his father so we can assume he's the one who came up with up the plan to kill him."

"For the money? Is that a motive for a young man to kill his father?" Escobedo paused. "But what we've learned about his father, the kid wouldn't have seen a penny of the five hundred million."

They looked down the corridor and saw Ann walking toward them.

"I just put Martín's copy of the Medical Examiner's report in room three with Cathy and her lawyer. I told them it was confidential and I would explain it when I got back. Is that legal?"

Guerevich smiled. "It's a confidential report. They don't have to look at it."

Ann shook her head. "What if they discover the change?"

"They haven't seen the original, yet. So if they do, I can always claim it's a mistake."

Ann nodded and walked toward Interrogation Room Three.

Guerevich put his arm around Martín's shoulder. "Marty, you're going to be my trump card when the time comes."

Escobedo smiled at Guerevich. "I think Peterson has had long enough with his client."

They entered the sparse, no frills room. Peterson and Franklin sat at an old conference table covered with water rings, coffee stains and cigarette burns. They were speaking quietly. Peterson stood as Guerevich and Escobedo approached.

"This is a waste of time.   My client doesn't know anything about the unfortunate death of his father.  Where's Mrs. Margason?"

"She's being held in another room.   Her attorney, Judith Westerly, is with her.  She's being charged with homicide."

"You're charging her with homicide?   It'll never fly. Especially since she was a battered wife. But that's Westerly's problem. My client doesn't know anything except what he was told, so he can't make any statements.   Either charge him or let him go."

"Why don't we ask him if he has anything to say?" Guerevich sat in a metal folding chair opposite Franklin. He placed a large manila folder on the table.

Peterson tapped Franklin on the shoulder.   "Get up. We're leaving."

"Not so fast," said Escobedo.   "Franklin Margason, you're under arrest for possession of counterfeit money.  You have the right to remain silent, and anything you say may be used against you in a court of law.  You have the right to an attorney, but you already have one."

Peterson looked at Franklin and regained his seat, sneering at Escobedo.  "Where'd you dig that one up?"

"I think it's called Title 18 of the United States Code," said Guerevich.

"Yes, I'm sure it is.   But you need some evidence before making a charge."

Guerevich eyed Franklin, ignoring Peterson.  "I think this discussion will be more productive than our others. No peeping from behind the curtains this time."

"Can the pleasantries, Guerevich." Peterson glared at the detective.  "Do you have any evidence or not?"

"Counselor, I'm surprised at your attitude.  I'm trying to be civil."   Guerevich opened the folder and shoved it across the table toward Franklin.  Three eight by ten photos of Franklin and Cathy slipped out.  "Are you and your stepmother lovers?"

"That's disgusting. You don't have to dignify that question with a response, Frank.  What the hell does that have to do with the counterfeiting charge?"  Peterson folded his arms, elbows on the table.

Franklin looked at the photos then sat back in his chair.  His eyes became wide with surprise, like a child caught throwing stones at a neighbor's cat.

Guerevich moved his hand over the pictures.  "It would explain these photos."

Guerevich separated the three pictures of Cathy and Franklin and placed them side by side in front of the young man.  The first photo showed them embracing on the front patio of her house.

"You can't be serious with these pictures," stormed Peterson, pushing the photos back.  "That's an invasion of their privacy,"

"Not so, Jack."  Escobedo shook her head.  "These were taken from across the street.  He and Mrs. Margason were in public view."

"Of course, we also have this mall picture."  Guerevich raised his voice slightly and pointed to the second photo.  "That's a good one.  Holding hands at a restaurant. As his stepmother, she has the right to hold his hand. But he's twenty-five years old, not five.  So I ask again, Franklin, are you two lovers?"

"What if we are," said Franklin, looking at the table and lowering his voice.  "There's no law against it, is there?"

"Franklin, keep quiet," said Peterson

"Yes, there is," said Guerevich.  "Incest and adultery are illegal as well as morally questionable, considering her husband was recently murdered."

"Incest? They're not related. And he was killed in self-defense," interrupted Peterson. "Nothing illegal here, since as you pointed out, she's no longer married. And she's only a few years older then he is. They're practically the same age."

Guerevich chuckled. "I bet a jury'll have some fun with the information."

"I still don't see any relationship between these photos and counterfeiting. Are you going to charge him with having sex with a slightly older woman and get laughed out of court? What's your point?" Peterson had a note of impatience in his voice.

"The point is I think Stanfield found out about you and Cathy. He confronted you, and you shot him."

"I wasn't even there, remember?"

"Right. You have said weren't there." Guerevich stood and leaned across the table close to Franklin's face. "But then we still have the problem of counterfeiting in Las Vegas."

"What the hell are you talking about?" Franklin shouted, turning his head away from Guerevich.

"No need for him to shout, Peterson," said Escobedo. "Just answer the questions. You were in Las Vegas recently, weren't you?"

"Of course. I was in Las Vegas to try to complete the casino purchase my father started. I don't know anything about any counterfeiting."

"So you didn't meet anyone in Yuma with a briefcase filled with counterfeit hundreds to take to Algodones, Mexico?"

"Absolutely not."

Guerevich, looked toward the mirror. "Send Marty in."

Martín opened the door and stepped into the room. He closed the door behind him and stood in front of it, saying nothing.

"Who's he?" asked Peterson

"I remember him," yelled Franklin. "He's one of the fucking Mexican illegals who worked at the casino. He wanted a green card so bad, he'd say anything. He barely speaks English."

"Wrong, wrong, and wrong," said Guerevich. "Martín Velez is a police officer and a computer expert. He happens to be from Colombia. Marty, introduce yourself to Mr. Peterson. You've already met Franklin."

"Good morning, Mr. Peterson," said Martin in nearly perfect English. He offered his hand to Peterson, who shook it weakly. "What Aaron has told you about me is true. And Franklin's right. I did work recently as a cook in the kitchen of the Lucky Nugget casino."

"I don't know what he's talking about," said Franklin.

"Well, there is that Las Vegas police officer," continued Martín. "Sergeant Leobardo Gonsalves, who, I'm told, is now in custody. He drove me to Yuma to deliver one hundred thousand dollars to you in counterfeit hundreds. I gave you the briefcase in the lobby of the Best Western motel in Yuma. I am sure the hotel security camera caught the entire transaction on tape."

"Then this whole thing was an entrapment of my client. You'll have to do better than that, or you've got no case."

Escobedo regarded the attorney with a sneer. "Come on, Jack. Marty never asked to deliver the funny money, nor did Franklin have to accept it. Marty was hired to deliver the briefcase by Ruben Vasquez, for which Marty was supposed to be paid a thousand dollars. He was accompanied by

Gonsalves, who was probably going to kill him after the money was delivered. He would have been just another dead illegal, right Frank?"

Franklin bit his lip and his face flushed red.

"Don't say another word, Frank," said Peterson. He turned to Guerevich. "Are you seriously charging him with possession of counterfeit money? You couldn't prove he knew it was counterfeit with ten eye witnesses."

Escobedo looked at Guerevich and nodded. "You're absolutely right. He's free to go. We have no intention of charging him with counterfeiting. That's for the Feds and the Nevada authorities."

Martín opened the door. Cathy Margason stood outside in handcuffs, accompanied by her attorney, two female officers, and Ann Berendt.

Franklin quickly sat upright, hands palm down on the table and shouted. "Cathy? What's she doing there?" He jumped up, overturned his chair, and darted toward the doorway. Escobedo blocked him from leaving the room.

Cathy glared at Franklin. "You son of a bitch," she said. "You lying son of a bitch. You were so goddamn clever. If you think I'm going down alone, you're crazy." She shouted through her tears as the two female officers pushed her down the hall. "Get your fucking hands off me. He's the one who killed Stan, not me." She wrenched her shoulders back and forth, struggling against the hands holding her as she continued to shout. "He's the one. He planned the whole thing."

"What the hell's she going on about?" asked Franklin, walking back into the room. His steps were slow and unsteady. He braced his hand on the table for support.

"I think she must have seen the Medical Examiner's report," said Guerevich. "The one that says the bullet that killed your father was the one she put through his heart. So technically, she's guilty of murder."

"I don't think she's taken the news lightly." Escobedo walked outside the room and looked down the hall. "In fact, she was pissed enough to tell us everything."

"It was self-defense," shouted Franklin, looking at the floor. Then in a lower voice, like a child insisting he didn't break the shattered vase at his feet. "She shot him in self-defense."

"Don't say another word," advised Peterson, standing next to Franklin.

"No, no," said Escobedo. "Your lawyer's right. Don't say another word," She turned to the lawyer. "Mr. Peterson, explain to your client it's definitely murder when you stand over a man who happens to be unconscious, but alive, and put a bullet into his chest and through his heart."

"According to forensics," said Guerevich, "there was no way she could have fired the final shot from the same position as the other four. And the lack of scratch marks on his arms and head indicates he didn't go through the window. In fact, he was lying on the floor unconscious when the window was broken, isn't that right?

"Franklin, don't say anything," admonished Peterson again.

"He doesn't need to. We have Cathy's written statement about what happened. It was all about the money. I'm sure she'll be more than happy to fill in any other missing details."

Facing Guerevich, Franklin's face was twisted in an expression of hate, his lips curled into a sneer. He kicked the chair he had knocked over. "It's because he was a mean, stingy bastard, who fucked up his life, and he was trying to fuck mine up as well. Do you know what it's like to grow up with a father who always acted like a child? He had money, but it took a court order for him to give my mother anything. Even when I went to live with him, I never had a real father. He was supposed to be the adult, but he acted like he was a goddamn teenager.   In forty-four years, what did he accomplish? Nothing. Now, suddenly, he wanted a career as a casino owner so he could inherit five hundred million.  He told me I could have a job helping to run the place.  With a salary, of course.   While he squandered my inheritance." Franklin walked back to the table, picked up the chair, and sat down.

"What went wrong?" asked Escobedo, entering the room and closing the door behind him

"What went wrong?  Everything.  When he found out about the counterfeiting, he got scared and backed out of the deal.  And where did that leave me? Back on the streets, waiting to see if the old man would pull something off in less than a year.   Like a dog under the dinner table, hoping to get some scraps. They were willing to cut him in just on the promise of his inheritance.   All he had to do was help launder the money.  It would have been easy with all the

traveling he does."

"So you shot him?"

"He did find out about Cathy and me.   And you know what's funny.  He didn't even care.  And she didn't have the nerve to do anything until she thought he was already dead.  She didn't even want to divorce him, because she'd have had to pay maintenance.  Imagine.  A man blows off five hundred million, and she'd have to pay him maintenance."

"But her money was running out."

"Not if we bought the casino that he didn't have the guts to do."

"How'd she get him to come to the house?" asked Guerevich.

"She told him she had the divorce papers for him to sign and she'd give him his maintenance. Then she called me. We were waiting for him. She already had an order of protection because of his temper. It was simple to make it look like he broke in and she shot him."

Escobedo shook her head. "So you shot him and then she put the bullet through his heart to give her residue on her hands."

"Just a bit of insurance. bShe had to have some involvement. Besides, we thought he was already dead. Even then, she didn't want to do it until I told her there's no penalty for shooting a dead man."

After Franklin had been led away, Guerevich remained in the room, alone with his thoughts. He breathed a sigh of relief and thought about the relationship he had with his father. *Life is too short to carry anger in your heart. The Talmud states that anger is a sin like idol worship which is so evil that a Jew must die rather then participate in it.*

Guerevich also knew that anger against his father was a violation of the second commandment to honor his father and mother. It was a transgression against both God and man. With Yom Kippur only a few months away, he knew he would feel pressure to ask his father for forgiveness. What better time was there to do something about his own anger.

# CHAPTER TWENTY-EIGHT

Cathy Margason and her stepson, Franklin, were remanded to the Scottsdale Detention Facility on 75th street to await trial. This time they were not granted bail. The police fingerprinted them, took their mug shots, and inventoried their personal property. They were placed in separate cells while they waited to be transported from to the court by the Police Detention Manager. Their lawyers had successfully petitioned to try them separately.

The morning after the Margason indictments, Ann awoke early and made coffee. When the aroma wafted into the bedroom, Guerevich slipped on a robe and shuffled into the kitchen. He poured a cup and carried it to the table. "Better than the kitchenette in Vegas."

She joined him at the table where he sat staring into his cup, his hands propping up his head.

"So what're you going to do?"

"About what?"

"Don't play dumb."

"No one'll get that inheritance now. That young man killed his father for nothing."

"You think I can't tell what's really eating away at you? I know it's not just Danny. You should be elated at ending the case, but you're moping around like someone whose dog just died. You're thinking about your own father."

Thoughts of his own father streamed through Guerevich's head and brought him back to the happy memory of his Bar Mitzvah at Anshe Shalom B'Nai Israel in Chicago. This was one of the times he remembered with pristine clarity, as if it has happened yesterday.

In the religious community, he had become an adult. He made his first *aliyah*, the honor of chanting the blessing before reading a portion of the *Torah*. He even chanted a selection in the ancient Talmudic language. His father had chanted the *Haftorah*. Aaron had hoped someday he would be treated with deference, like his father, whom everyone admired, a respected teacher and writer.

A second memory flowed from the first. Not a happy one. The year following his Bar Mitzvah, his father Avram announced the family was moving from Chicago to Phoenix, where he had been offered the chairmanship of the history department at Arizona State University. The transition had been difficult for the fourteen-year-old Aaron Guerevich. It was not until his first full-time job at a police department that he began to understand the politics of the workplace, and comprehended why his father had left Humboldt University in Chicago. Avram had angered members of the administration as well as some influential alumni when he compared the National Socialist State to the university system in his book on the rise of Nazism. The chairmanship of the history department, which Avram desired, had been offered to a woman from the University of Iowa.

A third memory was a painful one, the time he told his father he was going to become a cop and had switched his college major to Police Science in his junior year.

The admission had happened on a Friday morning after breakfast. Aaron had come home for the weekend. Avram sat at the kitchen table reading the *Arizona Republic*, tie loosened, brown tweed jacket over the back of the chair, his feet still in corduroy slippers. The pinkness of his bald head was partially covered by his yarmulke, and his wire frame glasses had slid down his rounded nose. Aaron moved a chair and sat across the table from his father.

"I need to talk to you, Papa. I'm changing my major."

Avram dropped his newspaper to his lap and scrutinized his son. "You don't want to become a lawyer? First, you didn't want to be a doctor because it takes too long. Now you don't want to be a lawyer?" Avram stared at his son over his glasses. "So tell me. What do you want to do with your life?"

"I don't know. I'm not sure."

Avram tightened his jaw. His lips thinned in a grimace. "Aaron, don't play games with me. Tell me the truth."

After hesitating a moment, he said, "All right. I've decided to major in Police Science. When I finish my BA, I want to work in Glendale or Scottsdale. They're not big police forces, but either one would be a good place to start."

"You want to be a cop? With a uniform? And a gun?"

"Why not? Think of it as fulfilling my mitzvot. My mission to help others."

"By putting yourself in danger? Maybe getting killed? What kind of help would that be?"

"Maybe I could go to law school later. Once I get a feel for what life on the streets is really like. I know two lawyers who did that."

Aaron had thought his idea would soften the disappointment his news brought to his father, who once hoped his son would become a rabbi.

Disappointment had clouded his father's eyes. "It's your life." He raised the newspaper, a fragile wall between the two men. "Do what you want."

Those deadly words ended the discussion.

From that time on, Guerevich never discussed his occupation with his father, even when he passed the detective exam with the Scottsdale Police Department. A year after that, he had broken a troubling crime in which a young man killed his grandfather. For several months before the case had been solved, the Sackman investigation had made headlines in *The Arizona Republic.*

Even after that, the older Guerevich had said nothing, as if he tolerated his son's occupation, balancing the need for police with a disdain for the necessity to have police at all. He had once written an article in which he stated that those who joined the police were, for the most part, attracted to positions of power, the very power that corrupted them.

Ann interrupted his reverie. "Well, Aaron. Are you just going to sit there? What are you going to do?"

After a short silence, he sipped his coffee and looked across the table at her. "I think I'll go see him," he said. "Phone calls are too impersonal."

"That's a start. How long has it been since you spoke to him?"

"You mean argued? Almost three months. I haven't seen him for almost a year."

Guerevich called the university and found that his father had office hours that afternoon. At two o'clock, he knocked at the door to the office of Chairman of the History Department.

"This is a surprise," said Avram, his voice unmodulated. "To what do I owe this pleasure?"

Guerevich looked at his father, standing there in his customary tweed sport jacket and gray trousers. The jacket seemed to hang a bit more than he could recall. He saw deeper wrinkles in his father's face, and noticed that his skin seemed thinner, more papery, than he remembered.

"It's been too long, Papa. I just wanted to see how you were doing."

"I read about the Margason case. It's been all over the news this morning. Even NPR carried the story. Is that why you're here? A bit of gloating?"

Guerevich looked at the floor. "No," he mumbled. "I came to invite you to join me at services Saturday morning. There's a Conservative synagogue, Temple Beth Emeth in Scottsdale, with a new Rabbi you might have heard of. Like you, he's also a teacher and writer."

"Yes. Rabbi Rosenthal. I read his book. An interesting man."

"I also came to apologize for not treating you with the respect you deserve." He raised his head, his eyes shining with tears, and he looked down at his father.

Avram walked toward his son, opened his arms, and reached out to hug him. Guerevich bent down and the two men embraced.

Avram whispered, "No. You're wrong. It's I who should apologize. And I'd be happy to join you on *Shabbos*. Do men and women sit together?"

"Yes, they do. Ann will be able to join us as well."

"There's an interesting saying, popular with my students. It probably refers to my lectures. 'What you cannot cure, you must endure.'"

At the services, Avram whispered to his son that the liturgy followed orthodox procedure, which made him feel at ease. After services, Ann and Guerevich accompanied Avram to his house and joined him for a lunch of cold roast beef sandwiches with horseradish on rye bread.

A few months later, Guerevich and Ann gathered with Avram, his friends, and the rest of the family to eat potato *latkes* and applesauce at a traditional Chanukah dinner. There were teachers from ASU that Guerevich had never met, and when everyone was seated at the table, his father introduced him.

"For those who do not know him, this is my son Aaron, the well-known detective."    He looked at his son and smiled.